In the stunning conclusion to award-winning author Jewell Parker Rhodes's mystery trilogy begun in *Season* and *Moon*, Dr. Marie Levant, descendent of Voodoo queen Marie Laveau, must confront a murderous evil in New Orleans.

Dr. Marie Levant aka Laveau, great-great granddaughter of Marie Laveau, has achieved fame and notoriety for saving New Orleans from the wrath of a vampire. Now she's taking a break from the city, heading up the highway to DeLaire. She doesn't know this backwater town, but an elderly woman called Nana has been expecting Marie to arrive and save her and others in this God-forsaken place from sickness and death.

Yet all of Marie's powers can't bring life back to the corpses she finds in a house by the road. Nor can she force those who know how they died to say so or to confess. Were the crimes committed by shape-shifters, vampires, and ghosts—or by living men and women? And even as Marie searches for answers, a hurricane threatens to break the levees of Louisiana and cause unimaginable destruction.

Jewell Parker Rhodes blends magic and man-made evil and weaves New Orleans's past and present into a spine-tingling mystery that is masterfully crafted and deeply haunting.

HURRICANE

Jewell Parker Rhodes

WASHINGTON SQUARE PRESS
New York   London   Toronto   Sydney

WASHINGTON SQUARE PRESS
A Division of Simon & Schuster, Inc.
1230 Avenue of the Americas
New York, NY 10020

First Washington Square Press trade paperback edition April 2011

WASHINGTON SQUARE PRESS and colophon are registered trademarks of
Simon & Schuster, Inc.

For information about special discounts for bulk purchases,
please contact Simon & Schuster Special Sales at 1-866-506-1949
or business@simonandschuster.com.

The Simon & Schuster Speakers Bureau can bring authors to your
live event. For more information or to book an event contact the
Simon & Schuster Speakers Bureau at 1-866-248-3049
or visit our website at www.simonspeakers.com.

Designed by Jaime Putorti

Manufactured in the United States of America

10 9 8 7 6 5 4 3 2 1

The Library of Congress Cataloging-in-Publication Data
    Rhodes, Jewell Parker.
    Hurricane / by Jewell Parker Rhodes.
       p. cm.
    1. Laveau, Marie, 1794–1881—Fiction. 2 African American women—
Fiction. 3. Vampires—Fiction. 4. Voodooism—Fiction. 5. New Orleans (La.)—
Fiction. I. Title.
PS3568.H63H87 2011
    813'.54—dc22   2010037938

ISBN 978-1-4165-3712-0
ISBN 978-1-4391-8741-8 (ebook)

✷

Dedicated to the citizens of Louisiana
and to the New Orleans Public Library Book Club

HURRICANE

PROLOGUE

The Ibo say, "All stories are true."
Conjure women say, "Truth flies on the wings of dreams."

NEW ORLEANS

NIGHT TERRORS

Bodies were everywhere—limp, bloated, tangled in bushes, trees, floating in water.

Men, women, and children bobbed in the muddy current, interspersed with upside-down Chevys, shredded trees, snapped power lines, and mangled street signs.

Rain added to the river's rise. Hot, humid rain. Rain that tasted metallic and fell, like blades, pricking skin.

Marie was dry, parched. Awake inside her dream.

For weeks, she'd been having the same dream; she'd been trying to interpret it, break the horrific spell.

"*Water, water, everywhere, and not a drop to drink.*" The phrase kept rewinding in her mind. Coleridge. *The Rime of the Ancient Mariner.*

"*Not a drop to drink.*" Just dead, infested waters.

She moaned. Her legs were tangled in the sheets; sweat blanketed her skin.

She dove back down into her dream, through layers of thought, anxiety, and consciousness.

Inhale, exhale. Breathe.

The river was widening, swallowing, then spitting up more bodies.

The Guédé, the death gods, in top hat and tails, were standing on a bridge, pointing at the dead. No—at something else. Something within the water.

"Let me see," she murmured. "Let me see."

The Guédé heard her. In unison, they shook their skull heads and pressed their white-gloved hands across their hollow eyes.

"Show me," she demanded. "I am Marie."

The Guédé opened their mouths. They didn't make sound, rather, Marie felt their howling—an obscene absence of sound that terrorized, rattling her bones.

Both inside and outside her dream, Marie wanted to run, hide, burrow into a hole so deep, no one—tangible or intangible—could ever touch her.

Each night, this was when and where her dream ended—the Guédé howling, refusing to look deeper into the water.

If the Guédé were afraid to look, why should she?

Her body constricted; her respiration quickened; her legs grew rigid, tight. She rasped, "Let me see. I am Marie. I need to see."

She fell, hard, fast. Screaming, she clawed at the sheets. Her body jerked; the freefall stopped.

Parallel, weightless, she floated inches above the river water.

She recoiled.

Bodies bobbed so close she could touch them: a woman, her lips locked in a grimace, her arms flung over her head; a blue baby, covered in algae like a desolate infant Moses; and a man, twisted onto his side, insects burrowing into his exposed cheek and nostril.

Snakes greased through brown water. A baby crocodile perched on a dead body like a log.

She smelled waste—human and inhuman. She smelled decomposing rot and withered leaves.

In the polluted waters, there were layers of deepening darkness, darker than mud, darker than earth. Darker than any sin.

She heard: "Rise." It wasn't the Guédé—but the other spirit, the one, camouflaged, deep inside the water. She saw an outline—a face, human?—ascending. Then, it stopped; the spirit still cradled by deep waters.

"Rise."

Streams of white smoke rose from the dead, billowing like foam waves in the sky.

"Rise."

The dead were transformed into flying birds. Blackbirds. Thousands of blackbirds were flying south, escaping, soaring above the landscape, above cities, parishes, levees, and marshes. Flying toward a horizon split with orange, red, purple, and gold. Flying toward the river's mouth.

"Mama!"

The scream pierced sleep.

"Mama."

Marie jolted awake, stumbling out of bed, running. "Marie-Claire? Marie-Claire, I'm coming. Mama's coming."

The blue revolving lamp had stopped, its silhouettes of birds were dim and static on the ceiling and bedroom walls. The night-light, in the wall outlet, flickered, its power waning.

Marie-Claire lay facedown on the pillow.

"Baby." Fearfully, gently, she turned Marie-Claire over.

Marie-Claire was asleep; her lids closed tight, her eyelashes fanning long, delicately. She was hot, her face flushed, her brown curls matted on her brow and neck. But no fever.

She was asleep.

Wind lifted the bedroom curtains like birds' wings. Marie trembled with relief.

"Women hand sight down through the generations. Mother to daughter."

She and Marie-Claire were bound by tragedy, bound by love and blood.

They were imbued with *sight,* spiritual gifts carried from Africa into the New World, through Marie Laveau, New Orleans's famed, nineteenth-century Voodoo Queen.

Maybe Marie-Claire, too, had been awake inside some dream? Maybe she was still dreaming?

Marie prayed her daughter's dreams were sweet. No bloated bodies. Only rainbows, magnolias, and friends at play.

"Marie-Claire," she whispered, gently shaking her.

Marie-Claire's eyes fluttered, her breath smelled like almonds.

"Mama, go bye? Go bye-bye."

"Marie-Claire?" She held her daughter's limp hand.

"Bye, Mama. Bye-bye." Still slumbering, Marie-Claire turned, onto her side, her tiny fists curled beneath her chin.

Marie kissed the tip of her nose, then quickly turned, sensing a presence.

Baron Samedi, the Guédé leader, was solemn, all skeleton and shadow.

Cocking his head, he pointed a gloved finger at the night-light. It glowed, strong and bright, like a lighthouse guiding lost sailors home. He touched the lamp. The birds continued their kaleidoscopic flight across the ceiling and walls. Then, Samedi waved his hand.

"South. Birds flying south," she whispered.

In the Sleeping Beauties case, she'd learned the Guédé despised those who interfered with death. She learned, too, that if the Guédé refused to dig your grave, you wouldn't die.

Asleep and awake, the Guédé were guiding her.

"You coming?" she asked the baron softly.

Baron Samedi tipped his hat and shook his head. He sat on the bed, then leaned forward, his gloved fingers stroking Marie-Claire's hair.

The hair on her skin rose. From her medical training, she knew it was a chemical reaction spurred by fear, the fight or flight response. Adrenaline was raising her blood pressure, making her heart beat faster.

It was startling to see Death touching Marie-Claire.

Baron Samedi smiled, a grimace of a skeletal jaw, lost and rotten teeth.

"You won't hurt her." It was a statement, not a question. The Guédé were encouraging her to follow her dream to its source.

"You don't do oatmeal, do you?"

Samedi sat, cross-legged, at the foot of the bed.

Marie smiled. What better babysitter than Death itself?

She suddenly wanted to wake Marie-Claire. To see her smile and see herself reflected in her daughter's eyes. She bent, pressing her lips against Marie-Claire's cheek, inhaling her sweet scent.

"Thank you, Baron. I'm grateful."

Samedi kept mute.

Marie walked quickly out of the room. She needed to call the hospital, rearrange her shifts. She needed to call the sitter, Louise. She'd take care of Marie-Claire's temporal needs: fix her food, keep her warm, and read her a story. Without question, Marie-Claire would be safe. Baron Samedi himself would refuse to ferry her to the afterlife, the other world.

Marie let her drawstring pajama pants fall to the floor. She slipped on underwear, jeans, and buttoned a black shirt over her cotton tee. She pitched extra panties, shirts, a comb, and a toothbrush into an overnight bag.

What did it mean? Any of it?

The Guédé were telling her that the bodies in the river were only part of a mystery she needed to solve—there was still more to discover, more to dream.

She'd drive south. And pray she'd stay alive, her spirit whole.

She saw herself reflected in the mirror: thick brown hair pulled back in a ponytail; lean rather than voluptuous; bags beneath her eyes from working too hard as a mother, a doctor.

If the Guédé were here, her daughter was at risk. The balance between life and death was unsettled, unraveling.

Her life's calling was to heal—and her dream, even though it didn't make any sense, was, somehow, a call for her skills.

She snapped her overnight bag shut.

The river's mouth, the river's mouth.

There was only one place in Louisiana to go—the Gulf of Mexico. The Gulf was where the Mississippi drained.

South. Drive south.

I

Old ways, country ways,
Haints fly,
Everyone has southern roots.

ONE

A BAYOU ROAD

LATE AFTERNOON

As soon as she hit the road, her bravado faded. That was the problem with having spiritual gifts. She was still ordinary, only extraordinary when need demanded it.

But wasn't that true of any woman?

Marie pressed hard on the gas—her new Mustang, top down, carrying her into the unknown.

She was following the birds. Except they weren't black—mainly gray, brown, and mottled pigeons, some swallows. But as she traveled farther south into a landscape infused with water, streams, inlets, and tributaries, white egrets soared, pelicans arched bony wings, and hawks glided.

Her gift was following signs. Believing that all things animate and inanimate had life.

Still—some of the time, she thought she was crazy.

She worried she was becoming just another southern

gothic—an "eccentric"; a "haint"; a "black magic witch"; or "a Lilith demon," as some folks liked to call her. Once she heard, "*Ju-ju Whore,*" shouted by a French Quarter drunk who hadn't been sober in over two years.

She looked into the rearview mirror.

El.

"Damnit, El." She was chauffeuring a ghost.

Her palm slapped the steering wheel. That's it. She might as well get it over with—break down, lose her mind, and live in a padded cell.

El's ghost rolled her eyes, as if to say, "Whatever."

Marie laughed, releasing strain, the tension gripping her neck and back. She pressed hard on the gas, feeling the car adjust gears, gathering speed.

Bayou air flowed over her, layering her skin with sweat.

No more self-pity. No regrets.

Marie had always found salvation in her work. But in the months since El, Charity's head nurse, and Dr. DuLac, the head of the ER, had been murdered, being inside Charity Hospital had lost some appeal. As a medical resident, she'd been drawn to New Orleans, and hadn't known why. It had been DuLac who'd explained her legacy, and tutored her in the voodoo arts. DuLac—who'd become both her beloved mentor and father figure. El was the mother who encouraged her.

During her last case, DuLac and El had sacrificed their lives to protect Marie-Claire from the *wazimamoto,* the African vampire. She kept remembering El and DuLac dead, limp, their bodies twisted on the floor, drained of blood.

She hadn't seen DuLac since his death. El's spirit visited occasionally. She often brought women with her. Sister-friends. Ghosts from another age: slaves sold as breeders; quadroons contracted as mistresses to white aristocrats; and prostitutes who played sex games to buy milk and bread for their children.

El was reminding her that the world could be hard on women.

"What else is new?" Marie would say to El after failing to convince another battered woman in the ER to file a police report, run away, or spend the night in a shelter.

"It is what it is," El would reply.

Marie sighed, tucking a windswept strand of hair behind her ear.

The world was harsh, particularly Louisiana; steeped in conflict like rice in an unsavory stew.

She wondered if America ever regretted purchasing Louisiana from the French. In 1823, did America understand it was buying a landscape designed for fevered dreams: swamps that could swallow you alive; infected mosquitoes, insatiably draining blood; yellow moons heralding disasters; and weeping willows sheltering predators, large and small? Did they imagine hurricanes flooding rivers, streets, and with whipping wind howling, blowing houses down?

Still, there was a beauty to Louisiana, an otherworldliness and preternatural charm.

She was driving straight into its bayou heart.

El's presence was companionable. Marie felt herself relaxing. She could pretend she was on a road trip. Pretend for a moment she was free of responsibilities: work, motherhood, and miracles.

She turned the radio on, punched the buttons, searching for anything but static. Zydeco. Blues. Folk. Classical.

Nothing. Just static in the backwoods.

Inexplicably, the radio blared Marvin Gaye's "Sexual Healing."

Marie laughed again. Her car swerved slightly, then she straightened its course.

She looked at the backseat ghost. "What was I thinking, El? You weren't a mother figure. More like an R-rated aunt."

Alive, El had always encouraged Marie to get laid. "I'm too old for all that sweat. But you," she declared, her nails, outrageously long, her seventy-year-old skin, soft as magnolias, "should never sleep alone. It's not good for the mood. Or skin."

Apparently, death hadn't changed El.

Marie shrugged. "It is what it is, El. I can't chain a man to my bed."

The radio whined like a castrated cat.

"Unfair, El."

The radio snapped quiet, cutting off the bass line.

Sexual healing would've been great, but Parks, her ex-lover and the detective on the *wazimamoto* case, had grown tired of New Orleans.

"Not tired of you," he'd said with earnestness. "Tired of the murders. The never-ending crime. Come with me," he'd pleaded. "To Jersey. California. Wherever you want."

But he'd already known she wouldn't leave.

New Orleans was the one place where she didn't have to explain what it meant to be Marie Laveau's descendant. *Loas* and saints; drums and chants; African spirituality blended with Christianity—all of it made sense in the Big Easy.

Louisianans understood bloodlines. Women who spoke with ghosts.

※

Marie focused on the snakelike road. She liked the feel of the car beneath her—the engine rumbling, ever so sexy, feeling its tremors beneath her butt.

Drive. Fast. Leaning into the curves. Just drive.

El smiled. She was enjoying the ride, too.

Then El flicked her red-painted nails as if shooing some unseen fly; her lips thinned, as if seeing, sensing something distasteful.

Shaking her head mournfully, El faded, disappearing like a photo undeveloping, unraveling through time.

Marie refused to be shaken. Who knew what troubles El had on the other side? Death, like life, couldn't be easy.

Marie floored it and the Mustang responded.

※

Marie hadn't seen a truck stop for a hundred miles. Just bleak asphalt with a cracked dividing line. She was hungry. Low on gas. She needed to pee.

But she wasn't worried; rather, she felt exhilarated.

She kept driving, feeling her soul lift, knowing she was where she needed to be.

Her ancestor, Marie Laveau, was raised, here, in the bayou. Marie felt the spiritual connection, felt glory stirring in her bones.

She veered sharply, driving deliberately off the main road. The car rocked, jolted, and bounced as asphalt became gravel, became dirt, then mud.

Three oaks, their bark scored with insect warrens, blocked her path.

Three—the numeric symbol of magic, intuition, and fertility. Three—the sign of the trinity.

She studied the oaks, their old-growth trunks with gnarled roots delving deep into the soil, and their leaves, unfurling, blocking the blue, but darkening, sky.

Marie clicked off the engine and got out of the Mustang. She was in an alcove of green—sawlike sedge, angular cypress, and weeping willows. Moss and ivy spread like wild lace.

Mist clung to her body. Honeysuckle scented the air.

She closed her eyes, feeling her senses sharpen. She could hear her heartbeat, swamp mice rustling in grass, and a soaring crow's caw.

She stretched her hands high, feeling the urge to undress and dance. To celebrate unashamed.

Something shifted in the dense growth.

"El?"

She turned right, left, twisting round. Nothing. No one.

She stepped on a felled branch. *The snapping sound ricocheted, echoing in the dense alcove.*

She kept still.

She heard an unnatural quiet, felt an electric cold descending. Peering past oaks and tangled marsh, beyond rampant ferns and gnarled bark, she saw a darkness, bubbling up from the earth, hovering. A darkness, denser than any night, blacker than any shadow.

She heard a piercing cry. Human or animal? Or neither?

Death's scent assailed her.

Marie knew Nature encompassed death: rotting plants, predators feasting, and a continuous cycle of decomposition and renewal. Only humans perverted nature with suicide and murder. That's what she smelled now—an unnatural dying.

The smell was pungent, like an entire hospital ward filled with the dead. Not just any dead, but those brutally dead from festering wounds, gangrene, and bullets boring through flesh, muscles, and sinews.

Her tennis shoes sank in the murky soil, the white canvas turning black.

There. She saw a smoky thread weaving through the brush, then swaying upright, like a snake from a charmer's basket.

Sent by the dead? By her ancestress Laveau?

The black thread stopped inches from where she stood.

She trembled, sensing the darkness had consciousness. Malevolence? She didn't know. She only knew nothing had been an accident. There was no escape from *fa,* her fate.

"Shit." She slipped, her ankle twisting. Branches, small rocks dug into her palms. She bit her lip, wincing. She wiped her bloodied hands on her pants before limping onward.

She came to a small clearing. But instead of the sugar-bright cottage Hansel and Gretel had stumbled upon, she saw a dilapidated one-room shack. New plywood bolstered old wood; gleaming black tar patched the weathered roof.

Someone had tried to refresh what time had worn down.

The well had a new pail but the chain was rusted orange.

Brush had been hacked away—not much of it, it would have

been back-breaking work, but enough for a pitiful patch of vegetables: mold-covered green beans, a shriveled tomato plant, and yellow-spotted peas.

Through dirty windows, she saw a small table with a kerosene lamp, and cut lilies, hanging limp inside a glass, waiting to be watered. The kitchen was empty. There were hand-sewn curtains—gingham. A woman's touch. Someone had tried to make a home.

"Hello? Hello?"

Nothing. No cats, dogs, or people. Just a forlorn porch with a broken rocker. *And the smell—the death gods announcing their presence.*

Parked on the side of the shack was a gleaming blue truck.

She breathed shallowly to prevent herself from gagging.

She called again, "Hello? Hello?"

She touched the door of the shack. It swung wide.

Flinching, she fell against the door frame, bile rising in her throat.

She forced herself to look.

Two bodies. A man, splayed, on the floor; a woman, facedown, on the bed. Blood speckled the walls, floor. Human bodies held approximately six quarts of blood. The woman's remaining blood had soaked the sheets, the thin cotton mattress, and had dripped off the bed, making a small puddle.

She was a doctor. Heal.

Gritting against the pain in her ankle, she bent, checking pulses. None. The man was still warm; the woman, warmer.

The woman had been the last to die. The blast had lain open her chest, fractured her spine, muscle. In the city, most wounds were from a .45 or .38. These wounds were from a shotgun. Pellets littered the body and the wall behind.

What had these two done to deserve such rage? Or had it been a random theft? But what did they have worth stealing?

The woman was slim, medium height. Her arms disappeared beneath her torso.

Marie stroked the woman's hair. Then stopped. Extending outward from the woman's throat was a swatch of pink with satin trim. The knit blanket was damp, stained red.

"Strength," Marie murmured. She gripped a shoulder, turning the woman over, revealing an infant scattershot through the abdomen. Lead pellets had passed from mother to child, killing the baby instantly. Or at least Marie hoped so. She hoped the baby hadn't suffocated first, beneath her mother's body.

Marie dry-heaved, grateful her stomach was empty.

"It is what it is," El murmured.

"No, it isn't fair," Marie responded, fiercely.

If you didn't look below the neck, the baby appeared asleep. Rich chocolate skin, with black strands covering her head. She couldn't have been more than three months; her skull was still flexible, the bones hadn't fused.

Marie turned, sensing a disruption in the air, a chasm in time.

The dead man, newly alive, was an arm's length in front of her. Ex-military. He wore khaki pants, army-issue boots. He was muscular, fit. A warrior.

His wife and baby were crying, the woman softly, the baby, big gulping cries.

Marie couldn't see the assailant. Assailants? Half the room was dark, as if a curtain or shroud had been drawn.

"Let me see," she murmured. "Let me see."

The young man, his ax in his hand, was planted like a tree, protecting his family. He was talking angrily (his words, soundless) . . . talking, shaking his head. Shouting, enraged, he tensed, crouched, and leapt, his left arm lifting his ax high. Then his forward motion stopped, the ax falling from his hand, crashing down. That must have been the first shot. His body jerked back. A second shot.

Blood drained from two huge wounds. He was nearly dead.

To the left, someone picked up his ax, swung it wide, cutting into the man's abdomen, cutting deep through stomach, intestines. He fell forward.

But not before Marie had a clear look at his face. He'd been startled, incredulous. Like the youth she'd seen in Charity's ER. Young men—often gang members—who never expected to die or thought they couldn't be hurt.

In seconds, like a silent movie reel, a veteran soldier lay murdered. Blood flowed like water.

Marie blinked tears.

If she shifted her weight, turned her head ever so slightly, she'd see the mother and child die. She refused. As it was, she knew she'd always be haunted by their image, a bloodied Madonna and child.

She kept her eyes fixed on the curtain.

Why couldn't she see the murderers? The murderer?

For each hour dead, body temperature dropped eight-tenths of a percent. Bayou heat might have slowed the progress. Rigor mortis usually occurred within the first half hour to three hours. All the bodies were still pliable.

Marie shuddered. The murders had occurred as she was driving, being guided, here.

Instinct told her that the woman had been kept alive. Why? Had they interrogated her? Harmed her in some other way?

Curious, she looked again at mother and child.

The woman's floral dress was hitched high. The backs of her knees were locked.

She saw a latex-gloved hand raising the woman's floral dress, ripping her cotton panties.

Marie turned, snapping, shutting her eyes tight. She wouldn't let herself think of it. She wouldn't turn and stare into the vision.

Air still shimmered.

The murderer, murderers had to have known—kill the mother, kill the child.

"No more," Marie screamed, raising her hands to block the images, her thoughts. "No more, please."

The air calmed, stabilized. The shielding curtain dissolved; the vision disappeared.

Flies and mosquitoes feasted on blood.

Outside, on the porch, it was easier to breathe. But Marie knew death's smell was seeping into her clothes, her pores.

Gripping the porch rail, Marie's palms began bleeding again. She gripped harder, using the pain to focus, heighten her senses.

She heard creatures stirring—alligators, swamp turtles, and nesting herons. She heard a manufactured silence, an intention not to breathe, move, or speak.

She sensed no imminent threat. For now, she knew they wouldn't return.

Wonderingly, she shook her head.

How did she know that, *for now*, she was safe? How did she know *they* were still hiding in the bayou? Watching her.

She wiped sweat from her brow.

Night was falling fast. Her head ached from the rise in

barometric pressure. A storm was coming. "Rain washes away evidence," Parks would say, "destroys footprints, tire marks."

There were clues she was missing. Add it up. What did it mean? Poor, backwater people with new wealth? A new truck, a new pail, fresh wood, and tar to patch a falling-down house?

She couldn't shake the feeling that there was something else, here, outside, more horrific than the murdered inside. Something inhuman.

She looked skyward. The crescent moon was startlingly white. Stars blinked. No warnings there. She lowered her line of sight— the treetops stretched high, creating vibrant, moonlit silhouettes. Lower, she saw branches twisting in the breeze, and pockmarked trunks. Still lower, she saw the tangled undergrowth, and plants suffocating, straining for air.

Something else was here.

She stepped off the porch, crossed the dirt yard, and stared hard at the riotous growth beyond the shack's clearing.

An owl dove then rose skyward, a mouse clutched in its claws.

There. Not moving. Twisting in and among the brush, she saw the shadow, squiggly, thin as a garden snake.

The shadow, like veins in a body, elongated, stretching like black taffy, then thickening into a rope, doubling in size, until it looked like a stream, a river, then a bleeding black lake covering the land. It was a slick, viscous pool . . . a gleaming darkness, spreading toward the porch, the house, and Marie.

Appalled, she stumbled backward.

In seconds, darkness covered the entire yard, swallowing the landscape's colors—the brown and green.

Marie stooped, extending her bruised hands. Her hands hovered, inches from the ground, slightly trembling in the moist air.

Like a spring snapping back, the darkness coalesced, shrank itself thin, and curled, like a ribbon, about her hand.

The darkness split into tentacles, sliding high and higher, wrapping about her arm. Her shoulders. Her chest.

The smell was toxic. Organic mixed with inorganic. Nature tainted with the unnatural.

Rot was natural decomposition; this darkness was purposeful destruction.

She felt rather than saw images: darkness bleeding into the earth's warrens, seeping downward, then gurgling upward and bursting into flames. Swamplands were burning.

The darkness was rising, swirling, covering her throat; soon, her mouth.

Birds fell from the sky, vanishing, drowning in the slick pool.

She could run. But to what end?

"I am Marie."

Her skin was irritated, burning.

"Descendant of a Voodoo Queen raised on this land. This, too, is home." The words came unbidden; but saying them felt right.

The darkness had weight. It inched across her lips, seeping into her mouth. She gagged, tasting bitterness, feeling herself drowning, a heaviness suffocating, filling her lungs.

"Marie Laveau." She knew her name had power; and inside her head, she chanted: "Marie Laveau. I am Marie Laveau."

The darkness lifted, dispersed as if it had never been.

A mirage? A dream?

The stars and moon glowed bright again. Animals stirred. The water thrush sang, trilling more richly than a nightingale.

Had the murderers seen what she'd seen? She held her breath, listening again for movement.

She was the only person alive for miles.

Her ankle and hands ached. She looked back at the bleak house, hoping the newly dead didn't rise as ghosts. She wasn't sure she could carry the weight of the young family haunting her. But as soon as she thought it, Marie knew she lied.

"It is what it is."

She was who she was—part of the Laveau bloodline extending across centuries, across nations, to the *mambos* of Haiti, the shamans of Bahia, and the spiritualists of West Africa.

Visions, dreams, ghosts came to her because she could bear it, had learned to bear it without going mad. At least, not yet.

"El? You there?"

No answer. Only the shrill of cicadas. "Should I head north, back to the city? Or south?"

Again, no answer. But Marie already knew the answer. South— that's where the *loas,* the spirit-gods, wanted her to be.

TWO

Marie drove slowly, the Mustang's headlights overly bright, tires crunching on gravel. The night was pitch-dark—a weightless, normal darkness. No streetlamps. The town—if you could call it that—wasn't much longer than a city block. Squat, square buildings cast shadows. She didn't see road signs or designated landmarks. She could be anywhere. Lost in a rural wilderness.

Die here and no one would know she was gone. Marie scowled. Her imagination was spiraling out of control. Or was it?

Adrenaline spiked; her pulse quickened.

Truthfully, nothing could surpass what she'd already seen.

She squirted windshield fluid, clicked on the wipers to scrape dead bugs flattened on glass. In the rearview mirror, she didn't recognize her face, lit up by the green odometer's glow.

On the left, she could make out a no-name bait shop; just BAIT in cheap neon, dangling in the window. Next to it was Bebe's

Grocery, dark, with rockers and an old-fashioned Coke machine, shaped like a deep freezer, on the porch. A few feet down, on the right, was a mechanic's shed with a lot beside it filled with a seeming graveyard of Chevys, pickup trucks, and two high-speed airboats on trailers. Boats used for swamp tours. Extra income. Vivco Oil was next door, a two-pump gas station with a dull, spiraling, barbershoplike, red light.

Just a small town filled with working people, all in bed, because they'd be up at 4:00 AM for fishing, shrimping, salvaging, and trying to make old things work.

She'd driven to the end of the block. On the far left was a building with a dangling wood-burned sign, out of the old West: SHERIFF. A small glow radiated from inside. She parked.

Her need to pee came raging back in full force—her bladder urging, like the inevitability of birth water.

She half-skipped, half-limped across the street. Bars were on the windows. She pounded, then pushed open the door.

Someone—the sheriff?—had been sleeping at his desk, his head on his arms.

"Bathroom, please."

"That way." He pointed. She followed the direction of his finger.

Marie barely slammed the door, barely had time to pull down her panties and jeans, before her bladder let go. She hadn't even turned on the light. Face flushed, part of her felt shame. She tried to dismiss it. There was always a mind/body connection. Her body felt safe (now that she'd found someone to tell about the crime), so her body did what it needed to do.

"Police offices aren't public restrooms."

The overhead lights were still off. Marie watched as the officer leaned forward in his chair, his face moving from shadow to light in the desk lamp's glare. He was handsome, boyish, his cheeks still puffed with baby fat. A digital clock read 10:43 P.M. The fluorescent lamp buzzed.

"Sorry. I've been holding for a while."

"Not good for you." His voice had a southern twang.

"Tell me about it." She flushed.

"Looking for someone? Room for a night? Passing through?"

"I was looking for you." As soon as she said it, she knew it had come out wrong.

He walked toward her, an odd mix of easy, elegant grace with a hitch to his left step. She suspected a knee injury. He was young, barely twenty, she thought.

"Derek." He extended his hand. "Folks call me Deet."

She smothered a laugh. Only in the South would a nickname after an insect repellent not be an insult.

"Football. Tulane. Halfback." He smiled, cocky, his head tilted as if he were wearing an imaginary hat.

"No one could touch you," she said.

"Not 'less I wanted them to."

"Are you flirting with me?" Any second, she'd laugh, hysterical.

He had brown eyes, almost puppy dog. Tight, curly black hair. Why not burrow against him? Since motherhood, it had been sexual feast or famine. Making love to Parks—no, admit it, part of her had deeply loved him—had been good. But no one had touched her gently, sweetly, romantically for almost a year.

Why not let the day unwind and forget anything had happened? Marie scowled—as if sexual afterglow could wash away murder.

She reached out, her fingertips tapping the nameplate beneath his badge. "Malveaux? Sheriff Malveaux?"

He grabbed her hand, kissing her palm as if they were at a fancy dress ball. Even in a faintly lit dusty jail, this young man was all outrageous confidence. A country boy acting like a city man.

Marie slid her hand gently from his grasp. Without question, she liked handsome men. But she liked smart men better.

"I've come to report a murder."

"You serious?" His voice cracked, pitching high.

"What? No murders here?"

"Never." His affected charm gave way to thrilled awe. "Most we get is bait shop robberies. Rods and reels stolen. Coke machines busted up. Parts—carburetors, spark plugs, tires ripped from dead cars, airboats. Small town."

"Small-town cop," she replied.

He bristled. "Might as well say it—stupid. That's what you're thinking."

It was. But she didn't reply. She didn't usually stereotype. She knew better than anyone else how stereotypes demeaned. "Wicked witch." "Satan's child." "Devil." She'd been called all that and more.

She flushed. "I'm sorry. An entire family was murdered. About forty, sixty miles back. You'll need forensic analyses. A full postmortem."

Deet kept staring at her. Then he turned, his gait more stiff legged. No need to woo and appear smooth. The knee injury must have ended his football career. Her heart constricted.

At least Deet still had his life.

He flipped on the overhead light.

Marie winced. She knew she looked a mess—blood, mud, and

dirt on her jeans. Scratches on her arms and hands. She was angry for feeling self-conscious, vain. She shifted her weight, easing the strain on her sprained ankle.

Deet stared, openmouthed.

She grimaced wryly. He was probably regretting he'd given his best pickup line to such an unappealingly dirty, battered-up woman.

"Look. I'm sorry. I'm behaving badly. Rudely. I think . . . I'm in shock. I'd give anything to be back in the city," she rushed, words tumbling out of her mouth. "New Orleans. Start over. Have this day never happen. Three dead. Brutally murdered." She exhaled. Marie fidgeted, wishing she could sit.

Deet kept staring.

A drunk tank was in the far corner. An overweight red-haired, red-freckled Cajun was passed out on a cot, a flannel blanket twisted about his chest. His jacket was balled into a pillow.

The only chair in the jail was behind the cluttered desk. There was a second cell, now empty. There was a bookcase filled with old telephone books, field guides, and racing manuals. A bulletin board had layers of the FBI's most wanted flyers posted with thumbtacks.

"Sheriff, is there someone else I could talk to?"

"Deputy."

"What?"

"I'm the deputy. My brother's in charge."

Her fists clenched. She wanted to scream.

"You were in the papers," Deet said, stubbornly. "I saw your picture."

Can you even read? Marie nearly shouted. But that wouldn't be fair. This wasn't New Orleans. No urban crime or gangs. No modern police department. Who would expect someone to walk into a small town—no, not even a town, a ramshackle village—insisting that three people were unnaturally dead?

"Can you get your brother—?"

"You're that—"

"—the sheriff. Please. There's been a crime."

"You remind me of Nana."

"Don't you understand? There's been a horrific murder."

"She said you'd come."

Marie cocked her head. The boy was crazy. But she noticed that he'd stepped back, lengthening the distance between them, as if she was the crazy one.

"She told us. Told us. Said you'd come. Aaron didn't believe her. I did."

"Shut de hell up," came roaring from the corner. Marie, startled, clutched her chest. Definitely a shock reaction. Her hands and feet were growing cold.

"Shut up, Baylor." Then, to Marie, "Drunk. He'll be fine shrimping tomorrow."

Deet opened the front door. Night air laced with crawfish, algae, and salt wafted in. "Baylor!"

"What?" Baylor growled, pummeling his jacket pillow.

"I'll be back. Come on."

"You're talking to me?"

"You wanted the sheriff? Aaron won't mind me waking Nana. Least I hope not."

"What are you talking about?" Real people were sometimes harder to deal with than ghosts.

"Nana said the Voodoo Queen was coming. Said you'd be here. Nana knows. Knows everything," Deet said, his head nodding, his hand wiping sweat from his brow. "Aaron didn't want to believe her. I did. Wanted to see the famous queen. See the woman who'd taken Orleans's hoodoo, by storm." Even the *Times-Picayune* talks about you. 'Just like they talked about Marie Laveau,' said Nana. 'People, newspapers, spreading your glory.'

"Come on." He limped down the steps to a blue Ford pickup truck.

Marie smiled ruefully. Both of them were lame. Her right ankle had swelled to twice its size.

She got into the truck. Why not? The entire day had been her *fa*, fate. She was a doctor, solving crimes; a *voodooienne*, healing spiritual riffs. For both, you gathered clues, followed leads. Explored. Delved into the unknown. Not much difference in methodology, Detective Parks had taught her; and she had taught him that for a *voodooienne*, intuition could be divine grace.

The Ford turned right off Main Street and the gravel gave way to a narrowing, one-lane road. They bumped along, the truck rocking from side to side, past immobilized trailers on concrete blocks, shacks on stilts.

The Gulf was on the left and Marie could see mast lights, sparkling like Christmas, on shrimp trawlers, moored fishing boats. Not a single pleasure boat. But the boats with the lap, lap of the sea were more inviting than the dark, seemingly abandoned homes.

Deet didn't say a word and she didn't either.

In rural Louisiana, streetlamps, lights, and air conditioners were a luxury. Electricity was needed for freezing shrimp and catfish, and fueling backup generators during hurricanes. Unfortunately, decomposing bodies did just that, they decomposed.

She checked her cell. No signal. "Does this town have a name?"

"DeLaire. Used to be a plantation. Dating back to the seventeenth century. Most folks related."

The truck jerked; the front-left wheel hit a small crater. The truck made a sharp turn. Marie's head hit the side window. She cried out.

"What I tell you?" Deet's hand slammed the wheel. "There's Nana. She knew. Knows everything. Told Aaron. Told him. Nana knows everything."

The truck bounced, shaking erratically, its headlights glaring, appearing, disappearing, and zigzagging among trees.

"See. There she is."

"Where?" Marie peered. She saw the shack's outline. Steps. A porch. Then she sat back, unnerved by a rail-thin figure—a seeming white-haired ghost in a flowing, white nightgown. One hand was wrapped about the post; the other held on to the rail tight, as if fearing the wind would blow her away.

"Nana knows everything."

Marie kept silent, studying. The woman had Muskogeen in her—high cheekbones, long, straight hair. In Louisiana, slaves and native peoples had been intermarrying, intermingling blood for centuries.

Gears shifted into Park. Deet pulled the hand brake and cut the engine. "Nana," he shouted out the window. "You knew, didn't you?"

"Hush, boy. You want to wake the gators?"

Deet hop-skipped out of the truck, up the porch steps. Marie imagined that, as a toddler, he'd rushed toward his grandmother with the same delight.

She slid out of the car; her muscles had stiffened. She winced; it was difficult to put weight on her foot.

"You should be in bed," said Deet, lifting Nana off the ground, giving her a hug.

Nana slapped his hands, saying, "Let me see. Let me see her."

Marie hopped closer, wanting the woman to get a look at her. No surprises.

She stopped short.

Nana was blind, her eyes blue-gray with cataracts.

Nonetheless, Marie swore the old woman saw her. Saw her lean frame, her hair tied back, pants torn, blood and dirt on her clothes.

There was a portable oxygen tank on Nana's left, and, drawing closer, Marie could see the clear plastic tube twisting upward to the clip on her nose.

A small dog barked from behind Nana's nightgown. Marie stooped, patting its head. It was a pug with a wrinkly, smashed-in face, suede-colored fur, and black eyes. Its stubby tail wagged so hard, its whole body shook. Marie couldn't help thinking the dog was ugly enough to be cute.

"Beau," said Nana. "This be Beau."

"Two years ago, he just wandered into our yard," said Deet, "Attached himself to Nana."

Beau licked Marie's hand. She rubbed his ears.

"I dreamed you." The voice was barely a whisper, cracking and strained.

Marie straightened, stared into vacant eyes.

"Last three days. Dreamed you were coming." Nana gripped her hand. "Never expected you in my lifetime. Never expected the all powerful. To be here. In front of me."

Marie cupped Nana's wrinkled face. Beneath tissue-thin skin were spider veins, purplish, blue. Her palms felt the life inside the woman—the intelligence, the questing spirit.

Marie blinked: *She saw Nana dead. Levitating skyward, arms outstretched, with wires, tubes in every orifice.*

She gasped, stepping backward.

"You ain't seeing nothing that I ain't seen," murmured Nana.

"You know?"

"Know what?" asked a gruff voice. "What'd you see?"

Marie turned, seeing a larger man—Deet's uncle? older brother?—rising from behind Nana.

"You've scared Nana," said Deet.

"Hush, Deet, Aaron. No one scares me. Never thought I'd live to see this day."

The frail woman trembled, as if too much emotion had shaken her core.

Marie felt her magic. This woman was her—rather, who she'd be in fifty years. Similar height, weight, and spiritual gifts.

"I've seen my death," Nana said, flatly, her hands squeezing Marie's shoulders.

"What're you talking about?" asked Deet.

"No," said the other man, standing tall. Just a stubborn defiant "No."

Nana pulled back, the moonlight illuminating the map of wrinkles on her face. "Everybody dies." She caressed Marie's unlined face. "Seen you, too. You came before it was too late. We ain't the same, don't be thinking it. I'm just an old hoodoo woman. You're the Voodoo Queen."

"You're thinking of Marie Laveau, my ancestor."

"Laveau never died. Don't be thinking different. You're you. But *fa* brought you here, you're the bloodline that survived. You survived to put things right."

Nana opened her arms; Marie stepped into her embrace.

Fear, doubt drained from Marie, leaving her body limp, her soul elated. Since coming to New Orleans, she'd tried to honor her calling. Her mother, buried in a Chicago grave, had disowned her heritage; and her grandmother, whom Marie had disowned, sold tawdry spells for profit, pandering to every tourist's thrill-seeking stereotype.

"You were meant to do good in this world."

Marie wanted respite, wanted to feel forever this elder woman's love. She wasn't sure she was ready to solve another set of murders.

"Nana, you should be back in bed," said a gruff voice.

"My brother, Aaron, the sheriff," said Deet. "He'll help you."

"A few miles back," Marie murmured. "A family's been murdered."

Aaron stiffened, stone faced like Medusa's victims.

"Aren't you going to say anything?"

"We know," said Nana, softly. "Signs been everywhere. A bird's nest fell from that very tree. Even though I can't see, I saw it when it fell. Inside my head, the eggs rolling, rolling . . . them speckled eggs broken, cracked wide open. Baby birds dead."

"Sheriff, I'll take you to the scene."

Aaron raised his hand. "I'll get to it. Once I get Nana to bed."

"We've wasted enough—"

"Nana, let's get you into bed."

"Plenty of time for bed," said Nana stubbornly. "Every day's not like today."

Aaron grimaced. He was used to his orders being followed; but Marie could see his concern as he gently touched Nana's arm.

"He's right," she said, pushing aside her worry about the crime scene degrading. Delay or not, the outcome wouldn't change. The bodies wouldn't resurrect. "You need your rest."

"If you say so, child," said Nana, her mood lifting, her voice crackling with laughter. "Never thought I'd see this day. My, my. Maman Marie."

"You're chilled, Nana." Deet wrapped her woolen shawl about her shoulders.

"She wouldn't sit, relax, until you came," said Aaron. "Wouldn't let me care for her."

"Hush, Aaron. Sometimes I think you're the old woman."

Marie suppressed a smile.

Aaron led Nana, shuffling, into the house, as Deet followed, rolling the oxygen on wheels.

✳

At first glance, the home seemed as straightforward as Nana—uncomplicated, uncluttered. A rugged oak dining table with a tin coffee mug and a blazing kerosene lamp. A coal-burning stove on the left. A teapot on the grill. Smells of rosemary, thyme, and leftover roast chicken. The fireplace burned a small stack of green wood. Past the fireplace, in the far-left corner, was a cot.

"Over here," said Deet.

Marie, one hand on Nana's back, turned right. Astonished, she felt she was back in the ER. A hospital bed was raised high, like a metal crane, in the far corner. Beside it was a rotating tray with a plastic cup and straw. Next to it was an IV tree. A respirator. Even a heart monitor. A portable defibrillator was nailed to the plank wall.

Marie looked to Aaron for an explanation. His eyes were purposefully blank.

"My grandsons take care of me. Good care." Nana felt for the bed's edge. Marie helped lift and swing Nana's legs, then covered her with a blanket. Like a skilled nurse, Aaron unclipped the portable oxygen, clipped the permanent machine's tubing to her nose.

Marie looked back at the coal stove, the flaming lamp and unscreened fireplace. Portables were always hazardous; but a full oxygen system increased the danger astronomically. Any good doctor would have disallowed home use.

Aaron rubbed alcohol on the top of Nana's hand, then inserted a needle, linked to the IV, into a vein.

"What is it?" Marie pointed at the tubing.

"Saline," said Aaron.

"To prevent dehydration," Marie murmured.

"Nothing but the best for Nana," said Deet, lovingly stroking Nana's hair.

"I keep telling my grandsons I ain't afraid of dying. It's as natural as living."

Marie lifted a bottle from the nightstand. Codeine. Then lifted another. Tramadol. Weak opiates, usually the first wave of pain management. Then, the stronger opiates to relieve cancer pain. Oxycodon, fentanyl. Slow-release tablets of morphine. It was improbable that a doctor would prescribe them all.

"You've got a pharmacy here," she murmured.

"All I need is cod-liver oil," replied Nana. "And my water."

On the nightstand's bottom shelf was a glass brimming with water. Behind it was a small crèche of voodoo gods. Legba; a voodoo St. Peter; and Damballah, the snake god, were fashioned from clay. Marie recognized Erzulie, the goddess of love. Long hair, with bright red lips, she was kin to the mythic Venus. The other two spirits she didn't recognize. Blunt clay figurines: one was painted black, with black flowing hair, but it was a breasted figure with a penis, a creature not fully male or female. Some ancient totem? *She felt compelled to hold the statue, as if it were calling her name.*

She picked it up.

Blind Nana seemed to be watching her.

The statue burned in her hand, transforming itself: first, female, two breasted; next, male, flat chest, with a penis. Then it settled into what it was—double sexed. Both male and female.

Unsettled, she set the figure down.

The other figurine was decidedly female, painted teal, with lush breasts, but it didn't have any legs. The limbs were fused, like a mermaid's. Beneath the statues was another mirror, making it seem as if both figures were floating on water. In front of them were a small pitcher, a glass, and a blue bowl of water. Marigold petals floated in the bowl. Marigolds were the Virgin's flower. But they also symbolized grief, a woman's sorrow.

Marie stooped, feeling latent energy in the figurines, the echo of spirits.

She lifted the glass.

Nana, sensing her motion, said, "Water ain't for drinking. Slide the glass 'neath my bed. 'Neath my pillow, too."

"Like this?"

"That's just how she likes it," said Deet, on his knees, peeking under the metal frame.

"Connects me to the ancestors," said Nana.

Marie stood, clasping Nana's hand. "Water helps the ancestors move from their world to yours."

"Yes, yes. They visit me in dreams." Nana swallowed a moan.

"You're in pain," said Marie.

"Make no mind about me." Nana clutched Marie's T-shirt. "I've got so many things to tell you," she responded, her blind eyes fixed on Marie. "So many things to hear. I want to hear about you. Your journey. How you got here. Not just here. But back to Louisiana. The faith."

"You should rest, Nana."

"You rest, Aaron. Worry, worry, worry." Nana slapped the air, as if she could banish his worries like flies.

"I'll be here in the morning," said Marie, softly, locking the bedrail in place. "We can talk then."

Aaron nodded thankfully.

"Sleep now?" asked Nana, her voice wavering.

"Yes."

"Dream?" asked Nana, her voice reed thin, like a child's.

"Yes. Only good dreams."

"You'll make them good?"

Marie doubted she could, her own dreams were filled with trauma; nonetheless, she nodded, smoothing Nana's brow.

"You're the promised savior. Because of you, everything transforms, changes."

Marie was startled. Speculatively, Aaron stared at her, making her feel uneasy. As if she were an adversary, not a friend.

Deet only grinned.

Nana exhaled, letting her body go limp as Aaron pressed a button that caused the bed to unfold and lie flat.

The sheets and blanket were stretched tight. Marie bit the inside of her mouth, tasting blood. Nana's abdomen was swollen, as if she were newly pregnant with a misplaced child.

"Do you mind?" Marie kept her voice calm, noncommittal. She looked at Aaron. He nodded.

She laid her hands on Nana's abdomen, feeling the thickening of skin beneath bed sheets and cotton nightgown.

"Naw, child." Nana, her dead eyes fixed on the ceiling, lifted Marie's hands. "Don't worry about healing this. Just is. My time."

"Tumor? May I see?"

Nana nodded. Marie unbuttoned the nightgown. She swallowed a gasp.

Nana's stomach was distended, but thick veins, cords bluish-purple, crossed beneath flesh. She'd never seen anything like it. As if the veins were both nurturing and containing an unborn creature, as if something inside Nana were wrapped in stasis or else transforming.

Aaron kept watching Nana. Deet studied the floor.

"Was it biopsied?" Marie asked.

"Cancer," responded Aaron, quickly.

Marie cocked her head. What wasn't he saying?

"Nana, may I touch?"

"Your touch would be a grace."

Marie probed the skin; then she tapped the flesh, listening for depth. The texture was uneven, not solid like typical tumors. Rather, there seemed to be multiple tumors. Hundreds of them. Some were wide and deep; others shallow. Fingers trembling, she buttoned Nana's gown. She'd never seen or read anything about a rash of tumors concentrated in one place. There'd been people with multiple tumors—brain, liver, abdomen. But Nana seemed pregnant with a world of hurt.

She stroked the old woman's brow. "Nana, you should be in the hospital. You can't heal cancer here."

"You'd be surprised by what you can do, Miz Marie," murmured Nana.

"You need chemo, pain management. Radiation."

Nana sucked her toothless gums. Her head turned, her eyes staring past Marie. "A Voodoo Queen with full power can heal anything. Faith healing, faith healers. Some kiss poisonous snakes; some use prayer; some, like Christ, raise the dead. But every healing has a cost. I'm ready to go. All used up."

Then, abruptly, Nana lifted herself onto her elbows, flailing a hand toward Marie. Marie grabbed her hand. Nana clutched harder, her nails digging into Marie's wounds. "Remember—every healing has a cost. You're young now," she said, hoarsely, "but you need to parcel out your power, strength. Each miracle ages. Takes. I won't ask you to give. One day, you'll be like me—not much left." Exhausted, she fell back onto the pillows, her chest heaving.

"Sleep, Nana." Aaron kissed her brow.

"Yes. Sleep. Rest," said Marie, her voice unsteady.

Deet lifted the pug off the floor.

"Beau. That you?" asked Nana. "That you? Beau?"

Beau circled three times then plopped down, curling himself against Nana. As if Beau were a sleeping draft, Nana closed her eyes and sighed, her lips upturned into a slight smile.

"Do you want me to sit with you?" asked Aaron.

"No, she is," responded Nana.

"I'd be happy to," said Marie, reassuringly.

"No, the other one."

Marie raised her brows.

El stood at the head of the bed.

Nana, eyes still closed, chuckled. "Being blind doesn't mean I can't see."

"What does she mean?" asked Deet.

"She's got a spirit with her," said Marie, watching the two brothers. Neither seemed surprised. Marie marveled. Clearly the two had been raised as believers.

"It's a good spirit?" asked Deet.

"The best," said Marie, smiling at El, feeling more at ease.

"That's what she deserves. The best." Aaron caressed Nana's brow. Deet kissed her cheek. Beau snored.

Marie was deeply moved by Aaron and Deet, their big hands gently stroking Nana, patting Beau. Aaron laid an extra blanket on top of both, tucking it beneath Nana's chin, over Beau's feet. Saying good night was a bittersweet ritual. Any night, the brothers knew Nana might not wake in the morning.

"It is what it is," murmured Nana before turning onto her side, facing El.

Marie couldn't breathe. It was unsettling to hear Nana repeating El's words. She walked quickly, opening the screen door, and stepped onto the porch. Grief burned in her mouth.

Buoys, tolling in the Gulf, sounded like church bells. She was as far south as she could go.

A firefly blinked, darted, then disappeared. From inside the house, she heard the grandsons' voices—more bass timbre than words.

A sea haze was trying to swallow the moon.

Marie inhaled, letting the fog spiral deep into her lungs. She heard rumbling, then saw lightning pierce the sky. What did this day mean? Meeting Nana. A black haint, a will-o'-the-wisp—whatever it was, expanding, contracting—guiding? taunting her?—at the murder scene. Anatomically incorrect statues that seemed part of a prehistory, attuned to another world. Dreams of bodies floating downriver.

What did anything mean?

It was hot, the night filled with blood-sucking mosquitoes. An old woman was dying and she needed shawls and blankets to still the cold overtaking her body.

The screen door opened. Aaron gently pushed Deet onto the porch. "Go on back to jail, Deet. Baylor's gonna need his wake-up call."

"How come you always stay? Have fun?"

"Fun? Viewing a murdered mother and child? If you think you're ready to be sheriff, go on. Take my place."

Deet brushed past Marie, grumbling, favoring his right knee, down the steps. "I wasn't talking about that family. Talking about Miz Marie. Remember, I found her. I found her."

"You found her," said Aaron, his voice flat.

Marie looked quizzically at Aaron.

"My brother's bright enough." Aaron leaned against the porch post. "Just young. Lacks common sense."

Something bothered her, like a fly buzzing inside her mind. "He damaged his knee at Tulane?"

"His head, too," said Aaron, but Marie heard the joking undertone, the big brother complaining about his little brother.

Deet backed into the truck, butt first, then used his hands to pull his right leg inside. He pulled his left leg inside, then slammed the truck door.

"He hoped to turn pro. Get us out of this hellhole." Sadness infused Aaron's bones. Marie thought that if he smiled, he'd appear handsome. Warm brown skin, black hair, long eyelashes. But Aaron no longer seemed young. He had the weary air of someone much older. Of someone with a simmering bitterness that drained vitality. Of someone—guilty. As soon as she thought it, she knew it was true. Guilty? For what? About what?

Her thoughts didn't make sense. Aaron was the sheriff—the good man charged with kindness, keeping the peace.

"Sheriff?"

He turned, straightening, his green eyes gazing into hers. Cat's eyes.

Marie felt a connection. The understanding that both of them had suffered. Seen too much.

The truck's headlights sliced across their bodies. Then the glare disappeared, replaced with blackness and red taillights, like a monster's eyes, bouncing, retreating eerily down the battered road.

"All week, she's been telling us you'd come," Aaron said hoarsely. "Marie Laveau. The great Voodoo Queen. All she could talk about. Day, night, she wanted to stand on the porch, waiting, watching for you."

"It must've been hard."

"It was. Her sick and all."

"I'm glad that I got to meet her. To see someone who's lived," she paused, feeling overwhelmed, "her life honoring the gods—"

"Nana's done that. Said it was the one part of our African heritage that must survive—that had allowed us to survive. There's no church in this town, only Nana. Church services she's given right here." His finger pointed at the yard. "Might not seem like much, but, here, on this dirt, she saved lives. Saved my brother and me when our father died. When our mother, her daughter, turned to heroin. I was eight, Deet barely four. Nana cared for us, the whole community. She stayed, healing, birthing babies, doing ceremonies where spirits rode her."

" '*Monte shwal.*' Possession. 'Riding the horse,' so Haitians say."

"Yes. This old yard has seen its miracles." His voice swelled with pride, with gratitude for a childhood filled with miracles.

In the clearing, Marie saw afterimages of voodoo ceremonies dating back to slavery: spiritual ecstasy, swirling skirts, and drummers calling the gods. Here, women in white chanted; here men danced as Ogun, the warrior.

She saw Nana, young, standing tall, supplicants bowing, reaching for her hand, her touch.

"You love Nana," she said.

"I'd do anything for her." A shadow darted across his eyes. Aaron bent over the porch rail, his hands gripping the wood like a lifeline.

"Why not a hospital?"

"She won't allow it. Won't die anywhere but here. Won't have anyone else care for her except me and Deet."

"You know it's going to get worse."

"I know. Anything else you want to say?" he said, bitterly.

"I wasn't criticizing. You know how to work the machinery. The EKG, the defibrillator."

"I've learned."

Marie hopped on her stronger ankle, reaching for the rocker.

Aaron clutched her hand, helping her to sit.

"Thanks." Aaron was a contradiction—a smart man who believed in ghosts; a rational man led by sentiment.

"Smoke?" asked Aaron.

"Lung cancer, that's your choice. But even out here, there's a slim chance a spark might blow up the house. Worse, you might forget and light up inside."

Aaron stuffed his Marlboros back into his shirt pocket. "Drink okay?"

"I'd love one."

Aaron pulled a flask from his back pocket. "Want a glass? Some Coke?"

"It's fine as is." She clasped the tin, swallowed moonshine.

Handing back the flask, she asked, "Who's Nana's doctor?"

"Doesn't have one."

Her mind flashed back to the bottles—there'd been no record of a date, a pharmacy, a doctor. Just the potent medication.

"I didn't steal the medicine, if that's what you're thinking."

"I didn't say you did. Are you reading my mind? Or is it just your intuition?"

"Intuition."

"Deet said you didn't believe I'd come. Didn't believe Nana's prophecy."

"I believed. Just thought if I denied it, it wouldn't happen." He shifted, turning to face her, full on. "I didn't want you to come."

"I don't understand."

"No need to. You're already here." He offered her another swig of moonshine.

"No, thanks." She watched him carefully, searching his expression for an underlying truth.

Aaron kept drinking, draining the flask.

Torches lit, she saw Nana, older, bent, while supplicants, desperate, clawed, reached for her hand. Her face was a mixture of love and pain. Nana stumbled, and followers, like swarming ants, crawled over her, touching every surface of her body.

Marie didn't understand. She'd seen two images of Nana—one vibrant, triumphant, but the tenor of the second was—what? Draining, unsettling? The circumstances seemed somehow inhumane. Her visions didn't make sense.

Inexplicably, she thought: Was Nana's blindness caused by a tumor? Or was it self-enforced?

Marie felt a cold, shrill breeze slapping her face.

She said, insistently, "You know none of the machines will keep Nana alive." When Aaron didn't answer, she added, "Only a narcotic drip will ease the final pain."

"We've got that."

"You've got powerful friends. Narcotics are banned outside a hospital or hospice care. You know they require on-sight medical supervision."

Moonlight backlit Aaron's body. His face was in shadow.

"What's your payback, Aaron? What've you promised to do? Does the debt ever get paid?"

"I'll go and investigate those murders." His back was rigid. She'd pushed too hard, too soon.

Marie hopped down the steps. "I'm coming, too."

"Nana can't be left alone." Aaron got into his black-and-white Buick. "Please." He jutted his head through the open car window. "Stay with her."

"You're going to need help. It's seven, maybe ten miles back. Off the main road, near three huge oaks. Have you got a forensic specialist? If not, you're going to need NOPD's resources."

Aaron's gaze was as vacant as Nana's. Over the steering wheel, he stared straight ahead, at his family's home. An open bag of pork rinds was on the passenger seat.

She cocked her head, her voice rising, "Did you hear me?" His stoicism grated. "You don't like to ask for help?"

Aaron blinked, then started the engine. "Just don't believe the city has all the answers."

"Fair enough."

"I'll go to the scene. Figure things out."

Aaron looked like the saddest person she'd ever seen.

"There's a cot inside. I'll be back by morning."

"Good, I need to get back to the city."

For the first time, Aaron smiled. "I'm not sure you'll be finished."

"With what? I've reported the crime."

"By now everyone knows a doctor's in town." Aaron undid the parking brake. "Get some rest, Doc Laveau. You're going to need it."

"I don't understand."

Aaron turned, his right arm over the seat, his head twisted back, and pressed on the gas pedal.

"Hey." Marie jumped back from the car. "Hey," she repeated, her hand raised high, seeking acknowledgment that he'd heard her. Understood.

No response. His car, like his brother's truck, had moved in reverse, then executed a three-point turn.

The red taillights bobbled with each crunch of gravel. The police siren was silent; but the searchlight sprayed the landscape with moving spirals of blood red light.

As much as Nana had lightened her soul, Aaron had dampened it.

✖

Nana was sleeping, raspy air moving through her lungs. *El was by her bed, glowing like a luminescent butterfly.*

Beau snored. Amazing, even the dog was comfortable with ghosts.

Marie swayed, adrenaline rushing out of her like air from a balloon.

There were two cots, each with sleeping bags. Without undressing, or washing her face, she slipped inside one. It felt good to lie down. Didn't matter that she was overly warm. Didn't matter that her legs were bound inside the bag. Nothing mattered but lying down, letting go.

Shadows flickered across the wood-beam ceiling. Embers blew orange in the fireplace.

Sweat broke out on her face, behind her neck, in the valley between her breasts. It dawned on her, during summer, Aaron and Deet must've slept atop the sleeping bags for extra cushioning. Yet she couldn't wiggle her body out of the bag. She felt trapped, unable to move.

Random images flitted through her mind: the ax handle; the pool of blood; the mother and child.

Her body was shutting down. Aaron would identify the bodies. Collect clues. Strange, he didn't seem worried about locating the house and the bodies.

She was in free fall, falling toward a river of death, a slick, black pool. She tried to catch herself, grip a ledge, but there wasn't one. Flames burst upward, randomly, intermittently.

Her fall accelerated. She cried out. Her body slammed into muddy, tarlike water; she sank, ooze clogging her lungs.

Rewind.

She was falling again, her arms flailing, her fingers trying to grip a ledge. Her larynx constricted. She couldn't scream.

She woke.

Marie shuddered, feeling cold travel throughout her body. Falling was often a prelude to deeper sleep. Her brain was trying to release anxieties, solve problems. But she hadn't gone deep enough.

Disoriented, she focused on the concrete. She was alive. In Nana's house. The oxygen machine whirred and clicked, rhythmically forcing air through tubes, sounding, oddly, breathless. Startling light pierced her mind.

Aaron said, "Mother and child murdered"—how did he know?

All she'd said was that a family had been murdered. She didn't say "mother and child." Yet, if you saw the crime or crime scene, you couldn't help focusing on the woman and girl child. Had Aaron seen it? Known about it? Even Deet had said, "That family." He'd said, "I wasn't talking about that family."

She was missing connections. Clues.

She felt a weight pushing her backward. Down. Sleep. She fought to stay awake. She should be better than this—she was acting like an amateur. Parks, if he was here, would fuss: "Facts, Marie. Collect hard evidence."

She tried to rise.

Something lulled, tugging her deeper.

She looked across at Nana. She was still sleeping, wasn't she?

Inside the sleeping bag, she smelled musk and burnt wood.

How did she end up in the middle of nowhere with a dying woman? Without a car, exhausted and hurt. Hungry, and nauseous from moonshine.

A hand pressed against her chest, a curtain fell inside her mind, shielding her from—what? Her strength drained.

Moonshine. How ironic. Nothing but darkness and the reflected light of stars, millions of years ago dead.

She slept. *Hundreds of black tentacles, like snakes, wriggled across the underside of her eyelids. Moving inside her body, in sinews, in blood, leaving trails beneath her skin.*

THREE

DELAIRE

MORNING

Marie jerked awake, disoriented. She heard bees—thousands of bees, like a hive exploding, outraged by fire and smoke.

In her mind, like a child's flip book, she saw again the images of the murdered family.

Her clothes were sticky, damp with sweat. Dried blood, crusty brown, coated her pants and shirt.

El was gone.

She unzipped the sleeping bag, probed her ankle. The swelling was down. Nana's heart monitor pulsed a steady rhythm, a white wave spiking up, then down.

Beau was looking at her; his tennis ball head propped on Nana's knee. Like her, he probably needed to pee.

Wincing, Marie rose. In daylight, she could see neglect. Dust on the table. Spider webs with dead wasps. Dirty pans in the sink. Only the area surrounding Nana's bed was clean.

She heard bees again. The humming muted, then, rising high, higher and louder into the air.

She walked gingerly toward the window.

A small crowd—at least thirty black and brown men and women were in the yard, staring, facing the house. Their humming was repetitive, unnerving, like a tragic Gullah chant. It was a sound first voiced in slavery, a reverberating moan from deep, back in their throats.

Beau leaped off the bed, padded across the floor, and scratched at the closed door. Marie opened it, and the sound, and the light from the rising sun, washed over her.

The unifying hum ended as if on cue. Women wore Sunday-best hats with bows, pink and green ribbons, lace and silk flowers. Their shifts, though, were plain, frayed. Men wore clean belted pants and white shirts dulled from overwashing. Several stood erect, like deacons, in old-fashioned three-piece suits.

They reminded her of her band of followers in New Orleans. The poor, the uninsured. They were mainly elders who remembered the traditions of the drum, remembered tales of African shamans who healed with roots, spells, and ancestor prayers.

A man, bushy browed, hat in hand, looking as ancient as Nana, stepped forward. "Heard there was a doctor."

Deet, rounding from the side of the house, appeared, like an apparition. "Baylor's out shrimping. Said to say hi. I think you'll be needing this." He held out a brown leather bag. "Aaron should be back soon. Take it. He'll be back real soon."

"Deet." Her uneasiness returned. She didn't trust the brothers. She should have gone back to the crime scene.

"Here. Look." He snapped the brass lock. Inside were medical supplies.

"Where'd you get these?" Gauze, syringes, wipes. Aspirin, peroxide, benadryl.

"Did your ghost stay with Nana?" Deet's expression was smooth, without guile.

"Most of the time, Deet. The ghost stayed most of the time. Nana's fine."

He grinned, then pushed the bag into her hands. "There's a thermometer. That thing for listening to hearts."

"Stethoscope."

"Everything you need for doctoring."

"Deet, I can't practice here."

"We need you," said the man. He looked like an Ibo with his high forehead and arched cheekbones. He had the inherent dignity of an African king, but his body was thin, malnourished.

"I'm Nate."

Marie stepped off the porch, and as she did so, the small crowd edged closer.

Most of them were old, on the far side of sixty. Some, with yellowing skin; one, with a misshapen back; another, with a draining, red, infected eye. Another carried a tree limb turned into a cane, his trousers cut above his knee, his calf bandaged. Still another had a lopsided neck. A tumor? She guessed that anyone able-bodied, like Baylor, was working at sea.

Everyone looked at her, expectant.

She felt she was in the Third World. The nineteenth century. As if the DeLaire plantation had never closed.

"We need you, Dr. Laveau," said Nate.

There was a cascade of "amens," some grunting assents, some shouts of "hey'ya," while others nodded. Still others made the sign of the cross. A woman's voice called, "Speak the truth." Another responded, "You were sent, Maman Laveau. Sent to us here."

Faces, trusting, yearning, were all upturned, toward her.

Sunlight was hurting her eyes. Her body and soul ached. She needed to know if Aaron had found clues to solve the crime.

A gray-haired woman, the side of her face marked with possible cancerous moles, clasped her hand. "Help us."

Marie exhaled, reminding herself to be in the moment. She was a doctor. So heal. "I'll do what I can," she murmured.

The woman squealed and clapped her hands.

The crowd parted, hands pushing forward a girl, her hair in tight, interlocking braids. Marie guessed she was six, maybe seven months' pregnant. There was no gold band on her finger.

Beau barked.

"I'll do my best."

The pregnant teen was at the front of the line, and, amazingly, the others seemed to order themselves behind her, the sickest first, as if they had their own intuitive sense of triage.

"I'll get Nana," blurted Deet. "She'll want to see this."

Marie set the medical bag on the steps, pulled out the stethoscope. "What's your name?"

"Brenda."

"Let me listen to your heart. The baby's, too."

The girl's heart raced like a rabbit's.

"Take a deep breath. You need to relax. It's best for the baby."

"Yes, ma'am."

The baby's heart was strong, but slightly slower than the mother's. It should have been reversed—the mother's heartbeat slow and steady, the baby's fast, like a galloping horse.

"Are you taking vitamins?"

The girl's eyes remained wide, awestruck. "You're pretty."

"You should get to the nearest clinic. You need vitamins. Especially folic acid, the B vitamins. You need regular care."

"Clinic is fifty miles away."

"How old are you?"

"Fourteen."

Marie's heart constricted. In the city, at Charity, unwed pregnant teens were a familiar story. The world was askew with pregnant, underage girls. Was the sex consensual? Or was it rape, abuse?

"Is your mother here?"

The girl didn't answer. Her hands traced circles on her stomach.

"Is Brenda's mother here?"

None of the women in the yard spoke.

Marie didn't understand it. Was the girl's mother dead? How could any mother leave her daughter? She could never leave Marie-Claire. All the women in the yard were postmenopausal. Possible grandmothers. Yet none claimed Brenda as direct kin.

"I drink cod-liver oil every morning," piped Brenda, eager to please.

Marie smiled at her. "Good. Don't miss a day. Eat plenty of vegetables, fruit, and eggs. An extra teaspoon of cod-liver oil if you're ever faint. It's a good home remedy."

Cod-liver oil had fat-soluble A and D, and EPA and DHA fatty acids. Still, the girl was underage. Unmarried. A lot of complications could arise: preterm labor, anemia, preeclampsia, hypertension, and low birth weight.

"Whom do you live with?"

"Nobody," said Nate, stepping forward. "We all take care of her."

Marie wanted to argue, shame him that inadequate health care wasn't proper care for a pregnant teen, but she didn't want to scare the girl. She needed to do a pelvic. But she couldn't do an internal exam in a public yard.

Brenda had a dusting of freckles on her nose. A face filled with a teen's hopeful joy.

Marie said softly, gently, "Prenatal care is important for a healthy baby. You need to go to a clinic."

Brenda bobbed her head. But Marie could tell she was just trying not to be rude. She wouldn't go anywhere. In DeLaire, Brenda would birth the baby as best she could.

Marie watched Nate move back into line. Nana's neighbors, her parishioners, offered no other advice or explanation. They looked at the yard's dirt as if it were gold.

"Sit, Brenda. Rest," she said.

Brenda sat on the porch steps, holding her belly, murmuring over and over, "Maman Laveau's going to birth my baby. Nana said so. Nana said so."

Marie doctored, but she couldn't heal or adequately help. Her resources were too few—cotton pads, antiseptic cream, smelling salts.

The community waited patiently, as if outdoor doctoring was the most normal thing in the world.

Peter's eyes were red, and nearly closed with pus. Esther's blood pressure was 160/115. The doctor's bag didn't have any eyewash, antibiotics, or diuretics.

Next was "Tommy. Just plain Tommy." He was a ruddy-colored man with open wounds and abscesses on his legs and feet.

"Diabetes. You need hospital care."

"Can't you just fix it, Maman Marie?"

"You mean with spirits instead of medicine? It doesn't always work that way—on demand. The *loas* also want us to care for ourselves."

Tommy sneered as if he disbelieved her.

"I'm telling the truth. Faith healing isn't a justification for not seeing a doctor."

"Things are different here. Here, our country, we follow older ways."

"I can't help you."

Disappointed, Tommy staggered away.

Marie shouted at the followers, "Christianity, voodoo. In both, God, the gods, help those who help themselves."

Murmurs of dissent rippled through the crowd.

From the porch, Nana called out, her voice reed thin, "This here be Marie Laveau. What isn't healed now will be healed tonight in a ceremony."

Shocked, Marie looked back at Nana, standing on the porch, clinging to Deet's arm. In his left hand, Deet held a cigarette. Beau sat on the bottom step.

There won't be any ceremony!" she wanted to shout, but she felt bad about denying Nana in front of her community. She felt DeLaire was like the world beyond the looking glass, where up was down and down was up.

An elder stepped forward, and as if it was the most natural act in the world, she opened her shirt to show a lump, like a golf ball, inside her otherwise shrunken breast.

Surgery was the only option.

"Your name?" Marie whispered.

"Luella."

"You must see a specialist," Marie said. "Come to Charity Hospital in New Orleans. I'll see that you're well cared for."

"I'll stay right here," Luella said, smiling angelically. "Nana's done good with her herbs and such, but she says you're the best. The greatest Voodoo Queen. Nothing you can't do."

"That's not true, Luella. All of you, listen to me. For serious ills, you need to come to Charity. I can return, but many of you still need hospital care."

"No—a ceremony," demanded Nate. "Nana says you'll heal."

The mole-faced woman stroked Marie's arm, saying, "We believe in you. I believe."

Nana was sitting, smiling and swaying, in the porch rocker.

Marie looked back at the small crowd. Too-serene faces stared at her with simplistic faith. Faith that she could fix any wound.

Marie felt as if she'd stumbled into a mad world. A backwoods world with a raw belief in voodoo. Yes, miracles happened, like faith healing in Christianity. The blind saw; the crippled walked. Voodoo had its miracles, too. But faith wasn't a substitute for medicine.

She was nearing the end of the line. The "patients" she'd seen congregated around Nana and on the porch. She realized that, except for Brenda, they all had serious, life-threatening ills. The "less serious" were really those who were stable but dying.

A fiftyish man, his throat scarred, said, "Cancer. Years back, spent some time in the hospital. Now I come to you. Nana told us you were coming. Told us there's nothing you can't do." His voice was barely above a whisper.

"You need to go back to the hospital. See your doctor."

"Don't have a doctor. After Vietnam, spent time in a hospital. Didn't do me much good."

She was startled. The survival rate for throat cancer was in years, not decades.

The veteran patted Marie's hand as if he was comforting her. "I'll come tonight. Me and Tommy."

"I won't be here tonight."

" 'Course you will. Nana said a ceremony. A healing."

He squeezed her hand and went to the porch to sit beside Nana.

Marie did her best to counsel those with abnormal growths, with fluid-filled lungs and impaired breathing. Cancer flourished— lung, breast, blood, and skin. Most of the villagers claimed they'd been diagnosed. By whom? Nana's absent doctor?

When she insisted that a clinic or hospital visit was necessary, each patient responded, "I'll be here tonight."

"I won't," she began repeating, over and over. "I've got to get back to the city."

Everyone disbelieved her. Nodded as if she were crazy.

Nana preened on the porch. Amazingly, she was enjoying herself. Her head and hair bobbing, her blind eyes darting. The dying faith healer was exultant, presiding over a mainly dying flock. It didn't make sense.

Finishing her bare-bones exams, the villagers began humming

again. This time the sound was jubilant, as if acknowledging that Nana's promise had been fulfilled.

There was a call and shout: "Maman Laveau," "Dr. Laveau," "Marie Laveau."

Deet kept exclaiming, "Nana knew. She prophesied. Nana knew."

A juba began, a ritualized ring circle, an African call and response. Old bodies danced in Nana's yard—hands slapping knees, chests, and thighs; feet stomping; spinning bodies like dervishes. Brenda clapped her hands, her big belly swaying. Nate, arms upraised, shuffled with grace.

Everyone was celebrating, and all Marie could see was poverty's worst ills and she, a doctor, without the ability to heal.

Nana, her blind eyes open, was enthralled, seeing what only she could see.

She needed to escape. Marie pulled Deet aside. "Outhouse?"

"Round back," he said, clapping, shouting with the passionate others.

Marie shook her head as Nana, oxygen tubing attached to her nose, faced and blessed the dirt courtyard as if she were a queen.

※

Marie squatted in the outhouse; the pungent smell fit her mood and circumstances. She couldn't doctor effectively, and she didn't believe an on-demand voodoo ceremony would cure all ills.

Erratic flies, mosquitoes, landed, fed, then flew. She held her breath. Urine flowed.

Her skin itched; hives spread along her arms.

"Damn it to hell." Where was Aaron? As soon as she thought it, she heard a car, the juba quieting, and shouts of recognition.

Zipping her pants, hop-skipping, running as best she could, she rushed forward, rounding the shack's corner, eager for Aaron's assessment of the crime scene. Did he identify the victims? Collect significant evidence?

Slowly, too slowly, Aaron was exiting the car.

She stopped short. A willow branch slapped at her arm. Look at me, she thought.

Aaron's gaze was downward, focused on the dirt.

Look at me. Tension coiled in her stomach. Look at me.

Aaron looked up as if she'd shouted his name.

Marie saw ghosts, saw the murdered family standing apart from Aaron.

She started screaming, "What did you do? What did you do?"

Father, mother, baby. A trinity, lost and woebegone.

She collapsed onto her knees.

Deet reached for her.

"Leave me alone!" she shouted.

She saw it: *A canister of oil—thick, dripping like a black stream onto the floor. The bodies were dragged into the center of the cabin. The mother, faceup; the father, facedown. The baby wrapped in the stained pink blanket was picked up and placed on the floor between her parents.*

Gasoline mixed with blood, a greenish-black with red.

A match was struck. Flames and smoke shot upward.

She looked across the yard. "Why?"

Aaron looked like an undead, his limbs heavy, his face drained of emotion.

Stumbling from the ground, ignoring the pain shooting up her leg, she raced toward Aaron. She punched, scratched, his chest, shoulders, and arms.

"You watched," she wailed. "Why? Why didn't you stop them?"

Deet pinioned her arms.

Followers exclaimed, pushing forward, behind Aaron. Nana moaned, "Aaron baby, Aaron baby." Deet shouted back to the porch, "Everything's all right, Nana. All right."

She stopped fighting, twisting from Deet's grasp.

The bewildered crowd quieted.

Contemptuous, she glared at Aaron.

He murmured, "I'll take you back to your car."

Breathing heavily, she asked, "Why?" Then whispered, "Nana."

Suddenly, she understood—the pills, the high-tech gadgetry, all of it useless bribery.

"She's dying. None of the machines can stop that. Who paid for them, Aaron? Who paid you?"

Bodies pressed, forming a circle around her and Aaron. Anxious, worried faces. In the high-noon sun, she saw sweat beading on foreheads, necks, and arms.

She smelled her own dirt, smelled Death again. *Rank. Penetrating the damp air.*

"Forgive them."

The crowd parted.

It was Nana, untethered from her oxygen canister, gripping Tommy's arm. "For me. All for me."

Women cooed: "Go back," "Rest," "Don't fall." Luella put an arm around Nana. Deet supported her left side. Like an amoeba, the community shifted, fanning out to the left, right, standing behind Nana.

They'd drawn a line in the sand.

On the planes of Aaron's face, she could see the cottage burning to the ground. See Aaron standing apart from the murderers, the fire starters.

She blinked. Aaron knew she'd seen inside his soul.

Aaron hugged Nana. Nana patted his back. And when he stepped away, all the DeLaire residents—even Brenda—were scowling, stern and fierce, as if looks could kill or turn Marie to stone.

She shuddered. Nothing was as it appeared. Folks, in their impoverished Sunday best, were menacing, threatening. As if possessed by some unknown evil.

It was clear that anyone who imperiled Nana was the enemy. Her grandsons were protected as well. Whoever Nana loved, the entire town loved. Marie could almost admire the sentiment. But she couldn't keep from thinking, who had loved the murdered young family? Who had stood for them?

"My grandsons mean well," said Nana, her voice raspy thin without oxygen. "Always mean well."

"You let them do it. Bargain with the devil." As soon as she'd said it, she knew it was true.

Nana had known her medical care was both payment and bribe. For what? The murder of a new family? Clearing criminal evidence? Or something even more sinister?

She and Nana both trembled. A burst of hot air blew into the yard, rattling leaves.

"I'm a weak, foolish woman," said Nana.

"Why? Why did you allow it?"

"They needed to feel useful. To help my dying sit easier." Tears filled her cloudy eyes. "I chose my grandbabies over faith. I'm not proud of it."

"Aaron's committed a crime."

"He was just looking out for me. For the village."

Appalled, Marie looked around at the ragtag band of followers. "What did the village get out of this?" As far as she could tell, every resident lived well below the poverty line.

She turned to Aaron. "Only the Malveauxs have benefited from your sins and crimes. If you've been gracing the community with your largess, I don't see it."

Aaron's jaw clenched; unflinchingly, he faced her.

Marie screamed at the villagers, "How could you allow it?"

Nate, Luella, Tommy—all of the villagers stared blankly.

She screamed at Aaron, "How could you? Obstruction of justice. Accessory to murder. Imperiling public safety. Betraying one's oath to protect and serve."

Knees buckling, Nana cried out, wailing almost loud enough to wake the dead. Deet lifted her, carrying her away. Followers closed ranks, blocking Marie's access to the house.

There was no gratitude. No pleasure that a doctor and a *voodooienne* was here, trying to help, to set things right.

Faces were strained, almost feral. How far would they go to protect Nana?

Aaron raised his hand. "Y'all go home now. I'm going to take Dr. Laveau to her car. Time for her to go home."

There were murmurs of assent. Still, no one moved.

"Go on. This is upsetting Nana."

Nate stood his ground. Old men, fierce, protective, made fists;

women, thin lipped, crossed their arms over their chests. Only
Brenda turned and walked away.

"Get into the car, Miz Marie," said Aaron, then, more
adamantly, "Dr. Laveau, get into the car."

Aaron opened the passenger-side door. Marie touched the
glass-cage barrier between back-and front seats.

"I should be driving," she said, slipping into the car. "You
should be cuffed in back."

Aaron shut the door, and walked around to the driver's side.

Through the front window, Marie had a clear view of Nana's
faithful. All happiness had drained from them. They looked just
like what they were—a forgotten, dispossessed, and dying people.

Aaron sat behind the steering wheel.

"I'll tell the police," she said.

"No one's going to believe you. Ever."

"I'll make them believe. See you prosecuted."

He shrugged as if he hadn't a care in the world.

"You're all crazy." *Crazier than her now seeing ghosts in the side
mirror, seeing El and the murdered family standing by the side of the
road.*

"You'll pay," she said, hoarsely.

"Tell me something I don't know." Aaron turned the key and
the engine roared.

The townsfolk started humming again, like smoked, outraged
bees.

The car in reverse, Aaron pressed on the gas. His boots were
mud sticky, layered with burnt ash.

She couldn't wait to get the hell out of DeLaire, to drive north, back to New Orleans. To drive out of a world where up was down, down, up—a mixed-up looking-glass world where she didn't have the power to set things right. But she swore that soon, one day she would. Justice wouldn't be denied. Not for a baby girl who'd never experienced more than a month's worth of life. Not for a baby who had to die in her mother's arms.

Threatening rain finally fell—water would be flooding the crime scene. But the water was too late to prevent arson. It was just a summer shower, a prelude to a storm.

Marie bit her lip. She wouldn't cry, even though her soul felt battered, blown apart, caught in the eye of a hurricane.

II

New ways, city ways,
Folks die,
Everyone drowns.

FOUR

Marie stood in the police captain's office. He hadn't asked her to sit. But the overweight Creole glared at her, his feet on the table and his fat hands holding a cup of coffee and a pecan praline.

Everything about the cop was disrespectful—but his disrespect for her didn't matter compared to his disrespect for the murdered family.

Captain Beauregard had pig's eyes, little gray slits inside rolls of fat. Today, another man—dressed in an expensive suit—stood to the left of Beauregard. The captain had introduced him as "Agent Walker, Special Agent James Walker."

The albino man looked nothing like James Bond. She would have laughed if she hadn't been so angry.

For three nights, she'd completed her red-eye shift at Charity and instead of immediately going home to her daughter and bed, she'd come straight to the station, badgering Beauregard about the DeLaire investigation.

"Just time. It all takes time," Beauregard said, over and over.

Yet she realized he'd been careful not to give promises. "Time" was vague and elastic.

Now, four days later, Beauregard was introducing a strange officer who seemed inordinately calm, and Marie couldn't help feeling wary.

Beauregard fit the description of most Louisiana officers—prime candidates for cardiac arrest, stroke, and hypertension. Walker was so fit he looked like he'd come from another planet. Maybe he *was* an agent? FBI? But if so, why? Why now for, supposedly, a noncase? And why would Walker look at her as if she were the suspect rather than a citizen reporting a crime?

Beauregard nervously fiddled with his tie. "Dr. Laveau, there's nothing to substantiate your claims. Why should I believe you over a man of law?"

"Why would I lie?"

"I can think of a number of reasons. Self-importance. Fame."

She lurched forward. Beauregard flinched. His feet dropped to the floor, and his rolling chair skittered back.

"Assaulting an officer," said Walker, "won't win you any friends."

"I don't need friends. Just officers willing to do their job."

"Sheriff Malveaux found nothing," Walker answered blandly.

"The sheriff obstructed justice. Allowed the murderers to destroy evidence."

"That's a serious charge," said Walker, his eyebrow lifting like a hawk's wing.

Marie ignored him and glared at Beauregard. She could see the bulldog of a man he'd once been. Age and insensitivity had fattened him; but today he seemed especially uneasy, subdued, as though Walker were his superior.

"Malveaux's corrupt," she said, stubbornly. "I've told you that."

"Why should we believe you, not him?" asked Walker.

"Because I'm telling the truth. An innocent family was brutally murdered. It happened. I didn't imagine it."

Beauregard stood, looking like a top ready to tip over. "As I said, this case is outside my jurisdiction."

"You said you'd coordinate with the state police."

Beauregard shifted nervously. "I called the state police. No one's missing."

Something was awry. Her head ached. She felt animosity in the room—as hot as Walker was cool.

"We've got plenty of crime in New Orleans," answered Beauregard. "Please, Dr. Laveau, worry about what's here."

"New Orleans. America's murder capital. I know the statistics. Seen the victims in the ER. But that doesn't mean we should value any one death less."

Beauregard shifted his gaze.

Walker, deadpan as ever, focused on her.

Marie stepped closer to Walker. "Who are you? State police? Internal affairs? No, I don't think so." His face was angular, close shaven, almost gaunt. White haired, white lashes and brows, his eyes were nearly clear, tinted with pinkish red veins. "I doubt you're a law officer."

Walker didn't flinch. "I don't care what you doubt. Just stay out of my way."

"Are you threatening me?"

"Look, Dr. Laveau," said Beauregard, moving from behind the desk. "I did have the state boys follow up. The whole town says the L'Overtures must've moved on."

She spun around. "L'Overture? Was that their name?"

"L'Overture. John and Mimi L'Overture."

"And the baby's name?" She tried to still her trembling. "The little girl?"

"No word. There," Beauregard blustered, "I've told you all I— we"—he looked at Walker—"know."

If nothing had happened, why mention a name? Three days— finally a name. L'Overture. Finally, an admission that a family had existed.

Like throwing a bone to a dog, she was supposed to be satisfied.

"Let me see you out," said Walker.

"You're not from Louisiana," she said, emphatic.

Walker's jaw clenched. "Doesn't matter where I'm from."

Beauregard was sweating, wiping his sticky hands on his pants.

"You're not law enforcement. Not a Louisiana native."

"Neither are you. Heard you were a Chicago foster-care brat."

"Louisiana is my home. I care about it. My mistake was thinking Captain Beauregard cared. You, Agent Walker—you're not an agent of anything, are you? You don't care about a damn thing."

Walker sneered, "And you, Dr. Laveau, care about everything. Care about 'your people,'" he sneered. "Isn't that how they say it down South? 'Your people.' But you're a city girl. How did it feel to visit Louisiana's back roads? The wild swamps? To go country?"

He was baiting her.

"How did it feel to stand on that porch?"

Air whistled through her teeth. Walker had watched her in the bayou. Had committed murder.

She could see oaks, cypress, and Spanish moss, gray like rotten tinsel, see Walker watching her through long-range binoculars, watching her grieve.

She wanted to tear the sneer from Walker's face.

She looked at Beauregard. Shame flushed his fat jowls. She knew Louisiana was famously corrupt. Yet it still surprised her when she could put a face on it. Beauregard, somebody's husband, father, was another betrayer.

"You won't get away with it," she said to Walker.

"Threatening me with voodoo dolls?"

"I don't do voodoo dolls."

Walker was her adversary, at least one of them, and she'd need every skill to outwit, outmaneuver a criminal protected by the law.

She wanted, needed, to know—why? Why kill a child? Her parents? "Motive," Parks had taught her, "is key. Motive unravels everything. Motive is the hangman's rope."

Nauseous, she looked out the inneroffice glass wall at the busy police hive: rows of desks, the requisite water cooler, an overworked copier, worn computers, hundreds of mug shots posted on the smoke-stained walls. Officers—some uniformed, some in street garb—were typing reports, and handcuffing, transporting criminals—petty thieves, vagrants, and repeat offenders. How many of them knew that a criminal, by act or omission, was in their captain's office? How many knew Beauregard was corrupt? How many of them were corrupt?

In the reflective glass, she could also see Walker towering over the squat Beauregard.

Flesh rolling over his belt, ballooning his shirt, Beauregard sidled up to her. "Maman Laveau, let it go." His voice was low. Marie detected sympathy. Empathy?

He called her "Maman," her voodoo honorific.

"They don't want your interference in DeLaire. Keep at it and there might be consequences."

"Are you threatening me, too?"

"No," said the captain, his voice thin bravado. "There's no evidence of a crime."

"Liar."

"Dr. Laveau"—Beauregard opened his door—"let me walk you out."

"I know the way."

"You'll come back." It was a statement whispered as she passed.

Beauregard's body blocked the sight line between her and Walker.

She nodded slightly.

Beauregard looked relieved. What the hell did that mean?

Beauregard had played her all along, and when she didn't go away, Walker was called. Walker, who, apparently, intimidated Beauregard more than she did. But Beauregard seemed to be asking for her help. It didn't make sense. Some things she could divine, but with Beauregard, she'd hit a blank wall.

Aaron had said she wouldn't be believed. That wasn't quite right. She was believed, but that didn't stop the cover-up, the lies, or the likelihood of conspirators lying to each other.

"I'll go to the state police myself."

"I wouldn't do that."

"You should listen to Beauregard," said Walker, softly.

Marie looked at Beauregard's fat, guilty face.

Police and doctors were supposed to be kin, counterparts in a terrible yin/yang. Police handled robberies, incest, and murder; doctors handled the resulting gunshots, suicides, and knife wounds.

"You disappoint me, Captain Beauregard." Then she looked scathingly at Walker.

Walker was everything Beauregard wasn't—tall, thin, white, dressed in an expensive tailored suit.

"I'm not an idiot, Walker. I won't let this rest."

"You think you can hunt me?" His voice was taut, mimicking his body.

"I know I can."

※

Marie moved through the maze of office desks and chairs. Some of the policemen tipped their hats, others stared, curious, still others showed outright hostility to a civilian interfering with police work.

She could feel both Beauregard and Walker watching her back.

It was an odd choice of a word—"hunt." That's what it had felt like in the bayou, a hunt. The family had been hunted and killed as if they were animals. On their bayou porch, she'd been watched as if she was prey. But just as Walker had decided then not to harm or pursue her, she'd decided not to hunt or be a predator now. Timing was everything.

She looked back at Beauregard, standing in the doorway, diminished and unsettled, while Walker, deadly as a tiger, leaned nonchalantly against the door frame as if he hadn't a care in the world.

✖

Outside, in the bright sun, Marie blinked, shading her eyes. In seconds, sweat caused her shirt to stick to her breasts and abdomen; her pants hitched tighter against her crotch.

In Louisiana, every August was the same. Heat from the Sahara blew across the sea, the Caribbean islands, and into the southern United States. Hurricane season. The city was a giant swamp bowl, twenty feet below sea level.

Even the air was pregnant with moisture, making Marie feel as if she were walking through water. Swamp air, rather than swampland. Sultry, almost unbearable.

She needed to think, come up with a plan.

She stared upward at the blue sky—not a cloud on the horizon. But that didn't mean anything. Any moment rain would come, thundering, showering, and sweeping up from the Caribbean and into the Gulf. The radio said there was Katrina, a tropical storm. Most times storms were small or medium size, but there was always the tense expectation that the "big one" was possible, even probable.

It was a never-ending cycle during hurricane season. Will it or won't it become a hurricane?

The sky was sweet baby blue. A hurricane hadn't ravaged New Orleans since Betsy in '65.

✖

She was tired, spent. She could use a stiff drink—anything but a hurricane, the tourist drink of punch and cheap rum.

Last night—or was it this morning?—she'd lost two patients, an elder without insulin, a child with pneumonia. Beauregard had wasted four possible crime-solving days. Ninety-six hours. If Parks were here, he wouldn't have allowed it. She was merely a medical doctor who Beauregard had blown off.

✕

She felt a strong urge to see water. The Mississippi—*misi-ziibi*, named by the Ojibwa as the "great river," was North America's largest river road. At its mouth, river water commingled with Gulf waters. She couldn't help believing the L'Overtures, the viscious darkness, and the waterways were interconnected. Water usually signified amniotic fluid, rebirth. Did it mean anything that Brenda was about to give birth, that Nana appeared pregnant, and that the DeLaire newborn was dead?

She walked toward the river, stopping at the Café du Monde to order a café au lait to go.

New Orleans, despite sweltering heat, was not the land of iced coffee and Starbucks. Hot coffee laced with chicory and mixed with steaming hot milk was, for most residents, the drink of choice, at least when they weren't drinking Sazeracs, absinthe mixed with rye.

The outdoor patio was packed. A duo, a young man with a guitar, a girl with a violin, strummed and bowed, a G-rated, "Fire on the Bayou." They were entertaining the tourists, the local schoolchildren on summer vacation. Scattered among them were prostitutes and pimps, all-night blues and rock musicians drinking their "morning coffee" before going to bed all day, to work again all night.

She paid for her coffee, then walked toward the river, powdered sugar from the café's beignets sticky on the concrete and her shoes.

Pigeons sauntered, pecking fluffs of the sweet bread.

Occasionally, someone recognized her and tipped a hat, nodded a head, or made the sign of the cross to ward against her supposed evil.

The real evil was inside the city police department.

She kept walking toward the river, down the promenade where tourists strolled, lovers kissed, and hopeful fishermen tried to catch catfish. Leaning over the rail, she watched the swirling muddy brown water. No visible fish, no blue-green algae, only dirt and more dirt. The public health department warned about PCBs and heavy-metal toxins. Steamboats, cargo ships, and pleasure boats spilled their refuse into the water. There was the romance of rolling down the river as well as the poison. For poor people, unhealthy fish was better than nothing at all. Like New Orleans, the river was a contradiction—beautiful but capable of being deadly.

El strolled beside her. "It is what it is."

"And I'm going to find justice, El. Solve the crime."

The L'Overtures stood at the Riverwalk guardrail, staring at the waves and swirling brown currents.

It was the first time she'd seen the ghosts since the bayou. It was as if they were tourists, enjoying the city sights, a family vacation. If they were alive, they'd be chattering, eating taffy. The baby would be squealing gleefully; her parents would be showering her with kisses.

Marie turned toward El. *She looked fragile, translucent, and cold.* Not at all the warm, big-boned, and big-hearted woman she'd loved in life.

"I wish I could have saved you, El. You were so much more than a friend."

If El were substance, Marie would have embraced her.

El pointed at the water.

Marie looked. Nothing unusual. White seagulls diving, and brown, muddy water stretching toward a stormy horizon. "I don't see anything."

A shape rose from the water, spiraling upward, water dripping like a rough waterfall. She dropped her coffee. Beige liquid splattered, the cup rolled over the wharf's edge. *When the muddy Mississippi fell away, the shape, beneath it, glinted like diamonds, sparkling rainbows, revealing the outlines of a woman's face, with white foam-filled hair.*

A spirit-loa rebirthed in water.

Tourists kept chattering, leaning over the wharf's rail, walking, arm in arm, or staggering with their plastic cups of beer. A boy lost his balloon, wailing as it floated high. The *Natchez* riverboat churned watery foam while a quartet played ragtime, and passengers, their hands dirty with spice, sucked crawfish heads.

The vision was hers. And El's. And the L'Overture ghosts'.

"She's beautiful," murmured Marie. *The figure spun, facing the shore, facing Marie. Her breasts were teal, her legs fused into one.*

El whispered, "See."

"I'm seeing," she answered, awestruck. "I don't believe it, El. A mermaid."

El disappeared. But the water spirit was poised atop the water, her hands, droplets of coalescing water, rose upward, then lowered, stretching, reaching across the watery miles toward Marie.

The L'Overtures, too, had faded.

"Maman Laveau."

Startled, she turned.

Deet, eyes bleary, stubble on his cheeks and chin, stood beside her holding Beau.

She knew immediately that Nana had died. Her heart ached. "I'm so sorry." She hugged Deet. Beau, his small head pressed between their chests, licked her face.

"When did she die?"

"Last night."

"And you didn't stay? You drove here?"

"Nana wanted me to. Before her last breath, she told me to leave."

"How did you find me?"

"Told me where you'd be. Said you'd be right here on Riverwalk."

"She knew?"

"Even about your visits to the police."

Marie averted her gaze. The Mississippi was still dirty brown; the water was placid, flat like a mirror.

"Nana understood why you needed the city police." Deet set Beau down. The pug peed on the boardwalk's iron rails.

"You and Aaron ought to do what's right. Report, solve the crime."

Deet shook his head.

"I forgot," she said bitterly. "Tin sheriff and deputy. You don't care about victims. Take the money and run."

"We didn't take any money."

"Just medical supplies. You think that isn't money, Deet?"

Tears filled his eyes. "Aaron always looked out for us. Tried to do it right. For Nana. Me." The young man who'd confidently tried to woo her was gone.

"Sit. Tell me about Nana." She pulled Deet toward a bench. Beau waddled, and lay between their feet.

"Aaron said she'd live longer. But she didn't. He said she wouldn't have any pain. But she did."

Marie heard the child's wail in Deet's voice. She heard his fury at Aaron, his grief that his grandmother had left him.

"There were plenty of sedatives. Even morphine."

"She wouldn't take anything. Said it was her punishment. For betraying you, the faith."

Marie closed her eyes. Nana's death would have been brutal, filled with excruciating pain. She sat back, straining for air.

"That's why Aaron did it. To help Nana."

"Did what?" She kept her voice soft, her eyes fixed on the river. She wanted to hear Deet say it. Confirm what she knew but hadn't actually seen.

"Let them burn the bodies."

"Who?"

Deet didn't answer.

"Did Aaron kill the L'Overtures?"

"No. Aaron wouldn't kill anybody."

"Just cover up murder," she said, scornfully.

"DeLaire isn't like New Orleans."

"Why isn't it?"

Deet's eyes were dry, his voice brittle.

"Tell me, Deet, who committed the murders?"

"I don't know."

"You're lying."

"No, I don't know."

"But you can guess."

Fear settled on his shoulders like crows. He twisted his head, scanning the Riverwalk crowd, almost as if he expected someone to appear.

There was a panhandler shaking a Dixie cup of coins, a street preacher singing "Amazing Grace" and sounding like a foghorn. Everyone else was intent on trying to enjoy the too-hot, sunny day.

Beau's nose nudged her hand. She stroked his head.

"Only thing I could do well was play football," said Deet, continuing. "Got injured in my first season. I kept begging for coach to let me play. I was a rookie wanting to show off.

"'One play,' I pleaded." He swallowed. "My only play. Hit from both sides. My left knee buckled and I felt muscle tearing, the bone shattering. I'd nowhere else to go—but back to DeLaire."

"To Nana."

"Yes." He leaned against the wood. "Nana loved me. No one will ever love me like she did."

Marie wished she could hold Deet like she held Marie-Claire and soothe away his sorrow. But she already sensed nothing could ease him.

"I can't stop seeing her dying," Deet murmured. "Even when I sleep. Close my eyes." Compulsively, his hand clutched his khaki-covered knees. "Aaron's screaming 'cause Nana won't take the medicine. 'Take the medicine,' he's begging. 'Take the medicine.'

"At the end, she blamed me, too, because I supported Aaron. Not the murder cover-up. But him doing what he thought best to heal Nana."

Deet's body shuddered, as if a cold wind had curled about his bones. "At the end, she wouldn't look at either of us."

"Tell me about the L'Overtures."

"Can't."

"Won't?"

"It wasn't easy for Aaron."

"You think dying is easy?"

"They were already dead!" Deet shouted. Passersby turned, staring. "Aaron didn't kill them," he said, more quietly, "Everybody in DeLaire is dead."

Beau barked, tried to claw onto Marie's lap. A seagull dived, screeching and plucking a fish from water.

Deet placed Beau on Marie's lap. "Nana wanted you to have him."

"I can't."

"She made me promise. Said Beau needed to be with you. Needed to be with someone who had the sight. Said Beau wouldn't be happy otherwise."

Beau's pink tongue lolled. He seemed to be saying, "Take me." Her heart went out to the little dog.

"I'll take Beau if you tell me who—"

"I don't know."

"But you suspect someone?"

No answer.

"Who gave Nana her medical equipment? Who did Aaron barter with? Report to?"

Deet's face twisted with guilt.

"Was it Walker?"

Deet stood abruptly, his right hand, itching, sliding up and down his arms. "All I have left in this world is my brother. I won't get him killed." He patted Beau's head. "Beau, you be good for Maman Marie."

"Deet, if I don't press for the truth, who will?"

His eyes were bleak. For a moment, she thought Deet was going to tell her. Confess what he knew.

"Nana said she'd be seeing you." He'd regained control. "Told me to tell you that El was right. Something about the world being hard on women. You know El?"

"She was a friend of mine." Behind Deet, the sky was bright blue. "Did Nana say anything else?"

"Yes. But it didn't make sense. She was in pain, nearly dead."

"What did she say?" She hated pressuring Deet, but she needed leads. Needed to make up for the time Beauregard had wasted. He was Walker's lackey.

"Nana said, 'Mine the water.' No, I think, 'Mind the water.' Or was it 'mine'?" He shrugged. "I don't know."

What did that mean? "Mine," "Mind," either way, it didn't make sense. She leaned over the rail, watching the brown pools swirling about the pilings. Three years after acknowledging her heritage, she'd had enough death and dying to last a lifetime. In medicine, you generally knew why someone died. You fought a known enemy. Bacteria. Virus. Lungs perforated by knives and bullets. Yet, as a *voodooienne*, she was a detective in two worlds—one tangible; the other intangible. Complications were challenging.

"See you, Derek."

Arrested by hearing his proper name, Deet studied her. "Maman Marie, please. Don't come back to DeLaire. Stay here. Let it go. For my sake. For Aaron's and Nana's."

"I promised I'd return."

"They don't want you back."

"Not even Brenda? Her baby's almost due."

Deet's lids half-closed, hiding his feelings. He knew Brenda and her baby needed help.

He repeated, "They don't want you back. They loved Nana."

"In the afterlife, I can't imagine Nana resting easy. Can you, Derek?"

He turned, limping away like an old, battered man.

"Wouldn't she want me to support her community?"

No response.

The air shimmered; the water's surface rippled.

"Tell Aaron I'm coming," she shouted. "With Nana dead, I claim the community. Tell them. I am . . . I shall be their Voodoo Queen."

Deet kept walking, his shoulders hunched, his hands stuffed into his pockets.

In a voodoo ceremony, Deet would be Legba. Except Legba, with his walking cane, opened the spirit gates. Everything about and inside Deet was shutting down. Secrets did that, she thought— spoiled like cancer.

He'd reversed himself. In DeLaire, he'd been eager as a schoolboy to take her to Nana; now, he was warning, wishing her away.

Marie cupped Beau's little head, her thumbs stroking his furry jowls.

Beau's gaze fixed on her. He had an old soul.

"Time for me to set wrongs right? To do what Nana couldn't, wouldn't, do? Blink once for no. Twice for yes."

Beau's stare didn't change.

Marie sighed.

"Come on, Beau." Holding him by his belly, she set him down, letting his paws touch the boardwalk. "Let me know if you get tired."

Beau's stomach shook, his four legs moving twice as fast as her two.

※

If she forgot the day's beginning, she'd enjoy her stroll down Riverwalk. Her sprained ankle had healed. Her hands no longer hurt. She wasn't wounded, physically, just plain old tired. A tiny breeze wafted off the river.

Beau sniffed and peed at every post. Even when there couldn't possibly be any more urine inside him, he lifted his stumpy back leg.

"You know, I don't usually like small dogs. My last dog, Kind Dog, was big. Brave." She still had nightmares remembering Kind Dog's howling while Parks broke down the bedroom door. Marie-Claire was safe because of Kind Dog's fierce bravery against the vampire.

Beau barked, his baseball-size head jerking up.

"Doggy," shouted a toddler in a stroller, sounding just like her daughter.

Marie was convinced there was a rule in the universe that all children under five sounded the same. A child shrieked and every mother turned; a laugh, every mother smiled; a cry, and every mother grew anxious. She'd seen it happen on streets, in grocery and department stores. A hundred times she'd heard a cry and gone searching for Marie-Claire.

Beau kept pace beside her.

Marie watched a mother cooing to her baby, wrapped in a

sling; another walked holding her two children's hands. A mother-
to-be, uncomfortably pregnant during a steamy August, waddled.
Another woman wore a pink T-shirt with an arrow, pointing down,
and the words, BABY ON BOARD. And another pushed an expensive
stroller strong enough for a safari trek.

Marie stopped. Beau, not much higher than her ankles,
bumped into her.

Strange, she'd never seen so many pregnant women or women
with small children. There was a mother, kneeling, her arm around
her child's waist, pointing at the anchored cargo ships. Another
pushed a curly-headed boy, playing with plastic key rings. Two
friends, both pregnant, were buying IMAX tickets, two air-
conditioned seats for *Hurricane on the Bayou*.

Suddenly, Beau started barking, running in circles and chasing
his stub of a tail.

"Beau? Beau." She picked him up. The fur on Beau's neck was
raised, sticking straight up.

Marie looked around, snapping, scanning images in her mind.
At the trolley turnabout, mothers and mothers-to-be crossed and
uncrossed tracks.

To her left was the Mississippi; to the right the Audubon
Aquarium of the Americas with flags, billboards with painted
alligators, sea turtles, and fireflies. Behind her was St. Louis
Cathedral, its three spires piercing the clouds. In front of the
cathedral was Jackson Square, grass and cobblestones, filled with
street peddlers selling Mardi Gras trinkets and French Quarter
paintings, and tarot card readers encouraging tourists to "Buy
souvenirs"; "See your future. Mama Rosa doesn't lie."

Actually, Mama Rosa did lie. Marie knew she never gave a bad reading, even when the cards signaled danger or death. "If bad things coming, and they can't be changed, why worry someone?" Mama Rosa philosophized. But good or bad, Marie preferred knowing what was coming. She didn't like surprises, being left in the dark.

Church bells tolled. Nine AM.

Pigeons burst upward, flying and landing like a wave of mottled gray. Birds settled in the fountain; others landed atop the statue's cast-iron wings; still others, reassembled, like a small army, on the ground.

Beside the fountain stood Walker. His suit jacket folded over his arm, he dangled his fingertips in the water. He knew she saw him.

Watching tourists, peddlers, and locals flow around Walker, Marie knew no one recognized him as evil. People had a desperate need to see what they wanted to see. Everyday reality was, more accurately, a reality of multiple worlds—the lawful and the lawless, the fair and the unfair, the living and the dead. Mysteries abounded.

Some said the French Quarter didn't hide a man's sins. That was part of America's fascination with the Big Easy.

Except it was a lie.

Plenty of New Orleans's sin, courtesy of city government and the Department of Tourism, remained hidden. Sex and alcohol were abundant, but the extreme, soul-destroying sins were layered beneath a garish surface. Conference attendees could be naughty in New Orleans, but miss the clues to a more pervasive evil. The abusive desires hidden behind sly smiles. The addictions—alcohol, drugs, gambling, and sexual—that encouraged pathologies, and could be dressed up in leather, sequins, and feathers, or be veiled, more horrifically, by a businessman's suit, a priest's robes, or a schoolteacher's cotton dress. Police weren't necessarily always on your side; bribery was their mother's milk.

Agent Walker was concrete evil down to the bone.

Yet no one recognized Walker for who and what he was. None of the mothers or mothers-to-be thought to run. If they saw what she did, they'd gather their children, cover their abdomens, and run screaming. That was the problem with *sight,* seeing what others didn't see. Knowing what others didn't know. On the one hand, Walker was a thin, bloodless-looking man. White hair, sunglasses covering his nearly pink eyes; for some, he might be an object of pity. But he was deadly.

What did it all mean? Pregnant women; Nana's death; a mermaid spirit; and Walker, a human predator.

She scooped Beau up and kissed the top of his head. "You sensed him first, didn't you, Beau?"

Beau licked her cheek.

She slowly smiled.

Given all the unknowns, the confusing symbols and signs, Marie felt a perverse joy in knowing with certainty that Walker was her enemy.

FIVE

HOME, NEW ORLEANS

MIDMORNING

"Momma!" Marie-Claire squealed, her finger-painting hands high in the air.

Construction paper and bottles of red, yellow, and blue paint were on the kitchen table.

"Doggie," Marie-Claire shouted.

"Who's my baby? My, oh, so pretty baby?"

"Me." Marie-Claire, her fingers still sticky blue, wrapped her arms about Marie's legs.

One hand held Beau; her other hand hugged Marie-Claire, relishing her daughter being healthy and well.

"Let me see," Mare-Claire squealed. "Doggie. Let me see."

Marie stooped, lifting Beau's paw to shake Marie-Claire's hand.

"Oooo," said Marie-Claire.

Marie's heart thrilled, seeing Marie-Claire gently stroke Beau's paw. Seeing Beau keep still, careful not to frighten Marie-Claire, his little big eyes watching her.

"You're going to have to pay me extra," yelled Louise, her hands, bubble covered, in the sink. "Walking a dog. Ain't like walking a child."

"How much, Louise?" Since she'd brought Marie-Claire home from the hospital, Louise had cared for her.

"A dollar a walk."

"You got it."

"No, fifty cents. I don't want to be greedy."

Marie winked, and tickled Marie-Claire. Marie-Claire laughed.

"Let's make it an extra hundred a month. Who knows how many times he'll need a walk?"

Beau blinked, as if to say, 'I won't walk that much.'

Louise whooped, ecstatic. Marie knew she'd use the money to buy lottery tickets and dolls for her grandbabies. She was also happy because she'd found a way to give Louise a raise. Louise was still amazed to be paid good money for raising children; Marie wouldn't have it any other way.

"Beau. Beau. Beau," Marie-Claire shouted, twirling around, her yellow skirt billowing, her blue hands high in the air. "His name's Beau."

"How do you know?" Marie asked, her hands on her hips.

"Just do," Marie-Claire squealed, her hands outstretched for Beau.

Marie was still, at times, caught off guard by Marie-Claire's *sight*.

Her first year as a resident, she'd performed a C-section on a woman she'd thought was dead. Only later did she discover that the woman had been alive. Conscious, but paralyzed; a zombie. A distant and up to then, unknown cousin. Marie adopted Marie-Claire, and her love was as powerful as if she'd carried her for nine months and given birth.

Marie placed Beau in Marie-Claire's arms and stroked her black curls. "You're my good, sweet girl."

"You don't mind blue paint on your clothes, then," said Louise sharply. "Or blue paint on a dog. How you expect me to wash that?"

Marie laughed. There were blue streaks on her pants. Beau's right paw and tiny belly were blue, too.

"Thank goodness finger paint is washable."

"Humph," said Louise.

"Sorry," piped Marie-Claire, grinning, not sorry at all. "This dog's funny. His nose's smashed."

"He's a pug," answered Marie.

"He's boo-ti-full."

"Ugly, more like," said Louise.

"Boo-ti-full ugly," said Marie-Claire.

"A perfect balance," Marie said, smiling. For the first time all day, she felt content.

"Want some food?" asked Louise. "Oatmeal's left."

"O'meal," squealed Marie-Claire. Oatmeal was her favorite food.

"No, thanks." Marie kissed the tip of Marie-Claire's nose.

"I could make you some eggs. Grits."

"No, thanks."

"A woman's got to eat," said Louise, scowling, standing tall, proud of her heft. She turned back to the sink, muttering. "Never could stand skinny women."

Laughing, Marie hugged Louise. "Thanks. I couldn't do my life without you." Louise had helped her since she'd brought Marie-Claire home from the hospital. Marie hadn't known a thing about babies. Louise, forty-eight, already a grandmother, had done nothing but raise babies. She'd been shocked when Marie refused to own a "child-distracting" TV. But Louise adjusted graciously, and as Marie-Claire grew, she'd come to love reading aloud, finger painting, and sandbox time.

"Come on, Marie-Claire," said Louise, picking up Beau, touching his paws to the ground. "Time for day care." With a wet cloth, she wiped Marie-Claire's blue hands.

"I want to stay with Beau. Is he a puppy?"

"No, full grown. He'll be here when you get back, Marie-Claire. Give me a kiss."

They both puckered their lips.

"Day care, Marie-Claire," said Louise.

"I want to stay here."

"Your mom needs rest. She'll pick you up this afternoon."

"I want to be with Beau."

"He needs rest, too. Look at him."

Beau, obligingly, lay down, his head between his paws.

"Have you got your lunch pail?" asked Marie.

"Forgot." Marie-Claire rushed to the counter, picking up her vintage Wonder Woman pail. "Beau, come say bye." Beau trotted after Marie-Claire.

Marie stopped Louise at the kitchen door. "I need to go away this weekend. Can you watch Marie-Claire?"

"That child needs more of your time."

"I know." Mother anxieties flooded her body. Being a good mother was the most important thing in the world to her.

Louise snorted sympathetically and patted her hand. "Only one Marie Laveau in this world. Just don't get yourself killed."

"Come on, Momma." At the front door, with her lunch pail, Marie-Claire rocked back and forth on her sparkly tennis shoes. "Come say bye."

Marie scooped her up in the hall, kissing Marie-Claire, holding her extra tight.

"Don't worry, Momma," said Marie-Claire. "I'll be okay."

Marie set her down. "Who says I'm worried?"

"Me."

"How do you know?"

"Just do," Marie-Claire cooed. Then she patted Beau, who was sitting, his ears down, his tail curled beneath him.

It was hard work being a mother and a healer; hard work being a mother, period. She was blessed that Marie-Claire was so well adjusted.

"Forgot. Momma, I forgot." Marie-Claire started to run back into the kitchen. "My picture's for you. I painted it for you."

"Thank you. But I'll get it, love." She hugged Marie-Claire again—feeling tiny hands patting her back as if Marie-Claire were the reassuring mother. Suddenly, Marie felt like crying, felt as if she never wanted to stop holding her daughter.

"Have a good day at school, sweet pea."

"You're a sweet pea." Marie-Claire kissed her mother's cheek, and followed Louise.

Marie watched them from the porch. Humidity was still high; clouds were rolling in from the Gulf. The horizon, once clear and sunshine filled, had turned purple with storm clouds.

"You got an umbrella, Louise?"

"In the trunk. Weatherman says a hurricane is headed for Florida."

"Not here?" asked Marie.

"Naw, it's probably going to turn. Blow out to sea. Louisiana's fine. Florida's just unlucky."

Marie sniffed the air. It was normal for the season—moist, pungent with Gulf odors of diesel, fish, and algae. She smelled bacon and strong coffee. If people were really worried about a hurricane, she'd smell fear.

She watched Louise buckle Marie-Claire into her car seat. Through the glass window, she could see Marie-Claire's pigtails, decorated with yellow beads, swinging. See Marie-Claire waving good-bye to her and Beau.

"See you at three," Marie called. "Have a good day." She kept waving, watching the car drive away. Kept wishing she had more hours to spend with her daughter.

※

Marie went back inside the house. DuLac had willed it to her and she was grateful. The Orleans parish house was much better for raising a child than her French Quarter walkup. It had front and back yards, three bedrooms—one of which DuLac had designed as an altar room to the voodoo gods.

DuLac's belle époque furnishings were a bit risqué for a child but Marie hadn't had the heart to change it. Sometimes she imagined DuLac, a handsome, elegant Creole, in the chair near the fire. It was DuLac who'd guided her to the faith she hadn't known was hers.

"It's your fate, your *fa*," he'd told her when she'd been most afraid. And for the first time in her life, he made her feel normal, part of a community.

Marie looked about the kitchen: a messy kitchen table; clean dishes in the rack; light streaming in through the oversize window; and a fan, above the sink, blowing hot air in from outside. The kitchen was the last place she'd seen DuLac alive. He'd been happy, cutting up chicken for gumbo.

"Beau."

The little dog looked at her, then stood on his hind legs, trying to climb onto Marie-Claire's vacant chair.

"Beau, come on, time for bed. I know you like the bed."

The little dog wouldn't move.

"Come on. I'll snuggle you." Rather, she'd take comfort from the little dog. If she didn't have a man, having a dog to snuggle against wasn't bad. "You want to be carried?"

Beau lifted his paw, scraping the air.

"You hungry?"

Beau barked, more fiercely, trying to leap onto the chair.

"What? The painting?"

She lifted Beau; he yapped. Marie swore he wanted her to see Marie-Claire's painting.

She stared at the glossy paper. Usually, Marie-Claire painted stick figures. She and her mama holding hands. She and her best friend, Susie, at day care. Sometimes, she painted El, DuLac, or Kind Dog. She remembered them all. Her surrogate family. All dead now. Marie prayed Marie-Claire didn't remember that each had died protecting her.

Marie picked up the painting. The color had dried and was already starting to flake. Three blue wavy lines, in layers, extended across the page.

"What's it mean, Beau?" The little dog, held, burrowed against her breast, had fallen asleep.

She kissed Beau's head. *For a second, she could see Beau curled against Nana.* Beau, loyal, steadfast, was more virtuous than Nana's grandsons.

"Hey." She scratched Beau's ear. The little dog opened his eyes and yawned. Then he wiggled his stub of a tail and fell back asleep. Carrying Beau, kicking off her tennis shoes, she walked down the hall to her bedroom.

She laid Beau on a pillow (he didn't wake), laid the painting on the nightstand, and closed the blinds.

She grimaced; working the night shift sometimes made her feel like a vampire. She pushed the thought away, stripped off her clothes, and slid beneath the sheets.

Inside her jeans pocket, her cell phone rang—the muffled tune, "It's Raining Men." A single mother's wish.

Marie-Claire laughed, hearing her mother sing the lyrics. For Christmas, Marie bought Marie-Claire the picture book, *Cloudy with a Chance of Meatballs*, and together, they'd giggled over raining meatballs. For weeks, they'd alternated singing "It's raining meatballs," "It's raining men. Hallelujah!"

In New Orleans, rain—like everything else—was a double-edged sword. Rain cleared the polluted air, encouraged the lush green, but during rough storms, it lashed like knives and caused deadly flash floods.

She burrowed in the sheets, letting the call go to voice mail.

She heard distant thunder.

Beau snored. Marie counted the seconds between the rumbling sounds to tell how fast the storm was approaching.

She sat up, turning on the nightstand lamp, and looked at Marie-Claire's painting.

Three wavy lines. Blue, horizontal, like ocean water? She thought of ships at sea caught by lightning, trapped by cresting waves. Did sailors believe in mermaids?

Did Marie-Claire know something she didn't? Innocents, supposedly, had purer sight.

Like a flash, she saw the second statue. Dual sexed. No siren lured it, rather, it had its own unique power. Both seducer and seduced.

Strangely, she thought of Parks. They'd been good together.

Marie exhaled, punching the pillow before settling her head. Beau shifted his weight closer to her, his short back against her shoulder.

A family of ghosts. A river siren. Darkened pools. A face in the water. Country. City. Water, earth. What did any of it mean?

She refused to worry. Today, she needed to rest. Needed to be ready for the future. Needed to do what Nana and her grandsons couldn't do. Make peace, find justice.

Her skin broke into a sweat.

Liar, liar, pants on fire, she thought, remembering the childhood chant.

When the *loas* called and signs appeared, she felt blessed, grateful. She also felt anxiety, and sometimes, fear. With the spirit world, anything could happen, including emotional and physical wounds that no medicine could fix and the creating of consequences beyond her control.

She thought she saw Baron Samedi in the corner, but she decided it was just another shadow. Her mind playing tricks.

Let me dream, she thought, and, in the next second, she thought, Don't let me dream.

She opened the nightstand drawer. She lifted a photo of herself and Parks on the Riverwalk. Asleep, Marie-Claire was slumped in her stroller, a huge rainbow lollipop still in her hand and sticking to her hair.

For a little while, they'd been a family. Just like the murdered L'Overtures.

She looked at the Jersey boy, blond, sun-kissed handsome like a surfer boy. Not her usual type. A Korean tourist, crazy about jazz, had taken the photo. Too bad Parks hadn't loved her enough to stay. Maybe it was because she hadn't had the courage to ask? Maybe asking would have made all the difference.

She punched the pillow.

Beau, dreaming, stretched, rolling onto his back, exposing his soft belly. Amazing, she thought, how dogs could trust and make themselves vulnerable.

She stroked Beau's belly, his little legs twitched.

"Parks," she murmured, "touch me." She stretched her toes and threw her arms above her head. She tried to imagine Parks lying beside her, stroking her belly and breasts. She felt nothing but humid air.

Beau snuggled closer. She kissed the little dog's head.

She slept, long, hard, and deep.

SIX

Marie stood beneath the parking garage's overhang. The world was gray. She'd brought an umbrella, but the rain was heavy, the wind brisk.

She scanned the sky, hoping for a lessening of rain, before dashing across the street to Charity for another twelve-hour shift. Thunder cascaded, and lightning, like a jagged knife, ripped the sky.

Built in the nineteenth century, Charity Hospital looked like a fortress; the original two-story building had grown helter-skelter into four huge towers, each thirty feet high, with hundreds of brightly lit windows, eerie in this weather, like a castle's malevolent eyes.

Charity Hospital was its own world as much as the wetlands, the bayou and marsh, except that it was enclosed, recycling stale air through linking hallways, surgical theaters, and overcrowded wards. Ages ago, the Sisters of Charity, mainly Irish-Catholic nuns, had battled yellow fever, tuberculosis, and venereal disease. Now an army of multiethnic men and women fought the good fight against human frailty: flu pandemics, cancers, West Nile virus, HIV and AIDS.

It was a universal law: bacteria, viruses, damaged cells were ever morphing, creating new ways for people to die. Her job was simple—outwit death.

Snapping her umbrella open, Marie sprinted toward the ER's glass doors. The automatic doors slid open, then shut.

"Hey, Doc." Sully, the security guard, handed her a towel. Big and big hearted, Sully had been at Charity for as long as anyone could remember.

"Thanks, Sully." She snapped the umbrella shut, wiped her hands dry, murmuring, "I've got a new dog."

"Big dog?"

"A little one with a big heart."

Sully looked disappointed. "What's the dog called?"

"Beau."

"Can I bring him bones?"

"Small ones."

"Take him for a walk?"

"You bet."

Impulsively, Marie kissed Sully's cheek. She remembered how much he'd loved Kind Dog.

"Beau's going to like you."

"You think?" Sully lit up with a smile. He looked like a serene Buddha, his hands clasped over his stomach, his feet turned outward, graceful, like a dancer's.

Sully's landlady wouldn't let him keep dogs, so he'd borrowed Marie's. Kind Dog had been a gorgeous black Lab mix. A perfect companion for a kind black man.

"How small is Beau?" asked Sully. "Terrier small? Or Chihuahua small?"

"Pug small."

"Ah," he sighed, weighing what it would look like for a big man to be seen with such a small dog. "I'll buy a new leash. Red, I think." His metal chair teetered on two legs.

Marie felt a rush of joy. She felt at home again in the ER.

Loss was what being a human and a doctor was all about—but she hadn't lost everything. She still had friends in the ER, her health, and her family. A new dog, Beau.

She surveyed the waiting room, a multiracial mix of desperate, uninsured people—Cajuns, Creoles, Hispanics, Vietnamese, African Americans, and more.

Charity, despite perennial deficits, turned no one away; the well-endowed Tulane University Hospital, next door, served the city's insured.

New Orleanians didn't seem to mind the irony of two unequal hospitals side by side. Didn't seem to mind the de facto segregation based on color and class. One hospital was a rainbow world, while the other was predominately white.

Marie waved to her colleagues Huan and K-Paul. K-Paul was a diagnostic genius who hadn't been tempted by Tulane's lure of more money and better equipment. Huan was an expert at caring for traumatized and abused children. Marie was the generalist with intuitive gifts. She was the one who sought out the worst cases.

In the doctors' lounge, Marie opened her locker, slid on her white coat. Her name stitched above the breast pocket used to say Levant; she'd had it restitched, changed to Laveau. She was convinced her mother, if alive, would approve. Though her mother had been afraid of her heritage, Marie, once she'd discovered her ancestry, couldn't bear dishonoring the ties.

She clicked the metal locker shut.

Her cell started ringing, singing about rain and men.

She slipped the phone out of her jeans pocket and flipped it open. She didn't recognize the area code. Probably a sales call. She placed the cell in her coat pocket, then wrapped the stethoscope around her neck and tightened her tennis shoes. Time to stop mourning El and DuLac. Tonight, she'd focus on the here and now. Tomorrow, she'd travel to DeLaire.

"Are you ready?" asked Lillianne, Charity's new head nurse. She was almost as good as El had been, professional and caring. El, though, had been short, her fashion tacky and loud. Lillianne was tall, always elegant, with her black hair tucked beneath an old-fashioned white nurse's cap.

"Ready," she responded.

"Coffee's still hot."

"Thanks."

"Huan brought some of her steamed buns."

"Great. I'll have some for midnight lunch." Marie redid her ponytail, stretching her hair tight, behind her ears.

Lillianne watched her, as if straightening, corralling flyaway hair was akin to a miracle.

"Anything else?" Marie asked.

Lillianne shook her head, poured a cup of coffee.

Marie knew Lillianne was curious about her powers. Marie

preferred Lillianne's reserve to colleagues whispering behind her back. Nearly five years at Charity and some still believed her spiritual work was evil.

"*It is what it is.*"

"Hey, El."

"Did you say something?" asked Lillianne.

"Just talking to myself." Marie pushed open the door. She winked at El's ghost.

One day, she'd have pity on Lillianne and answer all her questions. But not tonight, tonight she was just a doctor. Dr. Laveau.

✖

"Incoming," shouted Huan. "Just got a radio call."

Marie exhaled. Her shoulders ached. Twenty patients in less than three hours. She would have thought the rain would keep everyone but the sickest away. But Charity's ER filled with the usual—flu, kitchen burns, a spousal beating, heart attacks, gang beatings, and undertreated chronic conditions such as lupus, diabetes. Unfortunately, when they got busier and busier, it became easier to categorize patients by their conditions and symptoms.

Marie caught a whiff of jasmine. Only Huan smelled of flowers after hours of exhausting work. Only Huan, with her belief in ancestor worship, suspected Marie saw ghosts. She'd invited Marie and Marie-Claire to Vietnam. "Meet my family," she'd said. And Marie had understood she'd meant meet both the living and the dead.

"Did you try my *bánh bao*?"

"Not yet."

"There's pork and chicken. If you like, I'll make some for you and Marie-Claire."

Everyone knew Marie didn't cook much or well. Irritatingly, the nurses often wondered aloud if her daughter was plump enough and well-fed.

"Thanks. Marie-Claire will be happy. She loved your noodle soup."

"*Bún bò húe*. I'll bring some of that, too."

"Only if later you let us treat you to dinner. Po' boys with French fries. Marie-Claire's favorite. We'll go to Roger's Café."

"Can I come, too?" asked K-Paul, coming to stand beside them in front of the ER glass doors.

"Girls' date," answered Marie. "Any more news?"

K-Paul shrugged. "Another fight on Bourbon Street."

"How many?" asked Huan.

"Five, maybe six, hurt."

"Could be anything then," answered Marie. Knife or gunshot wounds. Broken noses. Cracked ribs from a fistfight. Rain had pushed the tourists indoors. Add in drugs, alcohol, gluttony, and lust enflamed by strip clubs and you had a perfect recipe for disaster.

Lillianne quietly ordered nurses to check crash carts and available beds.

Sirens whooped, repetitive, spiraling wails.

In the ER lobby, a drunk, a bloody rag twisted about his hand, started hollering, "I was here first. Don't take no more. Shut the doors. Can't care for us here." Some murmured agreement. Others, yelled "Drunken slob," "Troublemaker."

Lillianne went over to the man and spoke quietly. Whatever she said, it calmed him. He sat, hands folded, quieted, as if he was in church.

K-Paul chortled. "El would've shouted, 'Sit your ass down.' She didn't suffer fools."

"Including you, K-Paul?" asked Huan, deceptively sweet.

Marie laughed. K-Paul grinned. Humor calmed nerves. The three of them had become good at it.

The spiraling wails were coming closer. Eight, maybe six blocks away. For Marie, each high-pitched scream caused an adrenaline rush, a quickened pulse.

Marie saw the three of them reflected in the glass doors, herself and Huan, like twins, both average height, in white coats with brown skin and ponytails. K-Paul, six feet, ruddy and red haired, towered over them. Inside, she saw technicians, nurses moving with hurried grace; outside, rain still fell, seeming to bounce upward from the asphalt.

The three of them—herself, Huan, and K-Paul, the doctors on call—stood waiting, wondering if their skills were going to be good enough.

K-Paul glanced at her sideways. "How's it going, Marie?"

"Fine, K-Paul."

"Marie-Claire?"

"Fine."

"Thought you'd never ask," said K-Paul. "I'm fine, too. Right as rain."

"Don't start, K-Paul." Last summer, Marie had flirted with K-Paul, and every day since then, she'd regretted it.

"You've been ignoring me—"

"Not funny, K-Paul."

"—since your affair with Detective Parks. That's what it was, wasn't it? An affair? Temporary pleasure."

In the reflecting glass doors, Marie noticed nurses had slowed, stopped moving behind the counter. Teddy, who did blood draws, wasn't even trying to listen discreetly. Huan dipped her head, trying to hide her smile.

"Is Parks fine?" asked K-Paul, grinning like a Cheshire cat, deepening his accent, the twangy Cajun sounds. "Though why'd you'd want a northern boy . . . ," K-Paul paused, shaking his head sorrowfully. "Cajuns more fun any day."

Lillianne stepped forward. "Back to work, everyone." Teddy and the nurses dispersed from the station. "Doctors, time for you to meet the incoming. If the EMTs can get wet, so can you."

Marie turned to Lillianne, mouthing, "Thank you."

Huan slipped her arm through Marie's, whispering loudly, "K-Paul's cute."

"You date him, then."

Huan giggled. "I'm waiting for a Vietnamese man."

Walking backward, K-Paul crooned, "Cajuns better than them, too."

Huan slapped at him.

"Cajuns, best lovers on the planet."

The siren wails were loud, searing. Abruptly turning, K-Paul, serious, shouted, "Let's save lives."

The glass doors slid open and steam rolled in. Rain soaked skin.

One after another, three boxy red ambulances arrived. Sirens stopped midscream. Nurses rushed forward. Paramedics jumped out of cabs. Van doors swung open, gurneys lowered, their wheels unlocking, then locking in place. Disembodied voices shouted status reports:

"Head wound, probable concussion, pulse seventy-seven"; "broken nose, possible cracked ribs, one thirty-eight over ninety-eight"; "blunt trauma, unresponsive."

"Saline and restraints," said an EMT, his lip swollen, rolling a cursing, struggling patient past Marie. "This idiot wants to keep fighting."

Huan and K-Paul were effectively doing triage, shouting orders for ER placement.

Marie stood still, feeling for the worst case. She was in the middle of the vortex, the wet, swirling madness. The red and yellow ambulance lights seemed mournful. She wiped strands of rain-soaked hair from her face.

Then a police car, flashing red, pulled into the ER bay. An ambulance lagged behind it.

"K-Paul," Marie shouted. She sensed the patient in this fourth ambulance was critical.

K-Paul ran to Marie, not asking how she knew she'd need help. They opened the ambulance bay doors before the EMT.

"Fucking cops, fucking cops," shouted a bleached-blond EMT doing CPR. "They shot blind. Fucking blind. He's had two units of blood. The tourniquet isn't slowing enough."

The right leg was mangled, flesh open and scarred. Two bullet wounds to the upper thigh.

"He's not going to last." Marie scrambled inside the bay. "He's a beautiful boy." Maybe nineteen. Most likely an out of towner given his khakis and Dockers. Wrong place, wrong time. "Another blood pack. Any pain meds?"

"I didn't dare," said the woman. "Just a shot of EPI."

Blood pulsed through Marie's fingers.

K-Paul, dripping wet, crouching just inside the packed van, asked, "What do you want me to do?"

"I'm not sure," said Marie. "The artery is shredded by the bullet."

"Got a pulse," said the EMT.

"Let's move him," shouted the second EMT, standing outside in the storm.

The EMT started to lift the gurney.

"Wait," said Marie. "He'll never make it to surgery. Give me some silicone tubing, about an inch. Latex gloves."

"What're you going to do?" asked the EMT.

"You need sterile conditions," said K-Paul. "There's an on-call surgeon."

"Never mind, K-Paul. Do it," Marie shouted at the EMT, clean cut, not much older than the gunshot victim. He snipped a piece of tubing.

"K-Paul, hold his leg in case he wakes."

"I doubt it," said K-Paul.

"Wise guy."

"Cocky doc." Then, more quietly, "Surgery isn't going to like this."

"Then they can meet ambulances in the rain." Her fingers dug into the wound; the boy moaned, then quieted.

"He's out," said the EMT, checking his pulse. "But still alive."

Marie closed her eyes, letting her fingers feel for the artery, severed and lost in flesh. "Got one." She needed both ends. Her left fingers dug deeper. "Got it."

"Hand me some gloves," said K-Paul. He snapped them on. "Let me help." He squeezed beside Marie, their bodies close, their arms entwined.

Marie held the artery. K-Paul slipped the tube, like a bridge, over both ends. Blood flowed.

"That's amazing," said the EMT. "He's pinking up. Pulse is rising."

"Doc Laveau's amazing," answered K-Paul. "Aren't you, Doc?"

"Let's move him," she said.

"You learned that from the army field surgeon, didn't you?"

"Unlike you, I pay attention to guest doctors."

"Most are blowhards."

"Making miracles again, Marie?" Huan looked like a drowned cat, except a happy one. "He's the last one. The rest are recovering fine."

"Here," said Marie, handing Huan the IV lines. She flattened herself against the van as K-Paul jumped down, back into the rain, ready to receive as the EMT slid, then lifted the gurney.

The young man's eyes flickered open. "Dead?"

"You'll be fine," said Huan, bending closer, holding a pink umbrella over him.

"Angel," said the disoriented boy.

Huan giggled, and the lilting sound seemed to chase away rain. Droplets slowed to a mist.

"He's not Vietnamese," cracked K-Paul, pulling as the EMT pushed.

Huan, looking over her shoulder, smiled at Marie. Then she turned, jogging slightly, keeping pace with the gurney.

✳

Marie stripped, putting on dry clothes. Jeans. T-shirt. New lab coat. She shivered; she told herself it was the hospital air-conditioning. But it was really deflation from the adrenaline rush.

She checked her cell. The rain hadn't damaged it. But there'd been another missed call. She hadn't heard it ring. Hadn't heard the "raining men" melody.

A 510 area code. Where was that?

She pressed voice mail. She could hear Parks's soft, urgent voice: "Marie."

"Aren't we fine?" hooted K-Paul, entering the lounge, startling her. "Hey, you're fine. I'm fine. Everything and everybody's fine."

She pasted on a smile, shut her phone without listening to Parks's message. Why was he calling her now? She hadn't heard from him in nearly a year. Yet she couldn't deny her pleasure in knowing he'd been trying to reach her, hearing him say—"Marie."

"Let's go dancing," said K-Paul, grabbing, swinging her around.

"K-Paul, I've just gotten dry. Change before you catch cold."

"You were amazing. Me, you, Huan—we're all amazing."

She pulled away. "How's the patient?"

"In surgery. The surgeons, especially Bigelow, aren't too pleased you saved his life."

"Screw them."

K-Paul laughed. "We're—the three of us—a good team."

She smiled. "Yes. We are."

"You and I could be a better team."

"Let it go, K-Paul."

"This Cajun not good enough for you?" He twirled her like they were in a zydeco bar, explosive spins across the floor, then a final spin, arms apart, followed by a tight clutch, chest to chest. "Friends with benefits?"

"K-Paul!" she laughed. "Back to work."

He shrugged and winked, but not before she saw a shadow flit across his face. Cajuns were notorious for good humor, their laissez-faire attitude. But Marie also knew they were great at masking. A Cajun could be dying, his lungs flooded with fluid, and he'd still be cracking jokes, at his own expense, wondering how to ensure a good time. Not just for him but, also, for everyone in the hospital room watching him die.

"K-Paul—" Her hand caressed his face; for a second, she didn't know herself whether she'd kiss him or tell him again she wasn't interested.

"Thank you, Doctors. No one died." Lillianne, her hand on her hip, her body filling the door frame, stared curiously.

Marie let her hand fall to her side. K-Paul opened his locker, the door slamming against the metal next to it. He slipped his soaked shirt over his head; reddish-brown hair ran from his neck down to the small of his back.

When K-Paul started pulling off his pants, Lillianne murmured, "We'll give you privacy."

K-Paul responded, "Stay. You might see something you like."

Lillianne scowled. "I'll have maintenance mop the floor."

"Do that," said K-Paul, his face impish. "Sure you want to go?" Standing in his underwear, he looked fit and handsome. "You're going to miss a good show."

"We've seen this show before," said Marie, linking her arm through Lillianne's and exiting the lounge.

※

Two AM. Most of the night in the ER had been a mad sprint; now, it had a slow, steady rhythm. No life-threatening cases.

The storm had grown worse. Thunder and lightning rattled and brightened Charity's windows. Dozens of homeless trekked in. Junkies, alcoholics, veterans, a mother with a toddler and a preteen trailed rain and mud onto the linoleum and sat or slept wrapped in steaming hospital sheets. The air-conditioning system couldn't fight the humidity.

Lillianne let the homeless stay as long as they were quiet. Nurses handed out sandwiches—tuna, turkey, and egg salad, a bit stale, leftovers from the cafeteria.

The exam rooms were empty except for Exam Three where Will, a chronic asthma patient, was recovering from an attack. Just fifteen, Will was a frequent ER visitor. So frequent, his mother dropped him off, rarely staying.

"I've got four other kids to see to," she'd answered once when Marie had raised her brows. Sometimes, she returned to pick up Will; most times, he walked home after a debilitating attack.

※

In Exam One, Marie applied salve to a Haitian's arm, a new immigrant who probably hadn't quite learned the ins and outs of McDonald's deep-fat fryers. At least she thought he was Haitian. But he could be any islander from the African diaspora. The fast-food joints and restaurants loved immigrants, legal or illegal.

"You were lucky."

The solidly built man didn't speak. He'd left "Name" blank on the pink admissions form. For "Insurance," he'd written: "None." For "Work," "Part-time." Charity cared for anybody and everybody.

"Apply the salve daily. Then wrap it in gauze like this." She spiraled the gauze from his elbow to his wrist. "This butterfly clip holds it in place. Okay?"

Still he didn't speak; he just sat on the metal chair, dignified, impressive, his skin a glowing black. In New Orleans, boats arrived daily from the Caribbean isles—fishing boats, immigration smugglers, and independents, rafting in on makeshift crafts, seeking a better life.

"Here's a prescription for Vicodin. Just a couple of pills. Afterward, Motrin or Tylenol."

Nothing gave any indication that the patient was in pain. Of course, he had to be—burns were the most painful of wounds. Why else come to the ER if not for pain?

"Maman Laveau." His voice sounded like butter, deep, still mixing in the churn. Marie couldn't discern his accent. "Watch for the waters."

"Waters? What waters?"

"You know, as I do, there be no accidents." Standing, he undid his gauze.

"No, stop. You need to heal."

The white gauze unraveled, swinging and swaying, a windswept ribbon, or a kite's tail, or a wave's foam.

The wound was healed.

"Water needs to go where she wants to go."

Marie felt disoriented. The skin was smooth, like black glass.

Beyond the Haitian, she saw El near the automatic glass door, saw the ghost family, sitting, bereft, in the waiting area.

Lillianne and Huan were laughing. Nurses were restocking supplies.

K-Paul was leaning on the nurses' counter doing paperwork—sensing her gaze, he stopped writing, looked up, and winked.

Did K-Paul see the man? Had anyone seen her dressing his wound? Or did they just see her applying antibiotics to air?

The ER was often filled with craziness. Why not have a crazy doc, too?

"I'm here."

She looked at the man, (creature?) his eyes black pools, his face morphing, becoming more androgynous, both male and female. A turquoise bead necklace hung from his/her throat.

"Who—what—are you?"

"Mind the water."

"Marie," shouted Huan, pulling back the curtains. "Last dumpling." The dumpling looked pathetic on the paper plate.

"Try," said Huan.

She turned, for a second, but in that second, her patient disappeared.

The exam room was empty.

Marie bit into the bun. It tasted sour. But her mood altered everything. Even if Huan's dumpling had been pure sugar, it would have tasted sour to her. She hated it when her worlds, medical and spiritual, commingled. The rational and the seemingly irrational.

It still rattled her to have lesser gods, *loas,* medicine men, walk into Charity's ER.

She spit out the dough. "Damnit, Huan, I've got to go. Got to find him."

"Who?"

"My patient. Didn't you see my patient?"

"I didn't see anyone. No one's here."

"No, he was here. He was here, Huan. Didn't you see him?" She knew she was sounding wild, crazy. "I need to make sure he comes back for follow-up." Abruptly, she left, pushed through the curtains, rushing, searching the ER floor:

Technicians carrying pills, drawing blood; K-Paul completing paperwork; Lillianne smoothing her hair, repinning stray strands. A nurse wheeled a woman to the elevator; Labor and Delivery was on the fifth floor. The ER lounge was filled with bedraggled, sleeping patients. Some stretched across the folding chairs; some nodded in sleep, their chins grazing their chests.

There.

She saw a silhouette behind the green curtains of Exam Three. The Haitian leaned over a patient. She raced forward. *The silhouette changed—breasts enlarged, hair growing long, longer, tied into a ponytail.*

His/her outstretched fingertips touched a chest.

She dashed forward, swung back the curtains.

Will was resting on the bed. *The creature was gone.*

"Hey, Doc. I'm better. All better."

"Hey, Will." He didn't seem traumatized. He seemed healthy. Will's family was uninsured and too poor to buy inhalers. An ER trip often saved his life, but the visits were an expensive and inefficient use of resources. Worse, every time Will came to the ER, she worried he'd die.

Marie pressed her stethoscope to Will's lungs. The airways were clear, no irritated passageways. Air was flowing unimpeded.

"I'm cured. All better," said Will, sitting up like any healthy teenager.

"I'd like you to stay for observation."

"I'm fine. I could play basketball." Will jumped out of bed, stepping into his worn tennis shoes, tying the laces. "You really fixed me this time, Doc."

She was perplexed. "Will, did you see anyone?"

His brows rose. "You're kidding, right? You were here just a minute ago. I tell everybody Charity's got the best docs. You fixed me up." He grinned. "Hope I don't see you again, Dr. Laveau. Just kidding. Don't need the ER anymore.

"Don't you remember? You told me I could go. Told me I didn't need to come back. Said I was cured."

Jaw slack, she stared at the space that Will had just left.

Had the creature really manifested itself as her? Gone from invisible to visible? Had Will really been cured?

She started trembling. If a creature could manifest as her and convince Will, then it might also mislead Louise and Marie-Claire.

Huan pulled back the curtains. "You okay?"

"I need air." She couldn't bear her child being in danger. "Come with me, please?"

For seconds, Huan studied her. Marie knew she wanted to understand what had happened, wanted to get inside her mind. But, instead, Huan, a good colleague and friend, only replied, "Whatever you need."

Huan set down her empty paper plate at the admitting station and grabbed her umbrella, propped against the break wall.

"Break," she shouted, aggressively. "Lillianne, me and Marie need a break." Then Huan ruined her fierceness by giggling.

A few sleeping homeless stirred. One man turned, opening his brown, bloodshot eyes. A bored technician smiled.

K-Paul shouted, "Can I come?"

"Girls only," said Huan.

The ER doors opened and they were outside, the rain still falling.

Marie inhaled deeply. The fresh air was good for her. "Thanks, Huan. Thanks for covering me."

"No problem."

Inside, she wasn't sure she would have kept her composure. Bright artificial lights were too revealing. Outside, in the dark, she felt calmer.

The street was empty, the ER bay quiet. Secondhand hospital light made the black asphalt glow. There weren't any car headlights gleaming, inching and circling down the parking ramps.

She and Huan stood close together beneath the pink umbrella built for one instead of two. Their ponytails were still wet. Huan's was long and thin, a jet black rope to Marie's dark brown strands.

"It's all good," said Huan.

"What?"

"Everything."

Should she tell Huan that she'd seen something she didn't understand?

"You could be Vietnamese," said Huan.

Marie laughed.

"No, I'm serious. One reason I came to New Orleans is that people here believe in ghosts. You know, El and DuLac are both glad you stayed at Charity."

"Have you spoken to them?"

Huan raised her brows. "No," she whispered, stricken. "I'm not a shaman like you. Just ordinary girl. But I know you've been feeling bad since they died. I know they're happy that you're still here."

"And you?"

Bowing, hands pressed together, Huan answered solemnly, "Yes. Honor to work with you."

Marie, pressing her palms together, bowed in return.

Pop. It sounded like a firecracker bursting. Jerking upright, Marie staggered. Blood sprayed over her white coat. Huan's head tilted forward; then, knees buckling, she fell, her face and body slamming onto concrete. Her umbrella spun, splashing into the rain.

Marie dropped to her knees, her feet triggering the automatic door. She turned Huan over. Blood drained from her neck. "Help," she screamed. "K-Paul, help."

K-Paul kneeled beside her. "What the hell happened?" Lillianne, nurses, and an ER tech crowded around.

Sully, gun drawn, stood in the street, searching for the shooter. He shouted into his radio, "Ten-seventy-one. Ten-seventy-one. Charity Hospital shooting."

Huan's blood, mixed with rain, streamed into the storm drain.

"Hold on, Huan. Hold on," pleaded Marie.

"Move aside, Marie." K-Paul and the tech lifted Huan onto a gurney. Eyes closed, body limp, she seemed already beyond help.

"Call an OR attending," Marie shouted. In the trauma room, Lillianne added saline and IV blood drips. Marie clipped on the EKG monitor.

"Her pulse is slowing," said K-Paul. "Ninety over seventy."

"Where's the surgeon?" demanded Marie. "Clamp."

K-Paul handed it to her.

"OR is on the way," said Lillianne, her voice frayed.

Marie pressed against Huan's neck. The artery was like thin rubber; the metal clamp slipped. She tried again. Success. "Another clamp." Then another. The blood flow became sluggish.

"Pressure dropping," yelled K-Paul. "Do what you did in the ambulance bay. Come on, Marie."

"I can't," she answered. "Too much damage."

"Bullet?" asked Lillianne.

"High-powered rifle. Had to have been."

The EKG monitor whined.

"We've lost pulse."

"Compressions, K-Paul." He began compressing Huan's chest.

"More blood, Lilliane."

"She's already had ten bags."

"A hundred, if we have to. Is the defibrillator charged?"

"Charged to a hundred," said K-Paul. "Step back, Marie."

She stepped back, staring at the monitor, the waves of green lines.

"Charge to two hundred."

"What've you got?" asked Roberts, the surgeon on call.

"GSW. Neck. Carotid artery hit."

"Let me see." He pushed Marie aside, one hand on Huan's wrist, the other touching the wound. "Hopeless."

"No," insisted Marie. "Charge to three hundred. Try again, K-Paul."

"Charge."

Marie whispered in Huan's ear, "It's not your time."

"Stand back." K-Paul shocked Huan's chest, her torso lifting up, then down.

"Even if she survives," said Roberts, "she won't be the same. This is Dr. Huan, isn't it?"

"Don't say that," cried Lillianne.

The heart monitor flatlined.

"It's over, Marie," said K-Paul.

"No," she raged, knocking over a tray of medical instruments.

K-Paul looked at Roberts. The surgeon nodded, then left. The staff began mourning, some crying, others bowing their heads and praying. Lillianne wiped her eyes.

"She's lost too much blood."

"Another EPI," said Marie. "Charge again, K-Paul."

"She wouldn't have wanted it." K-Paul set down the electric paddles. "It's been a while, Marie. Brain damage is likely."

Lillianne murmured, "I'll get the chaplain."

Marie stared at her blankly.

"Father Roland has ties to the Vietnamese community. He'll notify the family. Do all that is proper."

Marie nodded.

The ever-modest Huan, her jacket bloodstained, her shirt and bra cut off, looked immodest in death. The overhead glare made her brown skin appear paler, yellow.

Marie covered her with a sheet.

"Want me to call it?" asked K-Paul.

Hours ago, she and K-Paul had celebrated their medical abilities. Now they couldn't even save a valued colleague.

"Time of death—4:38 AM."

Marie flinched. Brown skin. Dark hair. Similar height. "The

shooter thought she was me." She turned, leaving behind Huan, her startled colleagues, the few left in the ER waiting room.

"Marie. Wait up."

She didn't stop. The hot rain soaked her anew.

She saw it happening again, her bowing and the bullet entering Huan.

The shot could have come from Tulane University Hospital, across the street, or the garage, or even from one of Charity's labyrinth towers.

K-Paul grabbed her, his face fierce, twisted with grief. "Where're you going?"

"Leave me alone, K-Paul."

"Where're you going?"

"To track a murderer." She started sprinting toward her car. Never mind that her shift wasn't over—or that she wanted to cry for a good woman lost. She shouldn't have delayed a day. Shouldn't have let Beauregard delay her. If she'd settled the L'Overture murder earlier, Huan wouldn't be dead.

"Marie!"

"Leave me the hell alone, K-Paul."

Inside the garage, he blocked her path, moving right when she tried to move right. Moving left, when she moved left. "Tell me what the hell's going on?"

Fluorescent lights buzzed.

Breathing heavily, she said, "I've got this, K-Paul."

"That's your answer to everything. Self-sufficiency. Dr. Laveau knows best."

"Leave me alone."

"I won't." He gripped her shoulders, hard.

She almost winced, but she wouldn't give K-Paul the satisfaction. Biting her lip, she glared at him.

He released her. "I'm sorry," he said, plaintively. "Just tell me what's going on."

"It should've been me," she sighed. "It was supposed to be me."

"How do you know?"

"Something happened in the bayou."

"That's my territory. Home."

"It is, isn't it?" She looked intently at K-Paul. He was a rural Louisianan, through and through. A Cajun boy who'd come to the city to study medicine, but still spent holidays doing rural care. She'd never known him to let her or anyone else down.

"Let me help," pleaded K-Paul.

"It's not safe around me."

"I'll chance it. But you're not thinking clearly. The police are going to want a statement from you. It might help them find Huan's killer."

"I already know who her killer is."

"What if you're wrong?"

Marie looked at K-Paul disbelievingly. "You know me. Know who I am."

K-Paul flinched. The garage lights made his face sallow. "Call Parks, your detective friend. I bet he'll agree with me."

Marie sighed, "You're right." She could hear police sirens, more aggressive than ambulance wails. She'd give her statement. Maybe the crime scene investigators could confirm the weapon, fix the location from where the shot was fired.

※

Captain Beauregard, clownish, flesh ballooning out of his uniform, stood at the ER doors. Light spilling from the glass doors, police emergency lights strobing red and white made the scene look more like *carnivàle* than a murder scene. Rain dripped around the three-sided ER drive-through roof.

"They told me you left."

"I'm surprised you arrived," said Marie. "Aren't you usually hugging your desk?"

Beauregard flushed angrily. "Your mouth's going to get you in trouble, Dr. Laveau."

"Hey," said K-Paul. "Respect. She's a witness."

The three of them formed an unholy trinity. She and K-Paul were overheated, wet from the rain. Beauregard was sweating, his armpits soaked from nervousness.

Two patrol cars were parked in the ambulance bay.

She stepped closer, smelling Beauregard's fear. "What happened to you?"

He looked down.

Marie doubted he could see his feet. "Is your friend Walker with you?"

His beady eyes flitted up and sideways. She quickly turned, seeing the illuminated parking garage. The rooftop was dark, with space enough for a killer to hide and fire a scope rifle.

She suddenly understood. "Why?" she asked Beauregard. "Bribery?"

"We should take your statement," Beauregard blustered. "Officer Raymonde," he called.

A tall, muscular officer got out of the second patrol car.

Four cops, total, Marie realized. Two must be inside the

hospital, hoping to identify her body. Raymonde was Beauregard's driver and bodyguard. Another accomplice.

"Wait. You were expecting it to be me," she said. "That's why you're here. The police captain doesn't do random calls. Especially just before dawn."

"What're you saying, Marie?" asked K-Paul.

"The captain expected to find me dead. You had a premonition, didn't you, Captain?"

"What the hell?" shouted K-Paul, stepping forward.

Raymonde's hand shifted to his gun.

Beauregard raised his hand for Raymonde to halt, to back down. "Don't move," he told K-Paul.

K-Paul clenched his fists, his skin flushing red.

Beauregard said, flatly, to Marie, "You should get you and yours out of town."

"Would you kill me?"

"No. But these people don't play."

"What people?"

Beauregard grabbed Marie's arm, turning her, forcing her backward.

"Hey," yelled K-Paul. Raymonde twisted his arm up, behind his back.

Marie and Beauregard had changed positions.

"Your friend's going to get himself killed."

She didn't answer. Her back faced the ER doors; Beauregard's back faced the street. His huge body blocked hers.

"Not much time, Dr. Laveau. You should run." Beauregard tilted his head toward K-Paul. "Get her the hell out of here."

Raymonde released K-Paul.

"Walker," Marie breathed.

"My men can't search everywhere," answered Beauregard.

"Especially rooftops."

"It's business. Corporate resources are always greater than civic budgets."

"A company killed Huan?" demanded K-Paul, gripping Beauregard's arm.

"Get your hands off me. Else I'll shoot you myself." There was a flash of Beauregard as he'd once been—aggressive, youthful. "Damnit. Go. Both of you."

"Tell me why?" Marie insisted. "Who corrupted you? Why did you let it happen?"

"Don't be thinking anything romantic," Beauregard sneered. "Cash. Lots of it."

"Why are you letting me go?"

"The Laveau legacy. Either you're real and you'll be fine, or you're a fraud and you won't. This New Orleans boy is hoping for the best. Walker's a northerner," he spat. "A hired hand. Deadly, though. He'll come after you and yours." He bent, whispering in her ear, "Do us all a favor. Kick his ass." Then he smiled, straightened, and stepped aside.

Marie was exposed. She looked at the rooftop, a black, haunting plain.

It would take less than a minute for a sniper to re-aim and fire. Walker had had plenty of time. His sight was probably still aimed. He'd been watching her like a rabbit in a cage.

Thunder clapped, lightning, cracking the black sky, struck the ground.

Marie took off running. A rifle shot exploded.

"Marie," yelled K-Paul.

"Come on," she screamed to K-Paul, hoping the rain, the night, and the police car lights made her a difficult target.

Behind her, she heard pistols shooting high. Beauregard and Raymonde had no intention and no hope of hitting the garage roof.

"Where's your car?" K-Paul asked, gasping. They were inside the garage.

"Fourth level."

"Let's take mine. It's on the second." K-Paul punched the elevator button.

"Stairs are faster," said Marie, opening the stairwell door. It was claustrophobic—dark, bleak, smelling of urine. She reached for the handrail.

Steps echoed from above.

"Run." They raced up the stairs, one, then two steps at a time, their feet clattering on metal.

The door slammed open. Light flooded the stairwell. Steps echoed, closer, louder.

K-Paul pressed his key chain. Headlights awoke, taillights flashed red. On the left, in the last row, was a black Jeep.

"Come on." They dashed, not daring to look behind them. K-Paul grabbed her hand, pulling her forward, "Get in the backseat. Lie down."

The upholstery was torn; yellow foam stuck out like bits of popcorn. Marie lay on her back, staring at the soft top roof.

K-Paul started the engine, pressed the gas, and the Jeep jolted in reverse.

Overhead lights and concrete beams flickered in and out through the vinyl windows.

K-Paul shifted into First.

A bullet pierced the front-passenger side. If Marie had been sitting there, she would have died.

"What the hell." K-Paul pressed hard on the gas, circling his Jeep down the ramp to Level One.

Marie focused on her breathing, keeping it even, keeping her body from trembling. It was hot, close.

The Jeep stopped, and she knew K-Paul was inserting his key card to exit the garage.

The Jeep lurched, making a sharp left turn, bypassing the hospital. She could see a slice of Charity's upper windows, hear the swish of the car's windshield wipers. She propped herself up on her elbows, her eyes level with the window. She saw Beauregard and Raymonde. The unmanned police cars. Beauregard had wanted her to run. Whatever happened next wouldn't be his responsibility. Her death might even be outside his jurisdiction.

K-Paul downshifted the clutch and the Jeep accelerated.

Beauregard hadn't tried to save her; he was saving his own ass.

"Cops aren't even trying to help. What the hell is this?" K-Paul's fist hit the dash. "Who the fuck is after you?"

"Just get me out of here, K-Paul. Take me home."

"Your home?"

"No, yours."

"City or country?"

"Country."

"All right. I can do that." He checked the side and rearview mirrors. "I don't think we're being followed. But you should stay down, hidden. At least until the expressway."

She dug in her pocket for her cell and speed-dialed Louise.

Wake up, Louise, she thought, hearing the phone ring and ring. She clicked her cell shut and dialed again. "He'll come after you and yours," Beauregard had said. Panic started to build. Once again Marie-Claire was in danger and it was her fault.

"Pick up, Louise," she shouted into the phone; she clicked her cell shut then, speed-dialed again.

"Louise, Louise. Yes, it's me. Is Marie-Claire all right? Please check on her. Yes, now."

"Is Marie-Claire okay?" asked K-Paul, speeding up the expressway ramp.

"I don't know," she answered, her voice wavering. The seconds waiting to hear from Louise were tortuous.

"Good," Marie exhaled. "Take Marie-Claire to your house. Yes, now. Pack a few things. But get out of there, quick." She paused, hearing Marie-Claire in the background, waking. "Time for school? Time for school?" she heard her daughter's high voice say.

"Marie-Claire," she shouted into the cell. "I love you."

"Momma!" Marie-Claire shouted back. "Love you, too."

She could see Louise holding the cell to Marie-Claire's ear . . . see her daughter in her pink nightgown . . . see Beau curled on the bed next to her.

"Be good for Louise."

"I'm good. Beau, too."

"Let me speak to Louise." *She could see Marie-Claire giving Louise the phone, then patting, comforting, Beau.*

"Thank you, Louise. Don't let anything happen to my daughter."

Marie clicked the cell shut, wiping rain and tears from her face. She swore Marie-Claire would never be a victim.

She heard the windshield wipers rapidly whisking back and forth. Rain sounded like a drum on the soft roof.

She shivered, cold.

"This is weird shit," K-Paul bellowed. "I don't get this. What the hell's going on?" K-Paul was ranting, releasing stress. "Cops messed up. Rain flooding New Orleans. Who'd harm a child? Who'd hurt you? What the hell's going on?" She didn't need to answer. K-Paul was ranting, driving fast, changing lanes, and heading away from the city.

She closed her eyes. She didn't doubt K-Paul would get her away safely. Just as she didn't doubt that Louise, who'd cared for Marie-Claire since she was a baby, would do everything she could to keep Marie-Claire safe. But Louise was limited. A good woman with no special training, lacking, perhaps, El and DuLac's courage and selflessness.

She wanted to rush home and protect Marie-Claire herself. But her daughter wouldn't be safe as long as she was hunted, as long as the murder mystery remained.

"Help." She concentrated on the one word: "Help."

Her cell buzzed, vibrated. A text message, white words on a black screen, appeared like magic: R U OK?

It had to be Parks. All along, he'd been trying to reach her. The 510 area code was California, Pacific time—it all began to make sense. Parks must have had an intuition that she was in danger. Without question, they were spiritually connected.

She stared at the small screen: R U OK?

She texted: NO. COME PROTECT MARIE-CLAIRE.

Pressing Send, she felt worry lifting.

Whatever love there was or wasn't between them, Parks would come.

Even now he was holstering his gun, slipping on his leather jacket, and shutting his apartment door.

Parks knew nothing mattered more to her than Marie-Claire's safety. He would know, if he didn't find Marie-Claire at home, to look for her at Louise's.

Parks was in his car, driving. He was coming toward her just as she was being driven away.

After their last case together, Parks knew he might have to protect Marie-Claire from things both seen and unseen. With luck, he'd land at Louis Armstrong New Orleans International Airport in less than eight hours.

How much time did she need? How much time before she could safely return again to New Orleans?

If she didn't return—if she were threatened or dying—Parks would stay, steadfast, beside Marie-Claire. He'd know she'd want him to.

✕

Her adrenaline was spent. The motion of the Jeep lulled. The tight back space felt like a cave.

K-Paul, too, had quieted. The patter of rain, the slap of tires on asphalt made her sleepy. She didn't have the energy to climb into the front seat.

She curled her knees tighter, crooked her elbow beneath her head. She relaxed, letting her body sway with the Jeep's vibrations.

Pieces of memory floated in her mind.

She saw Huan, lying in her blood.

My fault, she wanted to scream, shout. Huan had been a better friend to her than she'd ever been to Huan. But she couldn't grieve. Not yet.

El was crying.

Then it wasn't El, it was Huan weeping . . . then Nana, her blind eyes filling with bitter tears . . . then, Mimi L'Overture, her cheeks wet, silent, holding her too-still baby. Images tumbled—the mermaid, the shape-changing creature, and the dead.

Part of her wanted to stop the pictures, but she needed more help than the concrete world could offer. Now more than ever, she needed to be the Voodoo Queen.

She knew there were layers to death, spiritual realms that stretched forward and backward in time. There were spiraling circles of cause and effect, links between women. Between blood and water. Between birth and death. Between transformations of self.

"Water needs to go where she needs to go." What did that mean? *"Watch for the waters."* Not water, but waters. Not a single body.

"K-Paul, wake me when we get there."

"You all right?"

"No, but I hope to be." She began shutting down, purposefully. They were on the highway. For the moment, there was nothing more she could do.

Hers and K-Pauls's damp bodies and wet clothes were steaming, clouding the Jeep's plastic windows. The defroster, like an asthmatic breathing, tried to suck dry the humidity.

Sleep, she told herself. Dream.

She sent her soul traveling.

✕

The Guédé sat on the riverbank. Wind stirred storm clouds in the Gulf. Mississippi currents tugged at bodies.

Beneath the bodies was the mermaid's face. Then the teal creature rose, her white hair lank, her abdomen swollen. Floating above water, she opened her arms to Marie.

In the embrace, Marie felt warm flesh and cool scales . . . a woman's beating heart.

As she returned the embrace, the spirit collapsed, exploding into sprays of water.

Water mixed with rain before falling back into the river of the dead.

III

City, country, north, south,
In the beginning, loas *create.*
Humans uncreate.

SEVEN

K-PAUL'S BAYOU HOME

MORNING

"We're here," chortled K-Paul.

She woke, her mouth dry, and sat upright. Her shirt and pants were damp and sweat soaked. There were sleep lines, ridges on her face from the backseat upholstery. She felt disoriented, lost, bereft of the mermaid's brief embrace.

"We're not in Kansas anymore," said K-Paul, opening the Jeep door, helping Marie out.

They'd reached Louisiana's southern coast. Like a wave washing over her, Marie felt Nature's grace.

They were in a shallow cove—colored with greens, blues, filled with loam, soft moss, and granite stepping stones. A rowboat, filled with fishing gear, was banked and anchored to a rock. Marie couldn't help thinking that Huck Finn had played here.

Spanish moss hung like gray cobwebs and tinsel. Wild ginger, foxglove, sweet william, and hundreds of irises dotted the land.

The sky was blue, the sun achingly bright, and the horizon clear.

There was a shack on stilts with the Gulf lapping within feet of the front door. A car tire hung from a swinging rope attached to a cypress.

K-Paul was grinning like a kid. He'd taken off his lab coat, T-shirt, and shoes.

A flock of white ibis cut across the sky and, off in the distance, Marie heard the cawing of pelicans and herons.

"That's Miranda," said K-Paul, pointing.

A yellow tabby, perched on a branch, cleaned her paw.

"Miranda, meaning 'worthy of admiration.' A vain cat. She's got to be at least sixty years old. Always been here, since my granddaddy's day—or, at least a cat that looks like her. I think maybe she's been reproducing herself."

"She doesn't seem too impressed with us." She stepped closer to K-Paul. "Thank you."

Unaccustomedly shy, K-Paul dipped his head.

"Thanks for letting me sleep."

"You needed it. Let me get you something to eat."

No more dumplings, Marie thought mournfully. No more Bánh Bao.

K-Paul didn't move, he was smiling, dopey and foolish, waiting for her to speak.

"Your home's beautiful," she said, knowing she'd said the right thing when K-Paul slapped his chest, exclaiming, "Best place in the entire world. Delta land, where the Mississippi ends." Excited, his hands swept the air.

"This has been my people's home for generations. Me and my father tarred the roof. See this knick on the porch post? That's where I banged my head. The house was a bit too small for three. But since my parents died, it seems too big for me."

The house couldn't have been more than six hundred square feet, a neat square box that proved K-Paul had come from poverty. It said a lot that K-Paul hadn't razed the house and its memories. He hadn't transformed it into a luxury cottage.

K-Paul cut across the yard to where pole beans and sunflowers grew. A vine was thick with tomatoes. He plucked two. On the deck, there was a box filled with a hacksaw, a hammer and ax, and snorkeling gear.

She'd been a poor friend to K-Paul, too. She hadn't known this side of him, his rural roots.

"Let me fix breakfast," she said. "You've done all the driving."

"You're a lousy cook. Huan told me so." He quickly turned from the threshold, his expression bleak. Marie knew he'd suddenly remembered Huan was dead.

"How're we going to manage without her?"

Marie didn't answer because she didn't think she could keep her screams at bay. Later, much later, she'd grieve more fully for Huan. But, for now, she needed to stay focused on the connections between the city and the country, between Huan's death and DeLaire.

K-Paul opened the front door.

"Don't you lock it?"

"No need. Everyone knows this is my place. If they need something or come to rest, they're welcome. Only city folks lock doors, even with themselves inside."

She didn't tell him that the L'Overtures might have benefited from locked doors.

She walked inside the house.

It was a large studio, a mattress on the wood floor, a basic kitchen with a table and two chairs, a potbellied stove, and shuttered windows to protect against storms.

"Shower?"

"Only upgrading I've done," said K-Paul, smiling, opening another door.

Marie stepped into a cupboard-size bathroom with brass and porcelain and a clear rain forest shower with a head-high, four-by-four horizontal window to gaze at the outdoors.

"Want me to join you?"

She did, but it wouldn't be right. Years of turning him down—then a yes out of grief, sorrow?

"Just kidding."

There it was again. The look that said he wasn't.

"Towels beneath the sink."

"Thanks."

K-Paul closed the door and she stripped down. Her body was cramped from stress and sleeping in the car.

The shower was like indoor rain, diffuse water washing away blood, dirt, and sweat. Looking through the clear window to the outdoors, she cried. The trees and sky blurred. She could blame it on the rain. Blame her tears on being startled by a crack of thunder, far beyond the inlet, the private shore.

✕

K-Paul had left a fresh shirt on the toilet seat. She hadn't heard him enter. She blushed, knowing he'd probably had a clear view of her body. She didn't mind being seen nude, she just preferred to choose who and when.

When she came out, the red-haired ER doctor was fully transformed into a country boy. He'd added a wooden crucifix around his neck; the cross lay in a swath of golden chest hair. Jeans that had seen better days rode low on his hips.

"Thanks for the shirt."

"You look good in it. I didn't peek, if that's what you're thinking."

"I am."

"Cajun honor." He raised his hand in a Boy Scout salute. He set a plate of scrambled eggs on the table. The tomatoes had been sliced and looked like lazy, blood-red eyes.

She believed him. "I could've cooked eggs," she said, sitting at the table.

"Really?" he asked, grinning. He pulled two beers from the fridge, opened both, then handed her one and sat across from her.

"Isn't it too early for alcohol?"

"Beer is mother's milk in the bayou. Breakfast, lunch, dinner. It'll keep you strong."

"Is that the medical doctor speaking?"

"Country boy."

"It really is different here."

"Didn't you know beer is one of folk medicine's greatest inventions?"

She smiled wanly. She couldn't bring herself to cut into the tomatoes and see red juice draining on the plate. The eggs reminded her of brain matter.

K-Paul lifted the plate and put it in the kitchen sink.

"You're different here."

"You bet. But it isn't paradise. When I was a boy, I used to think that." He straddled the kitchen chair. "But humanity always ruins paradise. It's our nature."

"Tell me about it."

"You first," he smiled. Then, he leaned forward, elbows on the wooden table. "Who killed Huan?"

"Walker murdered Huan thinking she was me. I'm sure of it."

"And who's Walker?"

"An albino, white-haired rat. Some kind of detective, I think. Or private agent, a hired assassin. NOPD's police captain was frightened of him, or else of the power he represented. Whatever, he had Beauregard wrapped around his finger."

Marie told him all the concrete, literal things. Everything she knew—about the murdered family, Nana and her grandsons, about Aaron's lying, Beauregard's stalling, and especially about Walker, threatening her.

"Why threaten you?"

She shrugged. "I'm not supposed to care about a murdered family? None of it makes sense."

K-Paul pulled another set of beers from the fridge. Freckles and downy hair, more gold than red, dusted his back.

"Tell me about it," he said again, his voice quieter. "What've you left unsaid?"

Through the front window, she could see the blue-green landscape. Paradise. Yet given the right circumstances, it could also be a rural dreamscape every bit as frightful as city terrors.

"I've seen visions, ghosts. Seen the murdered father trying to protect his family. Seen slick black threads shadowing, taunting me. Trails of viscous black spreading across earth, burying any green." Her breath quickened.

"Marie-Claire drew a trinity of waves. She's never done that before. Never made a painting of symbols, signs, before." She shook her head in wonderment.

"Afterward I saw a mermaid in the Mississippi. And just before the shooting, some kind of shape-shifter—male and female . . ."

"You mean a transvestite? Or someone transsexual, transgender?"

"No, a spirit, more like a mythic being. Prehistoric. It healed its own wound—" her voice pitched high; hysteria was creeping in. She was frustrated because of her inability to make sense of the spirit world.

"At the hospital, didn't you see me with a patient? It would've been just before Huan's death."

"I saw you with Will."

She swallowed a cry. "Will saw me with Will even before it was me. I know, I'm not making any sense."

Think, Marie, she told herself. Think. Breathe. She dug her nails into her palms.

"Prehistory. Nana had two clay statues—one was a mermaid. Except, nothing like western sirens, its body was teal; its face, brown. The other statue was dual gendered, with breasts and a penis. One side of its face, short haired and like a man's; the other, long haired and like a woman's."

"These were Nana's gods?"

"Yes, I think so. Neither is worshipped in modern ceremonies. Or at least not as far as I know. Not here in Louisiana." She swallowed hard. "Both appeared to me. I'm not sure why. I've had visitations from both."

"When did you see them?"

"The mermaid *loa* appeared just before Deet told me of Nana's death. The other appeared just before Huan's murder. It also knew about Nana, knew about her final words to me.

"In the hospital, it said: 'Watch for the waters,' a direct echo of Nana's 'Mind'—not 'mine'?—the waters'?"

"I'm confused."

"No more than me."

K-Paul reached for her hands. "Puzzle it out, Marie. DuLac had faith in you."

She closed her eyes, blocking out light so she could better see the interconnections, remember what she might have forgotten.

She spoke slowly. "Mythic systems, both western and eastern, posit that in the beginning, gods made humanity androgynous. Plato imagined the first humans as circular beings embodied with both sexes. He would've interpreted Genesis—'Male and female, He created them'—as meaning humanity was complete, dual gendered within itself.

"To be perfect, godlike, is to reconcile both sides of one's being—the feminine as well as the masculine."

"So the gods were dual gendered? Early humanity was made in God's image?"

"Yes. Historically and cross-culturally, androgyny resonates. Hindus, Aztecs . . . native cultures throughout the Americas embodied concepts of dual-gendered beings/spirits. One interpretation of the Judeo-Christian expulsion from Eden is that humanity, as punishment for its hubris, was split into two beings, creating the division of the sexes. Punishing humanity forever to search for his/her other half. For completeness."

"That's why sex, right? To fit your other half, to become a four-armed, four-legged creature again."

"Yes."

"I like sex."

"So do I." Companionably, she smiled and felt as if gloom had lifted, the sun had broken through clouds.

"What if this spirit Nana worshipped," she continued, "is primeval, from a time before humanity, a time when only gods, spirit-*loas*, existed?"

"A pre-western kind of spiritual shaman?"

"Yes. If humanity began in Africa, it follows that faith did, too, and I believe this shaman figure was/is ancient. Older than disaporic manifestations of African faith, older than known African and African-American spiritual traditions . . . older than the traditions normally practiced by slaves."

"So maybe it's an aspect of a legacy brought by a particular tribe—"

"Or a particular slave."

"A religious man—"

"Or woman. A spirit that's faded from cultural memory, except for DeLaire.

"DeLaire's an isolated community not quite in sync with modern times, more in sync with enslaved central and western Africans. Like the Geechee, the Gullah community off the sea islands. American slavery began in the 1500s; its estimated twelve million survived the middle passage. Of those millions, who knows exactly what religious variant they practiced? Or what obscure gods they believed in?"

"Such as double-gendered beings capable of shifting between genders?"

"Yes. Kin to shape-shifters, maybe. But legends suggest shape-shifters, with each transformation, find it more difficult to change form. They risk being stuck in one shape forever. The creature I saw was fluid. Transforming, changing features as easy as—"

"What?"

"Water." Arrested, she inhaled, trying to make sense. Her head ached.

The mermaid was dual natured—fish and human. But it hadn't transformed.

How were the spirits connected? What were they called? Why did Nana worship both?

She tilted forward, asking earnestly, "Didn't you see him/her at the hospital?"

K-Paul shook his head.

"He—it—had a wound on his arm. It healed."

"What else?"

"Then she—it—healed Will."

Elbows on the table, Marie rested her head in her hands. "Funny, I always see El. Never DuLac. I expect I'll see Huan." She looked up at K-Paul. "Did you know Huan believed in animism? As in voodoo, for her the world was brimming with spirits. She also believed in ancestor worship."

"The living should make provisions for the dead?"

"Yes. Especially for those who died violently. Otherwise, out of bitterness, the dead might harm the living."

"That's not Huan."

"No. But after her killer is arrested, I'll make provisions for her. I know her family will, too. Mine will just be extra love."

In her mind, she could see it. On her home altar, she'd add ponytail bands and ribbons for Huan's hair, bits of rice, a picture of Vietnam, and even a tiny pink umbrella, the kind used to garnish drinks. Even dead, she thought Huan would get the joke, bob her head, and smile.

Marie watched K-Paul. He'd gotten up, placed his untouched plate in the sink with hers, and grabbed two more bottles of beer.

"I'm freaking you out, aren't I?" She was still drinking her first beer; K-Paul opened his third and drank it down.

K-Paul never said anything, either positive or negative, about her spiritual abilities. He admired her hospital skills, understood the edge intuition and faith gave her. He'd been there when a vampire spirit had possessed her in the ER. And he knew DuLac and El, both trained in medicine, had been believers who believed in her.

He opened one of her untouched bottles, swigged deeply, and then laid his hands on the table. He had soft, magical hands able to feel a pulse, palpate an abdomen, and massage a heart. She swore he had his own special talents—extraordinary medical skills.

"My people been in Louisiana since Le Grand Dérangement, the Great Expulsion, when the British evicted us from Acadia."

"You mean eastern Canada. The Maritime provinces?"

"Yes. Acadia was a French colony. It was supposed to be our promised land." K-Paul's gaze unfocused, as if he were having an internal vision, seeing his homeland. Forced migration was ordered by the British governor and the Nova Scotia Council 1755 to 1763.

Today, we'd call it ethnic cleansing. Thousands of French colonists were maimed, killed." His expression bleak, he drank.

Marie waited, knowing she'd uncovered one of K-Paul's profound wounds.

He went on: "Most, but not all, my people escaped to Louisiana. We've been in America a long, long time. Through Spanish and American rule, we held tight to our native culture. Good food, good fellowship, and faith. Over time, us, French Acadians, became proud Louisianan Cajuns. 'Let the good times roll.' '*Laissez les bon temps roulez.*'

"Still," he turned his chair backward, and sat, his knees bent, his hands holding tight to the chair rails. "I'm a good Catholic boy, which means I believe in the unseen. Mysteries.

"Just cause folks paint God as white and male, I never bought it." He looked around, got up, and ambled toward the screen door. "I think God is right here. In Nature. This bayou."

"You've always worn that crucifix?"

"Since confirmation. My father whittled it for me. From cypress bark."

"Is he alive?"

"Died in a fishing accident. 'Bout ten years ago. My mother died two years afterward, never fully recovering from losing Pa. It was Pa's dream that I doctor. Said hardworking people, poor people, died too soon. Said I should help."

K-Paul turned from the screen, looked at Marie, and said earnestly, "Just because I don't see what you see doesn't mean I disbelieve."

Overwhelmed, Marie murmured, "I don't know anything. I wasn't a good enough friend to Huan. All these years, working together, I knew nothing about you. Nothing about your background, your past. I don't know anything."

"Plenty. You know plenty. I don't understand your powers, but I've seen how you use them. You always help."

"Everyone around me dies."

"Nature of life. Nature of evil."

She stretched her arms on the table, and laid her head on them. "It should've been me. Not Huan."

K-Paul stroked her still-damp hair.

She felt like Marie-Claire, getting comfort. It mattered to her that K-Paul believed her, believed in her. She hadn't realized how much strength she'd drawn from El's and DuLac's, even Huan's, belief in her.

Trembling, she sat up straight. "I've been warned. Over and over. But I can't figure out what it all means. Marie-Clarie's drawing, the mermaid, the oil slick—"

"What oil slick?"

"At least that's what I think it was. A kind of oozing darkness, threading like veins out of the ground, organic, yet not. A black oil-like substance covering the ground, pooling, where the L'Overture family died."

"It's either oil or it's not. Let's go see."

"We can't."

"What're you talking about?"

"It was a vision. An apparition. I didn't really see it. I mean, I did. But you couldn't see it."

K-Paul swung open the refrigerator, grabbed another beer from his endless supply, and snapped its tab.

"You think I'm crazy?" she asked.

Nonstop, he swigged beer, then crushed the empty can. He stared out the window.

"K-Paul?"

"Only two words I really understand. Oil and water. That's all Louisiana's ever been about."

K-Paul's shadow stretched behind him on the floor. Neither man nor shadow moved.

She'd seen this stillness in K-Paul when he was diagnosing a challenging case. He seemed entranced, like worshippers during her ceremonies. Except she knew it wasn't the spiritual infusing him. He was connecting with intuition grounded in scientific fact.

✕

She slipped on her tennis shoes, opened the screen door, and stepped outside, leaving K-Paul space to think.

Heat settled on her shoulders like melted butter.

She stared at the Gulf. This was where the Mississippi ended. The largest river slicing America for over 2,300 miles. A great river mingling with Gulf waters mingling with the ocean.

Mind the water.

She pulled her cell phone from her back pocket. It was reassuring to see Parks's text. Reassuring that even after a breakup, he'd fly to Louisiana.

She trembled, wondering whether Parks would reach Marie-Claire in time. Of course he would. He was Parks.

She pressed for voice mail. No cell signal. No disembodied voice coming through the small metal speakers. She tapped the tiny screen. The signal bars were faded, dead.

"You need a cell booster." The screen door slammed; birds fluttered out of trees; brush creatures scampered.

"You startled me."

"Here. Use my phone. I need to get Riley. He's a friend, a biologist. Used to work for public health. Did some environmental activism. Now he mostly fishes. Drinks." He stuffed his hands in his pockets. "But Riley knows this land better than anyone. Knows about water, oil. I think you need to talk with him."

"I'd like that."

"Riley doesn't have a phone. Or even electricity. I'll row down to him. If he's not at home, it might take a while. He's got a couple of regular fishing holes. We'll return in Riley's airboat. That all right? You'll be all right while I'm gone?"

"I'm a 'big girl,' as Marie-Claire would say."

"Yeah, one people shoot at." K-Paul winced. "Sorry. Didn't mean to remind you—"

She didn't answer.

"Huan's death wasn't your fault."

She stared at the blue waters.

"You should be safe here. I'll be back as soon as I can."

Barefoot, K-Paul headed for his boat, slipping the rope off its mooring.

He jumped into the boat, his back muscles rippling as he moved the oars. The small craft sliced through water.

※

Marie wiped her eyes with her sleeves. Mourn later, she told herself.

She opened K-Paul's cellphone, pressing numbers. At first, there was nothing but static, followed by silence, then, without a ring, she heard, "Parks."

"It's me."

"Are you okay?"

"Marie-Claire?"

"My plane's just landed. Need to pick up the rental car. I should be with her soon."

Relieved, Marie murmured, "Thank you."

"You know, everybody's leaving New Orleans," said Parks. "Few flights landing, mostly leaving. Did you hear? Katrina did major damage in Florida. Right now, she's back at sea."

"But she's heading west," she said, alarmed.

"Meteorologists think it could go either way. Katrina could become wind starved, turn into a storm or a tropical depression. Or she could catch her breath and turn inland."

"Heading straight for New Orleans." Her legs lost strength. She sat on the porch steps. Her dream was a foretelling of Katrina. Bodies, floating, flashed in her mind.

"Yeah, I didn't want to say."

"Get Marie-Claire out of New Orleans," she said urgently.

"If it comes to that, I will. Where are you, Marie?"

"On the Gulf."

"Delta land? I'd feel better if you were the hell out of there."

"Can't. Something else is going on. Something, but I don't know what—connected to Katrina. Get Marie-Claire out of the city."

"We'll wait for you."

"Don't. Go."

"We'll wait for you," he said, loudly, then, softly, "I'll wait for you."

"Parks—"

"We'll wait for you."

"Parks," she pleaded. She could hear his labored breath, imagine his jaw, squared and stubborn.

Were they true loves searching for each other? Her heart ached. She was running out of time. Maybe she'd never know. Never get a second chance. There were multiplying dangers—Katrina; Walker; warnings from ancient spirits; and the L'Overture murders not far from the Mississippi's mouth.

"I've got to go."

"What the hell are you doing, Marie?"

"Following leads. Isn't that what you taught me?"

"Let me help." It was Parks's turn to plead.

"You are helping."

"Whatever you say, Doc," he snapped, sarcastic.

Parks knew she hated being called Doc.

"Doc, do you think Marie-Claire remembers me? It's been nearly a year."

"She remembers you. She's got a good memory, like her mother."

"See you, Doc. I mean, Marie."

She knew she and Parks were both smiling.

"See you."

"Marie!" Parks shouted into the phone before she hung up. "Baton Rouge. If Katrina turns, I'll get Marie-Claire to Baton Rouge. I promise."

Too emotional to answer, she clicked the cell phone shut.

EIGHT

BAYOU WATERS

LATE MORNING

Marie heard the airboat before it arrived. It buzzed like a thousand wasps and bees combined. It came round the bend, a huge caged propeller, like a peacock's fan, at its rear.

K-Paul was standing, waving. Next to him, sitting high on the airboat, was a skeletal sunburned man wearing a New Orleans Saints T-shirt and a baseball hat.

She headed for the dock. The engine shut down and K-Paul, with a rope, jumped off the airboat, tying it to the dock.

"Marie meet Riley. Riley, Marie."

He looked like an emaciated Popeye. He took off his hat, flashing a freckled bald head. His eyes were jaundiced, his cheeks flushed from heavy drinking.

"Heard you wanted to see my country. The Gulf. Bayous. Marshes. Waterlogged soil."

"I do."

Riley stared at her hard, almost defiant. She could tell he knew he was dying.

She stared back, keeping her face neutral, her compassion dampened.

"Come on," grinned Riley. "I'll show you my kingdom."

K-Paul extended his hand, helping her climb onto the airboat's perch. "Put these on," he said, handing her ear muffs.

"Sit." Riley patted the chair next to him. Then he started the engine—a wild roar. K-Paul hooted.

The muffs only dampened half the sound.

The boat bucked forward, accelerating. K-Paul, still standing, held on to the metal stabilizing bar.

The boat swerved, almost like a jet ski, twenty, thirty miles an hour. Spray dashed her face; wind unraveled strands of hair. Riding high, the boat felt like a thrill ride, their bodies swaying into the curves. K-Paul and Riley grinned like crazy men. She held on tight.

There wasn't a single cloud on the horizon.

✖

This was the first time Marie had actually been inside the marsh, not just seeing it from the shore or trudging through it piecemeal. She could feel the struggle of predators and prey—cottonmouth moccasins and other snakes, small game such as rabbit and hare. Even cicadas, insects, catfish, and bullfrogs struggled for life.

By boat, she sensed the depth, breadth of water and soil blending for miles upon miles. There were warrens of water trails, marked by tall marsh grass, small islands of trees, and bush growth. Wisteria covered pines, moss covered oaks; pink trumpet vines and white spider lillies contrasted with lush greens.

Ibis flew overhead.

Riley cut the engine. The silence was jarring.

Marie took off her muffs, awed by stillness, Riley's serene expression, and her own desire that this moment would last forever.

Every sign of civilization was gone. She'd entered a primordial world where fowl, reptiles, and insects ruled, lurking in the bush, sky, and water. Here, in this vast wilderness, you'd never imagine that, hours north, a city like New Orleans even existed.

"Look there," said K-Paul.

A log floated in the water.

"A gator," said K-Paul.

"Really? Looks like driftwood."

"Look close."

Just above the water level, she saw the opening and shutting of a yellow eye.

"Alligators were almost hunted to extinction," said Riley. "Good meat. Hides became shoes, saddles for the Confederate Army. Oil harvested from them was used as a lubricant for steamship and cotton engines. They're protected now. Every first Wednesday in September, hunting season starts and lasts for thirty days."

"Have you ever hunted and killed one?"

"No. They're vicious. They'll eat anything, including each other. Besides," he said, smiling, "you can't help but respect a species that's been around for over two hundred million years."

Marie liked Riley. He was smart; his eyes glinted with irreverence.

"As a boy, I'd keep baby gators in pails," said K-Paul, squatting behind Marie. "When young, a gator's skin is softer than you can

imagine. Like velvet. But I always threw them back into the swamp.
Never kept them for more than a day or two."

Marie could imagine the young K-Paul, compassionate, curious
about nature and biology. It had never occurred to her that a bayou
childhood was the perfect preparation for becoming a doctor.

The airboat bumped up against a small island. A nest of birds, a
mother and her babies, was settled in the grass.

"These birds, green herons, are sweet to look at," said K-Paul,
"but they can roust your eyes in a second."

"You love it here," she said.

"Yes, and I'm losing it."

"Everybody in Louisiana is," said Riley.

"What do you mean?"

"See these waterways, canals?" Riley stood, pointing north,
south, east, and west. "For decades, oil companies have dredged
them. Look there. Pipeline valves." Rusted metal stuck upward
from the sluggish water.

"Canals were dug deep. So deep, roots and natural barriers
were destroyed. All this here"—he pointed up and down the
waterways—"used to be freshwater. Because of erosion, salt seeps
in from the Gulf, killing the wetlands. Destroying animal habitats.
Destroying one of the greatest wildernesses ever. Breaks my heart."

"We're losing what's impossible to get back," said K-Paul.

Marie looked carefully at the vista of marsh and swamp. K-Paul
and Riley had altered her sight. What she'd seen as a paradise was a
kind of slow dying. What else didn't she see clearly?

"New Orleans will one day go under, too."

"What do you mean?"

Riley stared at the water; his eyes squinting in the sunlight's glare. "In the 1890s the Army Corps of Engineers changed the direction of the Mississippi."

"You're kidding?"

"No. They wanted a more direct passage to carry oil and goods to the Gulf. The Mississippi used to birth tons of silt. Silt that became new land. There used to be thousand of miles of land between here and the Gulf, thousands more between New Orleans and the Gulf.

"Changing the river's flow, deepening canals, letting salt into the marsh has destroyed almost all the land that had once been. To make up for the land that's disappeared, the corps built levees, doing more damage to a damaged environment. Every half hour, a football field of land disappears. Floods wouldn't be a problem if land was still here. Eventually, even New Orleans won't exist."

"I find that hard to believe."

"I'll show you," said Riley, grimly. He downshifted the shaft. The boat moved forward in low gear, past trees, the fading landscape. The motor still growled but she kept her earmuffs off.

The boat veered south for a mile, then right.

She gasped. Hundreds of dead tree trunks, leafless, nearly branchless, were rotting in the water. The trees looked as if they'd been burnt and made barren by fire, but they were in and surrounded by water. The landscape was a nightmare world, as if Marie-Claire had painted sickly stick trees that needed a magician to revive them. The slow-moving, moss-covered water looked putrid. And the sun, drenching the world yellow, made it all seem a fevered dream. Just minutes ago, she'd thought the bayou wilderness was vast, but it was all an illusion. They'd turned a corner and encountered a landscape no longer green and vital, but black and disappearing.

Riley cut the engine and the world seemed more funereal, punctuated with articulate, almost mournful bird cries.

K-Paul murmured, "I used to hunt here when I was a boy. Now there's not enough land to walk on."

Riley grunted. "Used to be thousands of miles of healthy delta land. Nearly three thousand miles gone in my lifetime. And I'm not that old."

Marie guessed Riley was in his fifties, far too young to be dying.

"Land. Just gone," Riley went on. "The United Houma Nation used to grow medicinal herbs all along here. Now this stretch is just gone." Riley's voice choked.

"I haven't heard of the United—"

"—Houma Nation," K-Paul finished. "There's hard evidence that they've been in Louisiana since the 1600s. They're recognized by the state. But they're still waiting for federal recognition by the Bureau of Indian Affairs."

"In the meantime," said Riley, wiping forehead sweat on his arm, "they're losing more land, like all Louisianans, to erosion and hurricanes.

"Losing marsh, wetlands. Folks don't understand our marshes are a great big womb for shrimp, oysters, and crabs. These marshes have been declining, infected with oil and salt. Seafood production has been declining. Sons and daughters are abandoning family fisheries. And this area here is just dead. Plain ol' dead.

"Even the city of New Orleans used to be inland. Now it sits on the coast. Land mass used to buffer it from hurricanes. But as oil companies drilled, all along the coastline, acres of good land disappeared. Vanished."

"Water turns to salt. Oil turns to money," K-Paul said, mournfully.

Marie thought the landscape looked like a movie horror set.

"Why don't people stop it?"

"You think the government cares about habitats dying?" asked Riley scornfully. "Louisiana is a poor state. Poor, with corrupt officials. Oil companies are given cheap leases and have no incentive to give a damn about the land, water, or people. When the oil's gone, they'll move elsewhere. And to make it worse, the federal government barely funds environmental repair or rehabilitation. But it funded all the ways to divert the river, deepen the channels, and widen its mouth so oil could move from the Gulf up to city refineries."

"Is that why you quit?"

Riley looked bleak.

"K-Paul said you'd done environmental work. Public health."

"Yeah. I quit."

She'd touched his wound. K-Paul signaled her with his eyes. She nodded. She understood his work was what had driven Riley to drink.

"The environment's going from bad to worse. Decided I'd quit and live on the land until the erosion destroyed it all or a hurricane blew it away."

K-Paul squeezed Riley's thick shoulder. "You tried."

"The Clinton years were the best. Won a few court cases, settlements proving contamination. Environmental damage to land, animals, and humans. But, on the Gulf, good news doesn't last. We went back to the same old same old. Broken promises. Did I tell you there's a dead zone the size of New Jersey in the Gulf? Nitrogen, pesticides, animal waste, all wash down the Mississippi, depleting the water's oxygen. Nothing can live. Bribed officials don't care. Hell, America doesn't even know what it's losing."

"I didn't," said Marie.

"Oil men," hollered K-Paul like a circus barker, "just want you to think about how oil fuels America—"

"—our economic engine, some say."

"Our lifestyle. Hell, our American way of life," shouted K-Paul, his voice reverberating through the dead trees and grass.

"What's happening here can happen all along America's Gulf Coast. Oil poisoning will continue to threaten Texas, Mississippi, Alabama . . . even Florida. Who cares if fish and wildlife die?"

"I've got my gas," whooped K-Paul.

"Dredge the Mississippi. Slice it open. Put up another rig. Dig another well. Hell." Riley reached beneath his seat, pulling out a metal flask. His entire body was trembling. He drank his spirits, hard and fast.

Marie felt such sadness. She knew Riley and K-Paul had this conversation down to a ritual.

※

"Oil and water, oil and water," Marie muttered, gazing at the seemingly endless plain of petrified and rotted trees, dead grass and dry bushes. The landscape was like a body starved of oxygen and drained of blood. This bayou marsh had become a morgue.

"The apparition," she said, slowly, "the threads at the L'Overture homesite, were like veins in a body, spreading oil, destabilizing the soil."

"K-Paul told me you were special."

"Not spooky?" she joked.

"Spirits been haunting the bayou since forever," responded Riley. "I've seen native peoples, Creoles, Cajuns, African Americans call them. Hell, I plan on haunting this place myself. Expect to be doing it by the end of the year."

She and K-Paul didn't respond.

"Nothing wrong with oil itself."

"An organic substance," said K-Paul. "Exploitation spreads harm."

"Disease," coughed Riley.

"The river mermaid, the unstable soil—all of it's starting to make sense. Or, rather, I feel a glint of sense inside me. Feel a foreshadowing doom."

"You're feeling the tragedy of Louisiana."

Marie stared at the withered trees. "Why do I feel I've only scratched the surface?" she said. "Everything has life, spirit. That's the true message of voodoo. My role is to solve, to explain mysteries. To make sense of the connections between real and spirit worlds."

The heat and humidity were sapping her energy. Images of bodies—Huan's, the L'Overtures', and the river of dead—were making her feel unhinged.

The three sat on the airboat, K-Paul on the platform, she and Riley in the tattered upholstered chairs. Riley reached into a cooler and popped open a beer. He handed it to K-Paul, then reached for another. Marie shook her head. Riley kept the beer for himself.

She could feel death. This wasn't the Guédé's landscape. This was death outside the natural cycle—nothing less than murder.

"There's a phrase," she murmured. "'*Loas* created the world; man uncreates.'"

"Ain't that the truth," said Riley.

"Storm's coming," said K-Paul, pointing at birds in formation, dark silhouettes flying home to roost.

"Yes, I know." She could feel the air thickening, the rise in barometric pressure. Hairs rose along her neck. "It means something that all this is happening now. This time, this season."

"Hurricane season?"

"Yes."

"Katrina's out there, tearing up the sea. Maybe this season, all of this will be swept away. Like me. My doctor doubts I'll make it to the end of the year. Ain't that right, K-Paul?"

Marie looked at K-Paul. His shoulders were slumped. She knew it was hard watching a friend die. But she and K-Paul knew that some drunks couldn't stop drinking. Still, Riley's dying was as unnatural as the blighted landscape.

"Spirits—both water and earth—are calling me. I need to figure out what they're saying, what all this"—her hands swept the scene—"means."

"Can I help?" asked Riley.

"I think you already have."

"What about me?" asked K-Paul, masking his grief for Riley with a Cajun boy's enthusiasm.

"You were destined to help. What else would explain why you'd get me down to your home?"

K-Paul whooped. "It was all part of my plan. Cajuns don't take rejection easily."

"Romance going on?" boomed Riley. "K-Paul needs a girl. I been telling him that for years."

"Time to go, Riley," said Marie dryly. "Steer the boat."

K-Paul handed her the muffs. "Marie." His face was an open book. Expressive. For a minute, he let her see his longing, his desire, and affection for her. Then he shuttered his feelings, saying softly, "Let's visit where the L'Overtures died."

"Yes," she murmured. The engine revved and the wind-powered boat sliced through green, mucuslike water and all the creatures, ancient survivors, watched their passing. "And visit Sheriff Malveaux and all the other good citizens of DeLaire."

The airboat sped over muddy, slick water. Waves kicked up broken bark, tangled brown algae. "No good fishing here," said Riley. "No nothing." His voice was starting to slur. "Going fishing elsewhere."

K-Paul patted his shoulder.

Riley started singing, off-key.

Marie whispered into the whipping spray and wind, "Time's short, running out. Any grace I have, let it come."

NINE

L'OVERTURE HOMESITE

AFTERNOON

As soon as Marie stepped onto the homesite, she saw the ghosts.

John L'Overture was pulling pails of water up from the well, tasting, then tossing the water onto the ground. He kept repeating the sequence. Lowering the pail, pulling it high, tasting the water, then throwing the remaining water onto the ground. Water sprayed the vegetable garden—the moldy beans, the scarred tomatoes.

Mimi fed her baby at her breast.

El was leaning against a tree, flicking her red nails; she'd always been proud of her nails. Huan sat cross-legged in the dirt, her wrists on her knees, like a composed Buddha.

All of them had died violently, yet their spirit bodies appeared whole. No sign of trauma. But what about their souls?

"Do you see Huan?" she asked K-Paul.

"Don't see anything."

"El and the L'Overtures are here, too."

K-Paul made the sign of the cross.

"You're not scared?"

"No. Just recognizing the blessing. You're special."

She stepped closer to where the house had once been. Someone had set a raging fire. The only things left of the cottage were ashes, cinder, and scarred wood. The gleaming truck was gone, as well as the ax that had been propped against a tree. None of the split logs for the potbellied stove had escaped burning. They'd burned, collapsed like thick cigars, dead, graying and black.

"Look," said K-Paul, digging in the ashes with a stick. "Dog tags."

"Are you sure?"

"Sure."

"He looked like a warrior."

"When you saw him, you said he was dead."

"He was. I had a vision of him. But I'm positive he didn't have his tags on."

"Some vets, once they're home, take them off. Put them in a drawer."

At the hospital, she'd seen hundreds of veterans with PTSD, startled by noise, anxious in crowds, and self-medicating with drugs and alcohol. Louisiana had tons of poor boys who'd fought.

"L'Overture must've just returned from Afghanistan or Iraq," she said.

K-Paul kicked a pile of ash. "Damn shame to survive war. Then come home and die."

"Be murdered."

K-Paul rubbed the silver tags. "Blood type: AB negative. Faith: None."

"For a southern Louisianan, that doesn't seem right. No faith? Doesn't make sense."

Louisianans were famous for their faith; their churches might be a no-name, hole-in-the-wall, a converted storefront in a strip mall or a high-flying cathedral, but Louisianans always believed in things unseen. They had faith.

"At least he could be a holy roller," K-Paul remarked.

"A lapsed Catholic."

"Or one of your people."

Her lips thinned. "He would've been one of Nana's people. Maybe that's why he was living on the outskirts of DeLaire. Maybe he'd disavowed Nana and voodoo. Or at least the kind of voodoo as practiced by Nana. I'm still not confident that the community isn't involved in the deaths."

K-Paul slipped the dog tags into his pocket. "He probably disavowed the army, too. Some soldiers do."

"The only thing he didn't disavow was his family."

"Maybe they moved here to start a new life."

"To find some peace," responded Marie.

"I can understand that." K-Paul walked the crime scene, sticking a branch into ash, shoving aside crumbling wood. "Marie. Some bones here. And a skull."

"Let me see." With two hands, Marie gently clasped the hard bone. "It's an adult female. The mother's skull."

"Father and baby must be here, too."

Her fingers traced the eye sockets, the cheekbone arcs. She murmured, "Not quite a cremation. Too much bone is left. For some cultures, even a purifying cremation doesn't necessarily override a violent death."

"You mean like Vietnam?"

"Yes. But also in Japan, Nepal, and South Africa. Many cultures believe spirits can remain tormented and vengeful. Purification by fire isn't always enough."

"Two more skulls," said K-Paul, pointing with his branch. "Should we pack them up?"

Marie crossed to him, cradling the mother's skull next to the father's and baby's.

"A sad trinity," she said, yearning for Marie-Claire.

Inexplicably, Marie thought of "Goldilocks and the Three Bears." Small, medium, and large skulls; child, mother, and father.

"The baby's skull hadn't fused," she said. "I've never seen an infant skull without," she paused, "skin."

Fire and animals had scored, picked the bones clean.

She could see it—after the blaze, creatures waiting for the sight to cool. Then they did what creatures do, forage. Feed.

"I'm surprised bones are still here," said K-Paul. "Wouldn't murderers want to hide their crime? Clear evidence?"

"Walker came after you. Why? What do you think? Arrogance or stupidity?"

"Arrogance. And a complicit sheriff." She turned, studying the trees, the patches of cloudy sky. "Country people stick together. They didn't imagine that once burned anyone would visit the L'Overture homesite. The burning, itself, was a warning."

K-Paul sucked air between his teeth. "While the city is overflowing with unknowns. The unexpected. Though they failed, maybe that's why your murder was planned."

"Maybe they knew I wouldn't give up."

Marie and K-Paul stared at each other. Eventually, K-Paul said, dryly, "I can't imagine having you as an adversary."

Marie didn't speak.

Uneasily, K-Paul shifted his weight.

The good, honest doctor, the religious Cajun, Marie thought, was uncomfortable. K-Paul only knew her inside the context of the hospital. Just as she'd only half-known him until today, until she'd seen him in the bayou, he'd only half-known her.

"What should we do with the bones?" asked K-Paul. "Take them with us?"

"No, leave them. Parks would have already scolded me for disturbing the crime scene. But I have a feeling that no one is ever going to investigate this but us."

K-Paul laid the skulls gently on the ground, and placed the visible bones nearby. Marie squatted next to him. "Prayers, K-Paul. Let's say prayers."

Bowing his head, K-Paul made the sign of the cross. Marie spread her hands—high—above the bones, murmuring, "Peace. You shall forever be remembered, honored by me."

"Like Huan," K-Paul added, unashamedly wiping tears from his eyes.

"Like Huan," she responded, sorrowfully, thinking about how so many she'd known and loved had died.

"We should hide the bones," she said.

"You mean bury them?"

"Later. We'll bury them later. I don't know why, K-Paul, I just know it's right. We'll bury them later."

With their hands, and strong branches, she and K-Paul began

scraping dirt, fallen leaves, moss, and dried brush over the bones.

"Look, Marie." K-Paul pointed at a shallow trench, a foot behind them. "I bet it surrounds the house. Whoever set the fire knew what they were doing. The trench would've prevented the fire from spreading."

"A country technique? Something the sheriff would've been good at?"

"You bet. The bayou doesn't have sanitation drivers. Every kid learns how to burn trash, brush, even cook with fire without igniting a larger one."

Marie scooped soil. An inchworm crawled in the small mound. Marie knew that inside the dirt were seedlings, millions of bacteria. She dusted off the dirt, then stared at her palms. Dirt particles clung to her skin. Mud traced both lifelines.

K-Paul cupped her hands. "Traces of water and oil. Not just ordinary dirt."

"No. Not at all." She didn't tell K-Paul that she still felt a trace of the soil's energy in her palm. The ground they stood on was alive. "I'm missing something." She studied the desolate yard.

K-Paul wiped his dirty hands on his jeans. "The latent oil would've raised the heat by several degrees."

"And the added gasoline would've been perfect fuel."

"There's got to be a pipeline near," said K-Paul, studying the ground once more, trying to see patterns, subterranean trails, in the dirt. "Vivco probably leases this land. Maybe the L'Overtures were unwelcome squatters."

"But how would that hurt the oil? Or be reason enough to die for?"

K-Paul shook his head, plunging his hands in his back pockets.

"I don't know. This cloak and dagger stuff is beyond me. I feel like Dr. Watson."

"Maybe now that Nana's gone, Malveaux will stop lying."

"Maybe he'll lock himself inside his own damn jail. As in 'Physician, heal thyself.'"

"Policeman, arrest thyself?" Marie smiled.

"If the crime fits."

"I'm glad you're here, K-Paul."

"Even though I'm not a detective? Like your friend Parks?"

"No more teasing about Parks, okay? Parks was—is—a good friend. He's already in New Orleans."

"Well, you set this Cajun boy right," said K-Paul, loudly, slapping his chest.

"Stop it, K-Paul."

K-Paul reached for her; she stepped back, sidestepping his grasp.

"I need," she said emphatically, "Dr. Girouard's help. I need the country and city man who works in the ER. The Cajun Catholic who serves the poor."

K-Paul looked at the sky, the ground, then at Marie. "Let me say this," he said, his voice hoarse. "I've been attracted to you from the first day I saw you."

"Don't."

"I won't keep embarrassing you or myself. But tell me you've known." Vulnerable, he gazed at her. "Haven't you?"

"Yes, I knew."

The simple words satisfied him, and they confirmed her sense that she'd stayed away from him these past four years not just because he was a colleague, but because of his intensity and, maybe, too, because of her own repressed desires.

"What do you want me to do?" asked K-Paul, squaring his shoulders, his voice serious.

"Let's agree to stay professional. Both of us."

"Fair enough. Though from this Cajun's view, the flirting's been one-sided. Four years, I've felt like a frog trapped in a gator's throat. You don't give a man hope."

She couldn't suppress her smile. "K-Paul," she said, slightly scolding, "let's keep doing what we do well."

"Working together."

K-Paul smiled, extending his hand; Marie clasped it, and shook.

Though country, K-Paul had the soft hands of a city doctor. She studied their clasped hands, noting the contrast between her brown skin and his ruddy flesh. Black oil smudges were on both. Connect the clues, she thought.

"You said oil and water caused wetlands devastation. Could it have caused murder?"

"Historically, it already has."

Marie didn't quite hear him. She was distracted by the well, and the glare of the setting sun on the bright new pail. The sun striking it was bright and luminescent.

The ghosts were gone.

Rocks had been cemented together to form the well; digging, forming, then setting the stone would have been hard. But it would have been essential. And this well with the moss, weathered stone, and rusty chain had probably been built generations ago. Maybe during slavery? Or maybe, post slavery, as part of the L'Overture homestead? Without utility services, water would have been needed for any family's survival.

L'Overture's ghost had been fixated on the well. The new water pail.

What was it that Nana had said? "Mind the water."

She walked to the well. Turned the rope turnstile, pulling the bucket high, higher. It was heavy with water.

"What're you thinking?

"Not sure. Before she died, Nana said, 'Mind the water.' Deet delivered the message."

She dipped her hands into the pail. The water was clear, and she washed her palms clean. She cupped water in her hands, and smelled it as it dripped, disappeared through her fingers.

Plain water. No special odor. She tasted it. Just water. How did it connect with the shape-changing spirit's words: "Watch the waters?"

"What're you thinking?"

"I don't know. A hunch. We should take samples."

"Test the water?"

"Soil, too."

"I've got a medical kit in my Jeep. Some test tubes for blood. Urine cups."

"That'll work."

K-Paul headed toward the Jeep. He stopped, turning around, his hand sweeping, encompassing the yard. "This is where you saw the threads, isn't it?"

"Yes, and I'm certain now that it was malevolent. Not just earth, not just oil. The farthest thing from a benign, organic substance."

She saw it again, among the tree roots—taunting, like a charmed snake. Then, like a mirage, she didn't see it. She saw only shadows and light.

"Whatever it was, is," she corrected, "I think it would've affected the soil, and soil affects groundwater."

K-Paul nodded. "I'll collect samples." He walked to the car.

Marie let the pail drop. She could hear, but not see, its splash.

She leaned over the stones, trying to see into the black bottom of the well. In Marie-Claire's picture books, ogres or dragons always lived at the bottom of the well. Fearsome, furtive. Cannibalistic.

Did John L'Overture suspect something foul in the water?

That something had fouled the well? She looked at the scarred and charred house remains. "They had a small garden, K-Paul," she hollered. "Nothing was growing well."

"It could've been the oil."

"It could've been." But she didn't think so. Oil, despite all the troubles it caused, had a useful purpose. A balance of good and ill effects. Whatever corrupted the garden or possibly fouled the well was just wrong. Nature didn't survive without replenishing itself.

"A ceremony here," she stated flatly, knowing as she said it that it was right. "A ceremony here, in the L'Overture yard, on this hallowed ground."

A ceremony beside the victims' bones.

A gun fired. A startling, cracking sound tore through the trees.

"Marie!" K-Paul shouted. "Down!"

Shrieking egrets and herons flushed, flew high, streaking wings against the blue sky.

Marie stood her ground, feet firm, facing southeast.

"Are you insane?"

"It's Walker." She just knew: Walker, in the wild, with a rifle and a scope.

"Marie, please, we've got to get out of here. Back to the Jeep. I've got a hunting rifle in the trunk's gulley."

"No," she said sharply. She turned away from K-Paul and looked back into the marsh. Grasses swayed, curtains of gray moss trembled.

"There could be another shot. Please, we've got to go."

She kept staring toward the southeast. "Walker wants to frighten me," she said softly. "Cat and mouse."

A thin, hot breeze touched her face. K-Paul, charged with adrenaline, breathed heavily.

"We should go, Marie."

"It's okay, K-Paul." She bent, gathering soil in the plastic cup. "He's already gone."

"How can you be sure?"

"Just am." She thought of Marie-Claire. "How do you know?" She'd asked her daughter how she'd known Beau's name. "Just do," her daughter had answered.

"I just am," Marie repeated. "Sure."

She was in Walker's territory. His last shot was letting her know that he was powerful and in control.

K-Paul pulled up the water pail and held it as Marie filled two test tubes with water.

Her head tilted. *Mind, mine the water. She saw the words hanging in the air. Saw water changing into a woman's form.*

"You're sure you're all right, Marie? We've got to be careful. Cats usually catch their prey."

"Except when they're arrogant." Her voice, dry and harsh, she let the pail drop and splash into the water. "Walker should've killed me from a distance. His mistake will be to try and kill me up close and personal. He won't succeed."

She felt strength coursing through her, as if Ogun, the warrior god, was filling her up—but it wasn't spiritual possession or the memory of it. It was her strength—the part of her, as in all humanity, that could be courageous and cruel.

She stood erect, jaw rigid, her hands balled into fists.

"Where are you? What're you thinking?" K-Paul clutched her shoulder.

Her brow furrowed. She was starting to change. She was no longer just the book-educated doctor, but more Marie Laveau's heir. She recognized, here, now, that there was a link between Nature and humanity's failure to nurture.

DeLaire acreage and the bayou had been fouled, undone.

Her heart racing, she felt her ancestry rail and rebel. As a doctor, she had a passion for health and social justice, but her spiritual lineage, the memory of the gods who had possessed her, all fueled the heat in her blood. In her own right, she was a warrior, anything but passive.

"Who are you?"

She looked at K-Paul, her expression purposefully neutral. "I'm your friend, K-Paul."

She walked back to the Jeep. Parks had seen and accepted the fierceness inside her. She missed him. Maybe, for her, he'd be willing to give New Orleans another try. Out here, in the country, she was alone, with no DuLac, no El, no Parks to encourage and help her thrive.

She was strong, still human. But vengeance was rising inside her. Battle lines were being drawn. Between her and Walker. Between her and the evil awake in the world.

Any man who loved her would have to accept that.

She looked out the Jeep's front window. K-Paul pulled out his keys.

The bayou was an intense world. She was ready to be possessed, ready to find justice, ready to be the other woman she was—Marie Laveau, the Voodoo Queen.

TEN

DELAIRE PLANTATION

SUNSET

At dusk, they drove into DeLaire. Seeing streaks of sun, red, orange, and yellow, made it seem sad, unreal. A trick of the light, a rerun of a *Twilight Zone*.

The no-name bait shop; just BAIT in cheap neon, now turned off, dangling in the window. The sheriff's office looking closed, and rag-tag. The mechanic's shed with its graveyard of Chevys, trucks, and high-speed boats on trailers looked deserted. Only the spiraling, barbershoplike red light at the two-pump gas station suggested any life.

Had DeLaire ever been a vital community? She knew it was a community gone mad. Crazy, just like she'd felt when she first drove south.

Historically, Louisiana meant centuries of enslavement—backbreaking work, deaths, beatings, and rapes for African descendants.

What made newly freed slaves stay on the land where for generations they'd been persecuted? Why would a black person stay? Most didn't.

During Reconstruction, the newly freed migrated north, went west. To cities. Chicago. New Orleans. Tulsa. On foot, by horseback, or by train.

Those who stayed in DeLaire—why, why did they remain?

Were they too comfortable? Too passive? Or was it an act of defiance to stay? They didn't want to be run off their land.

This was the crux of the matter.

Thousands of acres of DeLaire land were bought and paid for with ancestral blood. Why should slave descendants leave the only American home they'd known, a homeland they'd paid for in sweat and tears?

Still, she thought, many slave descendants had left. That would account for why so many elderly remained in DeLaire. But why did the L'Overtures remain? Or come back? John had been a veteran. And the very pregnant Brenda, why did she stay? With no apparent immediate family, had she stayed because the town adopted her? Or because she feared doing otherwise?

Looking around the "town," Marie couldn't help believing that all the black folks were getting the short end of the stick. No doubt the DeLaire descendants were living in city luxury elsewhere, while the bayou land was still being sucked for oil, making money for a decadent, "good times roll" family.

No one living in DeLaire seemed to being having any good times.

K-Paul stopped for gas at the one-tank station.

Next to the station was Bebe's Grocery. Marie went inside, and paused, staring at the shelves of processed food, the glass freezer filled with frozen waffles and sausages, and the refrigerator section filled with scrapple and beer. Not a single fresh vegetable or fruit. She slowly walked the few aisles, grabbing sunflower seeds, candy bars, and a liter of Coke. She wanted to be seen.

"Sheriff know you're here?" asked the man behind the counter.

She recognized the grocer as Tommy, the diabetic. Khaki pants and the counter obscured the wounds on his legs. But she could tell that standing, he was in pain. A stool was behind the cash register.

"I've come to keep my promise," she answered.

"A healing? Healing ceremony?"

She saw the hunger in his eyes, the energy infusing his body, intent on worship, needing spiritual miracles.

"Medicine first. Then, afterward, yes, a ceremony."

"Nana's yard. I'll tell everyone." He reached for the rotary phone.

"No."

Tommy stopped dialing, quizzical.

"The L'Overture yard."

Shocked, Tommy wet his lips. He gripped his stool for balance. "That's where them murders were."

"Yes. Parents and their infant. Shot and burned."

Deadpan, Tommy stared straight at her, and shook his head. "A real shame." Then he blinked.

She watched Tommy weigh and value his own needs over the murdered family's. She couldn't help but feel disgusted. How many people would have to die before he'd think twice about a ceremony on their graves?

"You going to tell Aaron?"

"You mean the sheriff?"

He nodded.

"Why don't you?"

Glee lit in Tommy's eyes. She knew he'd spread the news like wildfire. Tonight, everybody in DeLaire would be eager to dance in the L'Overture yard. Her trap was modest. She hoped guilt would lead to revelations. But by springing the trap, she hoped she'd discover—the gods would help her discover—the combined mysteries of a dead dying people and an eroding, possibly toxic wetlands.

She left as Tommy started dialing his phone.

K-Paul was settling the gas nozzle into its carriage. He gave the attendant, a beanpole-thin man, thirty dollars. "Hate to do it," K-Paul said to Marie. "Vivco is part of the problem. Fewer oil wells, more land."

She handed K-Paul a Coke. "Follow this road to the end, turn right, and drive until you can't drive anymore. Then we'll be at Nana's."

K-Paul undid the Jeep's top. "Too much heat," he said, explaining.

"Couldn't agree more." Marie could see clearly and everyone could see her clearly.

Hot air and dust washed over her. Children were playing marbles by the side of the road. Pregnant Brenda was standing on a porch, her T-shirt, tight and rippling, inching up her bulging abdomen. The elderly Ibo-looking man—Nate, she remembered—stood, stoic, in his yard watching her pass.

Tommy wasn't wasting any time making his calls.

Other folks stopped, dead still, in the street; some, their screen doors slamming, stepped onto their porches, their hands shading their eyes. Men stopped fixing their cars, their boats in driveways; women stopped hanging clothes and sheets on lines.

K-Paul drove slowly, and in between the shanty houses, the boat docks, she saw slices of the Gulf, calm, deep waters.

"Not much here," said K-Paul.

"Not much," she replied. Or else too much of something sickening everyone.

She hoped Aaron and Deet would be at home. Waiting for her.

"There," she said, "Nana's house is there, the last on the street."

K-Paul parked the car. Both Aaron and Deet were sitting on the porch steps. The brothers looked like ghosts of themselves. Deet looked as if he hadn't slept in weeks; Aaron looked gaunt, as if he'd already decided to be dead.

"Heard you're going to do a ceremony," said Aaron.

"News travels fast," she responded wryly.

"Beau, is he all right?" asked Deet, pushing forward, wringing his hands.

"Beau's fine. My daughter loves him. She says thank you."

"That's all right then," answered Deet, grinning, while his brother scowled. "She'll play with him and love him."

"You shouldn't have come back here, Dr. Laveau," said Aaron, lighting a cigarette. "Want a cigarette? See, I don't have to worry about oxygen. No possible explosions here."

"Just elsewhere. At the L'Overtures."

"Funny," Aaron replied, studying K-Paul. "Brought a cop with you?"

"He doesn't look like a cop."

"You're right, Deet. Meet Dr. Girouard."

K-Paul offered his hand; Deet shook it, but Aaron ignored him.
Up close, Aaron reeked of alcohol, his eyes were scarred red.

"I'm sorry for your loss," she murmured.

"You don't know anything about my loss."

"I missed you, Sheriff," she answered, dryly.

"He's not a sheriff anymore."

"Shut up, Deet." Aaron looked uncomfortable, wounded.

Now she understood why Tommy had said Aaron, not sheriff.
"Fired? Surely not. Not an employee who's so easily bribed."

"Shut up."

"Hey," said K-Paul, ready to defend Marie.

"Guilty conscience?"

"Nana's gone, I've given up my work. What else do you want
me to do?"

"Tell me who killed the L'Overtures. Who set the fire."

"It won't make any difference. Two hundred years, this has
been our home. This land has held my family together. You
wouldn't understand that. Yes, I've read about you. Raised in
Chicago." He spat the city's name like a dirty word. "You didn't
even know your country roots. Know about Louisiana."

Aaron stood. "Come on, Deet. We need a drink to wash this
bad taste out of our mouths. Spoiled fish, throw the bastards back."
His hand on the doorknob, the screen door half open, his face
contorted.

Such sadness, Marie thought.

"Dr. Laveau, you don't know anything about the L'Overtures.
We're mourning them, too. Just leave us alone. Come on, Deet."

But Deet didn't move.

Aaron's face flushed red. "Suit yourself," he snarled before entering the house.

"I told you not to come here," Deet said, petulant, looking back at the screen door.

Marie couldn't tell whether he looked back simply because he missed his brother, or because he suspected his brother might be listening. Was Deet afraid of Aaron?

"Nobody wants you here, Miz Laveau."

"You mean your brother doesn't," responded K-Paul. "He's foul tempered."

"Don't be talking bad about my brother." Deet, his chest puffed like a rooster's, pushed up against K-Paul. He was daring for a fight, ready to pound all his frustration and hurt into someone's face.

"It's all right, Deet," she said, touching his arm. "K-Paul's sorry." K-Paul shrugged.

"We need your help."

"Not going to help that man with nothing," answered Deet, pointing at K-Paul.

"I need your help, Deet."

"No, I'm not going to talk to you, either. All you've brought is trouble." He turned, like a distraught child, taking his toys to go home.

"Please." Deet had been defiant when his brother wanted him to go inside. She just needed a bit more courage from him. "Please, Deet."

"No."

"Even if Nana would've wanted you to help me?"

"She's dead."

"But still here, Deet. I've seen her."

He stopped, not yet turning around, poised between going inside, joining his brother and his known world, or accepting her and the unknown.

She saw his shoulders slump. Saw him decide, turning quickly, coming toward her, stumbling down the steps.

"Where?"

Marie could smell his breath. Alcohol. But he didn't reek like Aaron. She felt sure Deet wasn't much of a drinker. But with Nana dead, she could imagine the two brothers spending their hours drowning their sorrow, staring at Nana's empty bed. Deet would nurse his whiskey; Aaron would drain one glass after another, rushing toward unconsciousness. Eventually, he'd die, like Riley.

"At the L'Overtures," she lied. "That's where I saw Nana. That's why I'm doing a ceremony there tonight. It's what Nana would've wanted."

"I don't believe you."

"You don't have to. I'd like to search Nana's altar, if you don't mind. I need some things."

"What things?" he asked, suspicious.

"Her water glass. The spirit statues she prayed to. The saints she favored will help me to conjure her."

Deet, his neck clenched, wanted to say no.

She rushed on: "All *voodooiennes* have aids, special spirit guides. You know that, Deet. I want my ceremony to honor Nana. To please her."

She didn't tell Deet she was also searching for evidence. For some clue about who doctored Nana, where the medical equipment came from, who supplied the medicines. Maybe she could connect them to who abandoned DeLaire's needed and necessary public health.

"Let me ask Aaron."

"You know Nana believed in me," she said, urgently. "You know it."

Deet didn't respond. Wincing, favoring his left knee, he climbed the stairs and went into the house.

Brows raised, K-Paul looked at Marie. "Torn ACL?"

"Football."

"Ah, every rural boy's dream to make it in the city. New Orleans. The big time. Big-time money. A million-to-one shot."

※

K-Paul strolled to the yard's southernmost end. "Come see, Marie. A backyard dock." He tugged a rope anchoring a small powerboat. Two fishing poles and a bait bag were inside. K-Paul opened the bag. "Look here," he said, holding up a jar as if he'd discovered gold. "Worms." He held the jar closer. "A bit lean, though. Need to be fat, juicy, to catch the best fish."

Worms squirmed behind glass.

"Even in the best places, fishing's declined. Still, it's beautiful here," said K-Paul. "Told you, nothing like the Gulf."

The landscape was beautiful. Warm, soothing air layered the Gulf. Every summer, breezes rushed in and over the Gulf, kicking up storms, hurricanes. But not today.

Waves lapping against sand sounded like a mother soothing a child, "Hush, hush, hush."

The horizon was now purplish-orange; some clouds floated, white, others were a dull yellow; still others were rimmed in gray. A

perfect landscape painting filled with depth and color. With beauty
and a touch of menace.

"Too bad evil exists everywhere," Marie said softly, not
knowing if K-Paul heard.

Shoulder to shoulder, they watched ships—motorboats,
shrimpers, a pleasure sailboat—all sail inland, harbor bound,
skimming across green, foam-tipped waters.

"Storm's coming," said Marie, echoing K-Paul's earlier warning.
"The weather service must've sent a warning."

"Everyone's racing home. Trying to make port."

"Except for the L'Overtures." She scanned the horizon for
ghosts, tried to sense if there was any prophetic vision she'd missed.

"If something happens, K-Paul, you'll have the samples tested.
Follow up with the Department of Health. With Parks, police you
can trust."

"What're you saying?"

"Just what I said." She wiped sweat from her brow. "Have you
ever been to a voodoo ceremony?"

"No. Only the French Quarter's voodoo tour."

"You didn't."

"Did."

She smiled. "Titillation and cheap entertainment, K-Paul. You
know those tours pander to tourists and their fears."

He shrugged. "What can I say? It was fun. Besides—"

"You got laid."

"How'd you know?"

"She was an out of towner."

"Exactly," answered K-Paul. "Northerners like being scared by
our voodoo. I had to comfort her afterward."

"Rogue."

Shouting sounds spilled from the house. A chair sounded as if it was being overturned.

More serious, she clutched K-Paul's hand, whispering hurriedly, "K-Paul, anything might happen tonight. Nana prayed to spirits I'm not entirely familiar with."

"That's why you want to search inside?"

"Yes. But the illnesses I've seen in DeLaire might be connected as well. There's something awry in the environment, I'm sure of it. But I'm not sure the illness isn't connected to the rituals.

"Voodoo communities aren't supposed to inspire fear, lies. Yet both brothers are hiding something. I think Nana was, too."

Her heart ached. It pained her to think that any voodoo community might be secretive, spiritually unhealthy. Such communities reinforced stereotypes. Yet given slavery's influence, it was amazing that voodoo as a sustaining force survived at all. She couldn't imagine, in the 1800s, 1900s, practicing her faith while being cursed, leered at, and pummeled with stones and shouts of "barbarism," "devil worship."

Americans bemoaned the Salem witch trials, but they didn't bemoan the attempted systematic destruction of African faiths. It was a miracle as surely as Christ turning water into wine that African slaves had blended their religion with Christianity and held strong to the good. Kept kindness, and fought off bitterness. Had Nana—no, Marie couldn't believe it—betrayed that?

"Marie?"

Far off, clouds were darkening. Rain threatened; somewhere, wind was beginning to swirl.

The brothers were arguing inside the house.

"K-Paul, if something happens to me—"

"Nothing's going to happen to you."

She shook her head. "Walker is dangerous. A concrete threat. But so, too, are voodoo ceremonies without proper protections. I don't have my drummers. Or any of the followers I trust. I don't have—"

"El and Duluc."

"Yes. I'm on my own."

"You've got me."

"You've never been to a ceremony."

"Still, I don't believe they're dangerous. That's all hype, isn't it?"

How could she explain? Each ceremony held spiritual danger, far worse than the bodily danger K-Paul was imagining.

She didn't answer but stared at the Gulf. Waves lapped the shore, adding soil but taking away far more.

You could walk into sandy waters, feel perfectly safe, only to have the ocean's shelf dramatically drop from beneath your feet. Ceremonies were like that, any second you could be lost among the unknown.

"Let's get out of here, Marie," said K-Paul urgently. "Let's go back to New Orleans. Attend to Huan's burial. Our patients at Charity. 'Sides, if a hurricane is really coming, this delta will flood. Folks should get the hell out."

"Cold feet?"

"No. I'm worried about you, for you."

"This is part of who I am—Marie Laveau."

✳

A door slammed shut. Aaron, head lowered, staggered down the porch steps. Willfully avoiding eye contact with Marie and K-Paul, he got into his car. It was still painted black and white, but the red siren lights had been removed from the roof.

"He's guilty as sin," said K-Paul.

"Nothing worse than self-flagellation," said Marie, pityingly. "Tonight, I'll delve for the spiritual, K-Paul. You watch for the concrete. Please. Stand by me."

"No need to ask again. I've got a rifle in the trunk. Walker won't get near you. Or Aaron, either."

Aaron drove off, his engine gunning, tires spinning, kicking up dirt and mud.

"I'm hoping the DeLaire community will reveal itself to me," said Marie sadly. "They act socially inbred, like they've known each other forever. They seem to act in unison, but they won't even take a young girl to a hospital or a clinic. I want to know why, K-Paul.

"I want to find out what secret this community is hiding. Find out who murdered the L'Overtures. Why Nana died protecting her grandsons and everyone here, especially Aaron. Why Aaron broke his vows."

She looked at the waves crashing against the shore. Swallows were rushing inland.

"Oil and water. I feel you're right, K-Paul. Both substances are so vital, so entwined. Nonetheless, there's been a history of lies, pain, and devastation. Odd, isn't it? Oil is still troubling the waters."

K-Paul spoke slowly, his eyes squinting, staring out to sea. "DeLaire. There was a case twenty, twenty-one years ago. Riley told me about it. Broke his heart. Started his binges. DeLaire Plantation and Vivco. Some federal investigation. Never went to trial. Heard there was a settlement."

"Against Vivco?"

"Both. Vivco and the DeLaire descendants. Some kind of environmental collusion. The federal government sued them both.

"The investigation had to do with waste, chemical by-products. Vivco and the DeLaires both paid damages for cleanup, remediation.

"Pa told me that they used to call oil 'the devil's excrement.' The DeLaires struck a no-win bargain. Look, even though there was environmental cleanup, you can still see the loss of land. Every storm, even the one coming now, will cause more and more land loss. The trees and marsh that protected the county and city, DeLaire and New Orleans, are reduced to the smallest number they've ever been."

"But the ex-slaves have stayed."

"And the owners have never given up ownership of the land, expressed guilt or remorse. Far as I'm concerned, they're beyond hope. Criminals."

"But you can help the living, the survivors. You'll see. The plantation descendants are still suffering. They're diseased and dying. Maybe John L'Overture discovered some connection—"

"Aaron said no."

Marie and K-Paul were startled.

Deet had slipped behind them, looking like a haint, his face pulled thin, his shoulders slumped.

"Aaron said he didn't want you touching Nana's things. Told me to tell you to go."

"It's okay, Deet. I understand."

Deet reached into his pocket. "When Nana took ill, Aaron changed. Even now he went to town to go drink. Said you disturbed his peace here."

"It's okay."

Deet looked about to cry.

"But Aaron doesn't have any peace. None of us do." He pulled his hand from his pocket, and opened his fist. "Brought you this, Maman Marie. Will this help?"

The water goddess. *Deep inside herself, Marie felt recognition.* The statue was the same spirit she'd seen in the Mississippi. Teal breasts, snakes entwined in her hair and neck. Except, in the Mississippi, the apparition had been bolder, three-dimensional. Water sparkled like diamonds.

"You can have the statue. I think Nana would've wanted you to have it. It was her favorite spirit."

"Thank you, Deet."

She couldn't help wondering why Deet hadn't brought both statues. Nana had had two gods on her small altar: the mermaid and the androgynous spirit. If the mermaid goddess was Nana's favorite, why honor the other? Altars usually favored one god, yet Nana had set her two spirits side by side.

Somber, Deet stared at the goddess in Marie's hand.

"Thank you," she repeated.

Deet had lost his chance for escape and glory. He'd lost his nana and was losing his brother, too. Still, he was trying to help her, trying to help because he knew Nana would have wanted him to, because it was the right thing to do.

Impulsively, she hugged him.

Deet's hands gripped her hard, as if he was using her body to hold himself upright.

"You're a good man," she said.

He shook his head, swallowing, his Adam's apple shifting up and down. "Water was always important to Nana. Said Mami Wata—"

"Mami Wata? Are you sure that's the name?" Puzzle it out.

"Nana said she was one of the old ones."

Marie thought hard. Three years ago, they'd been in DuLac's altar room. He'd taken a frayed book off his shelf. Inside were beautiful images of water goddesses. Some were line drawings, others were vividly painted. The book had discussed religion even before it was called religion.

DuLac had always insisted that she read with him, study old texts. Now she understood; he'd been preparing her for this moment. When voodoo wasn't typical, but atypical.

For the first time since his death, she saw DuLac. Not as a ghost, but as a vision.

DuLac was drawing three wavy lines, creating the symbol Marie-Claire had finger painted. He pushed the book toward her. Pages fluttered, sifting, shifting, through images of mermaids.

"I've seen this goddess before."

"Nana said when Africans were made slaves, this spirit, Wata, followed them across the ocean."

Marie turned the sculpture in her hand. Maybe a slave had molded it in the Americas? Or else clung to it during the horrific Middle Passage.

"Marie?" murmured K-Paul.

"Wait. Something's happening. I feel—"

Both Deet and K-Paul quieted.

She closed her eyes, squeezing the statue tight.

Inside her head, DuLac whispered, "Africans worshipped a multitude of water goddesses. First and foremost was Wata. All water spirits are aspects of Wata. Like Lucy is to flesh, so Mami Wata is to spirit."

She saw El. Mimi L'Overture. Her ancestor Marie Laveau. A trinity of women, three spirits standing, arms clasped, beside the water.

Marie Laveau, her voice a rich timbre, spoke: "Women hand sight down through the generations. Mother to daughter." El and Mimi echoed her.

Together, the three chanted: "Women hand sight down through the generations." The sound cascaded like a healing balm.

She understood. It was her time.

DuLac's disembodied voice, crooned, "You don't need me. You've never needed me. Or any man."

"You can do this," El's voice reverberated. "You can do this."

Marie exhaled. "Water goddesses," she said, opening her eyes.

Both men were staring at her—K-Paul, concerned; Deet, worshipful.

Water goddesses appeared in every culture. The divine feminine.

She stroked the statue's body, from her breasts to her tail. "European mermaids were more like sirens, sensual distractions, singing, sucking life from men. Most likely they were a myth, a manifestation of sailors' fears of feminine power.

"Mami Wata," she said, "was far more powerful than any mermaid or siren. Sensual, passionate, she was an ancient healer, encouraging prosperity and fertility."

"Doesn't New Orleans have a river goddess? Yemaya," asked K-Paul, "isn't she it? That voodoo tour mentioned her." K-Paul ducked his head sheepishly.

"The tour spoke true. Maybe it was Yemaya that I saw in the Mississippi. Maybe it was Wata."

"Why not both?"

"Yes, why not," she answered. "There's always been syncretism. A melding of variants of African-derived images and faith. More confusing, there have been changing names as slaves learned differing New World languages. Wata has become Yemaya in New Orleans. Both goddesses signify motherhood, pregnancy, and the rejuvenating power of water.

"But even in New Orleans, Yemaya is sometimes called Yemalla. In the Yoruba tradition, she would've been called 'Yemaja.' Elsewhere in Africa, she'd be known as 'Yemoja.' In Brazil, she'd be 'Yemanjá; in Haiti, 'La Sirene.' The fluidity of names goes on. But the image of water goddesses as healers, supporters of love and the fruits of love, remains sacrosanct. Water goddesses own all the waters: oceans, rivers, streams. Each of these goddesses, but especially Mami Wata, the oldest, is understood as the 'mother of all living things.'

"What if Wata has been restored? Not figuratively, but literally. What if Nana's worship reaffirmed, reenergized her in the New World? It makes sense that slaves transported by water would embrace, hold tight to Mami Wata."

"Ever since we were boys," said Deet, "Nana told us tales of

Wata. Said women took after Wata, birthing babies in rich, nourishing water. Said Wata healed by giving, never by taking away."

Deet wasn't making sense. How did one heal by taking away? Folk healers, like doctors, *gave*—medicinal herbs and soothing, palliative care.

"Nana said water was all about love, needing to journey, to go where a woman needed to go."

"Water needs to go where she wants to go." That's what the spirit in the hospital had said. But it still didn't make sense. How did it connect to folk healing? Medicine?

If she understood K-Paul and Riley, in drilling waterways, the Corps of Engineers had altered both fresh- and saltwater landscapes. What did that mean? To change the course of water? To force water to go where she didn't want to go?

It would be like telling a pregnant woman that her amniotic fluid had to flow upstream; her child couldn't be nourished and born.

"Deet, where's Nana's grave?"

"You don't want to go there. Too sad."

"I want to make obeisance," she said. "Thank Nana for her blessings." She gripped the statue. "Understand why she prayed to Wata. Help me. Please."

"You'll have to take the boat."

"I don't understand."

"I do," said K-Paul. "Where, Deet?"

"Southwest about ten miles. You won't miss it. Miz Marie, tell Nana I love her."

"You tell her. You'll come tonight to the ceremony."

He shook his head.

"Come. You'll be needed." *Why did she say that?*

"Hurts," said Deet simply, explaining his refusal.

Deet undid the dock slip, and handed Marie into the slim motorboat with K-Paul. The metal boat swayed, and she sat facing K-Paul as he used the rudder to guide the boat from shore.

"Deet," she called. "Where's the second statue? The one Nana kept beside Wata?"

"Don't know. Gone. Wasn't there." Deet, his hand raised, waved, growing smaller as the boat traveled farther.

✕

Marie held the figurine, thinking repeatedly, "Mind. Mine. Mind. Mine." Both could be right. Couldn't they? She looked at the round eyes of the blunt clay figure.

Most paintings rendered Wata as supernaturally beautiful, yet this figurine, so old, seemed to contain all its beauty inside the gray clay, behind its' pin-top eyes.

The boat bounced over the thin waves, breaking against currents.

K-Paul was quiet, intently searching for the graveyard. They were pulling farther away from land, motoring into the Gulf's wide arms. It didn't make sense. Nana hadn't been buried at sea.

Sunburned, K-Paul's cheeks and nose were red.

"Land ho," he shouted.

"Where?"

K-Paul pointed. "Oil and water. What did I tell you about land disappearing?"

She saw a small concrete roof half in and half out of the water. Then another. It was a sinking island of marsh. Maybe an acre, long and wide. Not all the tombs were sunken—several dozen were still upright on the land, but it was only a matter of time.

"Causeways and erosion separated cemetery land from the mainland. In another few years, maybe sooner if Katrina comes, burying Nana here will be the same as burying her at sea. In sixty-five, Betsey buried New Orleans under seven feet of water. I've seen plenty of cemeteries where bodies have floated right out of their tombs."

"K-Paul, where does the Mississippi end?"

His hands sweeping, he said, "This is all of where the Mississippi ends."

She saw more specks of land, isolated islands. Lush green, rich earth . . . then trickles, canals, small lakes of water.

"This here . . . where Riley took us, is all the river's end. The river's sediment—silt and sand—builds up, and the river breaks onto the surface, distributing fan-shaped deposits. New land. That's all the delta is."

K-Paul cut the boat's motor.

The boat gently smashed into the island, and soil fell away, crumbling, dissolving into the Gulf like brown sugar.

K-Paul swung his anchor rope like a lasso until it caught on a headstone.

"No disrespect," said K-Paul, making the sign of the cross. "Watch your step, Marie."

It felt like walking on an unsupported cushion—soft, bouncy, destabilized land. She held the rope, letting it guide her to the headstone's inscription: DELORES. HOUSE SERVANT. 1858.

"She must've been a beloved slave." By whom? Fellow slaves? Her master? Or her children?

"Most bodies were left in mass graves or buried with no signifiers," answered K-Paul. "Maybe a wooden cross. But that's it."

"So Delores was beloved by her masters?"

"You bet. Maybe she was a cook, a nanny? Didn't have a last name. Except DeLaire. She would've been Delores DeLaire, after her owners. No idea of her birth date or her age when she died."

"I wonder what she died of," murmured Marie, walking between the graves.

Class was clear in the cemetery. Some graves were bare or had minimal markers. Others had metal crosses soldered on their headstones. Still others had gates, with metal filigree encircling more modern tombs, raised by cement four feet off the ground.

"These tombs are like the ones in New Orleans," she said. "Aboveground."

"Makes sense because everything is sinking. The city is below sea level and DeLaire's slave descendants would've seen, storm after storm, land wash away. Like this here. I can't imagine why the Malveauxs went ahead and buried their grandmother here."

"Tradition," answered Marie. "But maybe something else. Maybe she insisted." Marie bent down before the freshly painted tomb of Ernestine "Nana" Malveaux. There were blank indented squares with the names Aaron Malveaux and Deet Malveaux and their birth dates, already chiseled in preparation for their deaths. Marie found it chilling.

"It'll be decades before the grandsons are buried," said K-Paul. "I doubt the land, the cemetery, will last that long."

"The tomb's cover isn't flush." The slab was slightly off-kilter.

"I can fix that."

"No, let's take it off. I think there's something I'm supposed to see."

"Grave digger?"

"Stop it, K-Paul. Just the slab. Okay?"

The two of them pushed; the gray concrete against concrete screeched like cats. They lowered the slab to the ground.

"Look." A cheap pinewood box held Nana. But on the tomb's cover, hidden on the underside, Mami Wata's portrait had been etched in stone. A huge snake hung from her neck. Beneath her were three wavy lines, like the lines Marie-Claire had drawn.

Marie laid her body on the slab. *She felt amazing power— creative as well as destructive.* She sat back on her knees, grave dust covering her pants and shirt. She didn't bother to look at K-Paul— he surely thought she was crazy. *Instead, eyes closed, she let her fingers study every inch of the slab, left to right, top to bottom. She felt such pain at the bottom-left edge.*

"Something's here." She opened her eyes, peering close at uneven cement, a scratched surface. She lay flat on the dirt, her face close to the edge. Everything was compressed into a three-inch space. There were scratches, not random, more like cave etchings. Figures, bent, holding their stomachs. Next, a figure lay prone. In another image, a figure, clearly a woman, laid one hand on the stretched figure; the other hand was raised high, to heaven.

"It's telling a story," said Marie. "A preliterate narrative. See. People are sick. One is near death, I think. And this figure with breasts must represent Nana. Nana is praying—"

"Or healing."

Marie stared, her heart racing. "You're right. Nana's trying to heal. One hand toward the gods. No, toward Mami Wata." Her hand embraced the portrait etched above.

"What's this last frame?"

The Nana figure was on her knees, holding her stomach. Black lines were drawn, depicting vomit, expulsion from her mouth. Figures stood tall around her. A small pool was drawn, colored with charcoal, beneath Nana's mouth.

"I don't understand it. It seems to tell the tale of Nana healing villagers and herself becoming sick."

"All true, right?"

"Yes, the villagers and Nana were both sick. But in this frame, the villagers seem healed. There aren't any prone figures." She sat, rubbing her brow, leaving trails of dirt.

"After Nana was buried, someone came here and drew these images," she said. "Why? Why underneath the slab? Why is Wata drawn boldly?"

"And the story small, like some secret?"

"Exactly." She stood. "Help me lift this, K-Paul."

Arms and backs straining, they lifted the slab, sliding it in place while Marie murmured, "'Night, Nana. May Wata bless you and keep you."

※

Circling all sides of her, Marie could see water churning, lapping hungrily at the cemetery island. It was almost as if the waves were pregnant with potential, feeding on earth.

The horizon was growing bleaker as gray clouds seemed to fly in, striking out blue sky and chasing birds to ground.

"Some folks are grateful for the levees—especially those

surrounding New Orleans, but I'm not one of them. They choked the river, keeping it from producing."

"Her," said Marie, "kept her, Wata, from producing." She touched the crumbling earth. "Levees, dams, kept her from creating, from birthing new land."

Marie clasped K-Paul's shoulder. The good-natured Cajun boy had grown sad and bitter. For K-Paul, the environmental struggle was as tragic as the closing of Charity's hospital services to the poor.

"In the drawing, the dark pool beneath Nana reminds me of the apparition at the L'Overtures'. Some kind of malevolence, poison."

"Used to be called Cancer Alley. Here and about," murmured K-Paul. "All the time, industrial chemicals, solvents, petroleum by-products "accidentally" spilled where black people lived."

"That accounts for why so many DeLaire elders have tumors. Nana was pregnant with multiple tumors."

"Funding was supposed to go for clean up and public health clinics."

"Didn't happen around here," she said, looking about. "No one's given me a doctor's name. Not even for Nana. Brenda said a clinic was over fifty miles away. Imagine, in America, having to go over fifty miles for prenatal care."

"The fate of the rural poor," K-Paul said wearily. "I wouldn't be surprised if much of the settlement money was diverted. Typical for Louisiana. Bribery, back-room politics, public funds becoming private slush funds. Remember Huey Long? Pretend to care for the poor, then rob them, and everyone else, blind. Look how Charity is perennially underfunded."

Marie, unsettled by the landscape, sighed.

"Louisiana, as much as I love it, is a cesspool. Polluting oil, diseased water—both salt and fresh. And New Orleans," said K-Paul, his voice rising, " a city beneath sea level, with inadequate landmass, and poorly maintained levees, is a disaster waiting to happen. I love this place. Louisiana. But even I can understand why your boyfriend, Parks, left. I'm more likely to turn out like Riley, unable to leave the dying state's bedside."

The temperature was falling.

"Sun's going down," she said.

"But the water's rising. The moon's almost full, sky high."

She and K-Paul held hands, comforting each other, looking out to sea, across the expanse of graves. Normally, she knew water signified life, but here, everything was turned upside down. Even the rainwater that refreshed the air, and fed flowers and plants, could, in an instant, go from shower to storm to destructive hurricane.

"K-Paul, is it possible that Vivco is still involved? Still poisoning the area?"

"Possibly." He whistled sharply. "That'd be a secret worth hiding."

"And one worth killing for."

"You bet," said K-Paul.

"Destroy the land, destroy the people. Maybe that's what the apparition was signifying. Unnatural substances poisoning the soil. Like the dead zone in the Gulf. Dying land, dead waters. A world falling apart."

"The history of Louisiana."

"This is what the Guédé were warning about. A rotting world incapable of regeneration."

"End of the world. Scientific fact."

She shuddered. She'd traveled from Chicago to Louisiana, following the Mississippi River south, to practice medicine at Charity. Amazingly, the trail had led her back to herself, her heritage.

But was this how her journey would end? Katrina erasing marshes, flooding the Mississippi, the streets, with bodies? A natural disaster.

She could accept that.

Oil drilling and processing, damaging what was left? Men— engineers—changing the Mississippi's course? An unnatural disaster.

Humanity's hubris was harder to accept.

ELEVEN

The Jeep rocked, its struts moaning and straining through the unsettled marsh. Occasionally, its wheels spun ineffectively, sucking up mud, trying to right itself as it moved over uneven soil—land, at times, more wet, more oil than earth. For hundreds of years, plantation owners, settlers, and oil companies had tried to tame the land but it remained raw with power.

Tonight, more than ever, Marie felt the bayou's nightmarish beauty.

The Jeep turned left, its headlights sweeping across the L'Overture homesite. Then the beams cut through the humid night, illuminating the small band of DeLaire residents. They were captured in the light's stream and were startled into inaction, stunned, still, like zombies.

"Have we gone back in time?" asked K-Paul, pressing hard on the brake.

"Seems like it. Old school, K-Paul. Like a ritual from an earlier time."

The yard was transformed. Someone, with yellow chalk, had drawn a dividing line between the L'Overture home burnt to ash and the rest of the cleared yard.

They'd made a square of earth for the ceremony, raked a square of dirt and pebbles where the invited *loas* would be safe. In the middle was an outraged bonfire, trying to lick the moon. Extra fuel, logs and brush kindling, were off to the side.

Marie's lips thinned. She was pleased yet displeased. The townsfolk had been busy as bees. They'd even raked away the arsonist's trench.

Small stones, painted white, were placed around the bonfire to look like waves and sea foam. She blinked. Shadows and firelight made the stones appear to undulate.

She focused on centering herself. Fire, oil, and water were intermingling elements. It was her job to understand the spiritual give-and-take.

K-Paul cut the engine, turned off the Jeep's headlights.

The DeLaire residents began moving again, fire-lit silhouettes dressed in white: old, wrinkled men, shirtless, in drawstring pants; women in scooped, ballooning blouses, shuffling in rustling ruffled skirts, their hair bound in cotton scarves.

"These are the same people who turned against you, aren't they? When you accused Aaron of destroying the crime scene."

"Yes."

"Makes them hypocrites, not divine believers. Sorry, Marie. This looks like a bad B movie."

Marie nodded. K-Paul was right. The entire scene had an

old-fashioned black-and-white-picture quality: deep night; glowing fire; men and women of color in bright white cotton; trees and bushes cast in shadows. Still, she felt an extraordinary latent power.

"Don't underestimate them, K-Paul. Hollywood has conditioned us all. They might look less authentic, too, because so many of them are elderly. They're direct descendants of slaves, perhaps only two generations removed. They're dying—yet incapable of leaving."

"Tied to the land."

"Yes. Tied physically, psychically, and spiritually."

The small community, a few dozen people, began swaying. Left, right. Left, right. An old two-step. A hum, guttural, heartfelt, yet less insistent than what she remembered from before, rose from their throats.

Tommy and Nate walked toward the Jeep.

"K-Paul," she said, hurriedly. "Help me. Help assess the people's health. It's all connected. Then I'll do a ceremony. Please. Help me add it all up."

"I don't have much medical equipment. Just the basics."

"For now, that's all you'll need. I want to know if you agree with my earlier assessment. Later, we'll bring more supplies. More colleagues."

K-Paul reached into the back, behind the passenger seat, and grabbed his medical kit. "My rifle's here, too. Health insurance."

"You won't need it."

"Someone tried to kill you, Marie."

Tommy and Nate, at the passenger door, interrupted them, their somber faces framed by the window.

K-Paul clutched Marie's hand. "Be careful."

She squeezed his hand, then swiveled as Tommy opened the passenger door.

"Maman Marie." The wounded grocer was gone, replaced by an eager, needy supplicant. "We've arranged things as Nana would've wanted it. She always wanted you here. Said you'd be back."

She took Nate's proffered hand, stepping out of the Jeep.

"We didn't have much time to prepare. Hope you approve." She could hear Tommy's pride. Nate grasped her hand as if he were leading her to a dance floor.

Followers milled about; some, their eyes closed, hummed to the gods; others smiled at her; some, humbled, looked away; and some, intensely curious, stared. But they all had a greedy desperateness. She'd seen it before. Country or city people, it didn't matter. Everybody had needs to be fulfilled.

And yet, she felt uneasy, as if some other unidentifiable need was being expressed. She imagined—or did she?—furtive glances, some unspoken communication being exchanged among followers. Like they had a secret to be kept from her.

K-Paul, the medical kit in his hand, veered right. Charming, smiling, he wooed an old woman, asking her to step aside.

"This is our altar," said Tommy to Marie.

She nodded.

"These bowls were carved," added Nate, reverently, his fingers circling the edges, "by ancestors who survived the Middle Passage. They didn't have mahogany, so they used oak."

"They wanted to keep faith," murmured Tommy. "After all they'd suffered."

"Praise be," she said, feeling reverence and humility for her ancestors' sacrifice.

She touched the altar. It was a weathered picnic table, but on it were the most intricately carved cups and bowls, wooden crosses, and statues of the Virgin and St. Peter. Plates were filled with beans, rice, and corn to feed the spirit-*loas*. Baby catfish were splayed on a platter, cut almost in two, their spines removed. There was a cane for Legba, a hundred small snakes cut deeply into wood; a wooden sword for Ogun, the warrior god. For Erzulie, the voodoo Venus, there was a wooden mirror without reflective glass. It was said that Erzulie was so beautiful, even glass couldn't capture her glory. Followers would use these props during possession. On the bench seat were sheer, blue-green cloth, seashells, and seaweed, all props for water goddesses. But there weren't any statues of water spirits or a statue with both male and female anatomy. It all seemed strange, especially given Nana's adoration.

Beneath the picnic table was a wooden crate filled with someone's prized chicken. She'd never sacrificed animals but most of the world's religions required blood sacrifices. Catholicism had taken it to an extremely ritualistic weekly communion, *"This is my body . . . this is my blood . . ."* to honor Christ's ultimate sacrifice, his crucifixion.

She bent. Dozens of water-filled bowls—all shapes, colors, and sizes—were beneath the table.

Nate stooped beside her.

She smelled him, warm, wet, with a hint of decay.

He whispered, "Said we were taken from water. Said water's fury would set us right."

"Who said?"

Nate shook his head, intently watching for her reaction.

"Nana said," she said, answering her own question.

Before her eyes, Nate's smooth, obsidian skin became fluid, without sinews and bones. Then the male features became more feminine.

"No, not Nana," said Nate, standing, walking away.

If not Nana, who?

Watching Nate's retreating back, she suspected the creature that had healed itself in the ER possessed him. Amazing. How could the spirit be here? It reminded her of the *wazimamoto*, the ancient vampire spirit that came without being called.

She needed more time. More study. She knew there were often schisms between western medical traditions and folkways rooted in spiritual traditions. She knew it was best to question every assumption, to be open to large and small miracles.

She looked skyward. Dead stars, sending down light, seemed alive.

The air was filled with static, electrical, yes, but filled with magic, too.

She shuddered.

Nature was becoming wilder, mirroring older spirits that seemed beyond her control.

The community's hum was intensifying, a wild, passionate sound, filling the night air.

"Tommy, take me to the drummers."

K-Paul was doing another vitals check, this time on a short, compact man with a concave chest and protruding ribs that seemed to have healed crookedly.

Tommy passed torches. Rags soaked in oil were elevated on stakes. Night lighting as it had been done centuries before. Burning oil sent black plumes floating into the sky.

In her city ceremonies, she used halogen bulbs and white mini Christmas lights. She had two drummers, teenage twins, Renee and Raoul, graced and touched by the gods.

Here, there were six drummers, a line of thin black men with large, calloused hands. Unlike the rest of the DeLaire residents, they were extremely fit. Old men with muscular shoulders and arms. She didn't remember seeing these men before. She stood, nodding in turn at each, then bowing, curtseying, honoring them all.

"Maman Marie." "Eh, yé, yé." "Maman Marie." Their voices overlapped and they sounded like six proud fathers offering unconditional love and grace.

She embraced each man. She tapped each drum, shaped from hardwoods and cow skin.

During ceremonies, drummers were the honest brokers. They articulated the call-and-response between the *voodooienne* and the spirit world. Depending upon which *loas* arrived, and in what order, they managed the rhythms, the herald, the spirit's passage into a concrete realm. Drumming, during a ceremony, required the same intuitive, improvisational skills of a jazzman.

The last and lead drummer was the eldest. His face was lined as intricately as a spider's web. His arms were as tough as knotted cords.

She cocked her head. "From the beginning, you served Nana."

"Up until her death," the drummer replied.

"You'll honor her tonight." It wasn't a question.

"You as well."

"What do I call you?"

"Gabriel. Call me Gabriel."

Gabriel was the messenger of God, the archangel who told Mary of her immaculate conception, of Jesus's expected birth.

"Do right by me, Gabriel."

He touched the charm hung arond his neck. "I always do right by the true."

"May I see?" Her hands quivered, holding the charm. She was certain it was Nana's androgynous statue. Gabriel had taken it . . . stolen it? and created a necklace. Black threads had been tied about the statue's neck, then the threads were tied to a thin black rope.

"Who is this?" she asked.

"Shape-shifter. Medicine man. Medicine woman. Shaman. Healer. Priest. Priestess. The shifter is known by many names. It only matters that it heals, transforms. Inside and out."

"Transfiguration?"

Why did she say that? Was there a metamorphosis?

Christ transfigured. She, herself, transfigured, becoming more than human when it was required, needed. Becoming a vessel for spiritual grace was an honor. She wasn't a goddess or Christ or Buddha, she was a human being. Frail and imperfect. Nonetheless, she knew the beauty of spiritual possession.

Tommy was pulling her arm. "Normally we have our ceremony on shore. Next to water," he said, dragging her away from Gabriel.

She ignored his implied criticism; it worried her more that Tommy had purposefully separated her from Gabriel.

She touched the Mami Wata statue in her pocket, feeling the cool wood, feeling the contrariness of water goddesses versus the earth.

Did the other spirit, the statue, "take" away? Heal by taking, not giving?

She looked back at Gabriel. He was cupping his statue, staring, smiling smugly, as if he were the *voodooienne,* not her. As if she, Marie, was lesser, beholden to him.

She was far enough away to see drawings on Gabriel's drum. Stick drawings. Cave drawings. Drawings like those on Nana's grave. There was a large spirit—perhaps the no-name spirit? Trembling, she focused on the stark figure of the woman, on her knees, ill, clutching her abdomen.

✖

She looked across the yard. K-Paul, his stethoscope around his neck, the buds lodged in his ear, was monitoring Brenda's and her baby's heart.

"Leave me," she said to a shocked Tommy. "Please." She needed space, air, time to escape Nana's small band of followers.

Reluctant, Tommy left her, but he still watched her, following her movements.

Oddly, here, under the open sky, she felt caged.

What was she missing?

She crossed the chalk line, crossed from the ceremonial space near the mound cradling the L'Overtures' remains.

Seething oil moved beneath ash.

She saw the L'Overtures, mourning. The infant wrapped in her mother's arms. A family, a trinity of ghosts.

Behind her, the bonfire raged.

Her arms were damp, slick with sweat. She turned, circling,

trying to understand where she was—how she'd come to this—how supplicants and drummers could both unnerve her. How Nana's world had been frozen in time, populated by ancient *loas*. *Loas* she was unfamiliar with; *loas* who, during the African diaspora, transformed; *loas* who only in this remote corner were still vital and worshipped.

"El?" she whispered. "Are you there?" She wanted El's pragmatic comfort.

Beyond the bonfire and torches was a ravaging darkness. And silence.

No echoing spiritual call.

K-Paul came to stand beside her. "You were right, Marie. There's too much illness to be explained by random circumstances. Active pollution, that's what you're thinking, isn't it?"

Was it? She focused on K-Paul's mouth and words.

"If Vivco is releasing solvents again, it'd be in violation of environmental law. It'd be repeating criminal behavior. Penalties would be severe, not just financial, but prison time."

John L'Overture had been murdered by Vivco. She felt certain. Someone in authority had ordered it and Walker had executed him. Walker had taken pleasure in executing the entire family. Her nails dug into her palms.

K-Paul started to walk away, but he turned back, adding, "Marie, some of these illnesses could be long standing, long maturing. But given their condition, not so much their age"—his hand swept toward the DeLaire residents—"most of these folks should've died long ago."

"What're you saying?"

"I don't know. I mean . . ." He scratched his head, stuck his hands in his jeans pockets. He inhaled, blurting, "Some of these folks said they've been sick for decades. I mean it's not possible."

"That they survived so long?"

"Yes. Luella, the woman with the lump in her breast, should've been long dead. The cancer should've spread to her lungs, abdomen. Another man, Simon, has an open wound on his side, inflamed, with pus. Said it was bad now, but Nana, before she took ill, fixed him up . . . always. For the past thirty years."

She knew they were both thinking the same thing. In medicine, doctors knew there were miracles, individual miracles. But an entire community postponing death? In a rational world, a single miracle was one in a million, a group miracle was one in an infinite number.

Inexplicably, her mind made a leap and she thought, "Sin eater."

"What?"

"Like a sin eater."

"The Vatican has banned such claims. There's no such thing as a sin eater."

"Just because the Vatican denies it doesn't mean there isn't truth. In medieval times, it was believed that the rich could pay a sin eater to swallow their sins so they could go to heaven. What if there was a way to delay disease—"

"You've got to be kidding."

"It's a metaphor, K-Paul. What if there was a way of transforming diseased cells, delaying the growth, taking away the impact of the disease?" Her head hurt. What was she thinking? *Take away.* That had to be it. It was illogical. Yet she knew, in her spiritual world, logic didn't necessarily triumph. K-Paul was looking at her as if she was crazy; she didn't blame him.

She turned quickly, raising her hands high. The humming stopped. She could see their pinched, hungry faces, sense their unfulfilled desires.

"You've suffered a great loss. Tonight's ceremony is in honor of Nana."

Followers nodded, clapped. Tommy was as eager as a boy.

"And in honor of the L'Overtures."

There was silence—stillness, as if air had been sucked from their bodies. Residents stood dumbstruck.

A bird caw-cawed and something slithered through the underbrush.

"This, too," said Marie, "is hallowed ground." She searched faces. Most were uncomfortable, wary. A few betrayed grief. Tommy appeared, furious.

"Tonight," she went on, "we honor Nana and the L'Overtures."

"Eh, yé, Maman Marie, eh, yé, yé." The roar was loud and magnetic. She blinked. Hard to believe that a ragtag band in poor health could sound so vibrant and alive.

She raised her hands again.

Silence.

"Damballah, creator of the universe, *loa* of infinite knowledge, guide me. Make me special." She opened her eyes. "Spirits, enlighten me. Especially the ancestral spirits honored by Nana. The old ones. Wata. The elders."

"Amen," rose from the crowd.

"Especially those spirits who came from across the ocean. Spirits I have not met. Spirits I have yet to meet."

Followers were rapt.

El stood with the L'Overtures, ephemeral forms hovering outside the ritual square, on the edge of the marsh.

Animals were attracted to the bonfire. Deer, mosquitoes, grackles, snakes were all hiding, lurking in the woods. *But Marie sensed them—she could see them, in her mind's eye, slithering, inching forward.*

Gabriel pounded the drums.

Energy, like electricity, trailed down her spine. "Make me special," Marie murmured. "Spirits come. Fill me with grace."

She took nothing for granted. Damballah, the snake god, was her special *loa.* But here, in this bayou world, Nana had worshipped other spirits. *Loas* who were less familiar to her, yet more familiar to slaves two centuries ago. Wata. And the shapeshifter, the dual-gendered creature.

Boudom. The drums' rhythm increased, the timbre grew louder.

To the left was the well. After dipping a cup into the shiny pail, Brenda was drinking water.

She wanted to shout, Stop. But she suspected it was already too late. If the town's water supply was toxic, the damage had long been done.

El stood beside her, reminding her that the world was hard on women. Hard on Brenda. Hard on Nana. Hard on her.

Gabriel pounded again and the other drummers echoed his insistent rhythm. Soon, Papa Legba, like the Catholic St. Peter, would appear to open the spirit gates.

She swayed, her body and mind both felt lighter than air, both responding to the drums' call.

With her roots and herbs had Nana kept sickness in abeyance? She remembered Nana saying that she, Marie, "could heal."

Yes, she'd healed as a doctor and as a *voodooienne*. In both roles, the price, anxiety and exhaustion, had always been worth paying. She'd never regretted a single healing, but, somehow, she was beginning to suspect Nana had. Decades of healing, being selfless, would exert a toll.

The drums were calling her. Gabriel, she imagined, was warning her. Or was he?

Why did she need to be warned? Yet the world, both tangible and intangible, seemed upside down. Hurricane season—would a hurricane ravish New Orleans? Would it even come? This season or the next? And Nana had died in pain, distraught as a *voodooienne*. Would that happen to her? Ten, twenty, thirty years from now, would she be embittered like Nana?

She held her head. What was wrong with her? What in this world—in this time and place—was making her weak? Tentative?

Inhale, exhale. She was Marie, intent on healing both medically and spiritually. She was Marie-Claire's mother. And being a mother, like a water goddess birthing the universe, was the most powerful position in the world.

Parks and Louise were caring for, loving Marie-Claire.

She needed to love and care for the world, the time and people she'd been given. As a Voodoo Queen, she served where she was needed.

"Damballah, Wata, give me faith. Give me strength," she whispered to herself.

Time to begin. Swaying before the fire, Marie prayed for *sight*, for possession.

Luella brushed against her and swooned.

Quickly, as if a floodgate had opened, followers were pressing against her, gripping, pulling at her arms, clothes, screaming, "Heal me. Heal . . . heal me."

She fought to steady herself, screaming, "Get away. Get away."

Followers fell back. The air was still too close. It was hard to breathe.

Strangely, she felt as if the followers intended her ill. Felt as though they wanted something that she couldn't give. Felt as if they wanted to suck her dry, like the *wazimamoto* she'd slain, and they wanted more than was acceptable to give.

She looked over at Gabriel, talking to her with his drum.

She didn't understand.

Nothing about the ceremony was as it should be. Luella wasn't healed. Papa Legba hadn't opened the spirit gates. She wasn't possessed with divine grace.

At the back of the crowd, closer to the trees, Nate watched her, his eyes lit like black jewels.

The air around him, trembled, seeming fluid, like water.

Marie knew it was a spirit—one not beholden to Legba, not beholden to the faith as she knew and understood it.

Nate's appearance was changing, shifting forms: from male to female, then back again.

No one else seemed to see what she saw.

She saw age—beyond ancient, wrinkled, and scarred flesh. Then Nate's skin became smooth, handsome. His face transformed again. It became the Haitian's face, the man she'd seen in the hospital. Then, like a mirror image, it became her.

She cried out, disbelieving.

Drums vibrated, followers chanted: "Maman Marie, Maman Marie. Heal me."

No one heard her scream.

K-Paul, entranced by the ceremony, was looking everywhere and nowhere.

Gabriel intensified Legba's call: a staccato rhythm with the left heel of the palm sliding. The other drummers were entering the conversation, adding new beats to the call, creating an urgent, insistent cacophony.

A man, screeching, "Open, open," was possessed by crippled Legba. Another follower handed him Legba's cane. Someone else gave him Legba's pipe. *The man limped, jutting his neck forward, screeching, "Open, open."*

Two women, their steps lively, danced and flirted with Legba.

Luella rose from the dirt, clapping, shouting, "Miracle." She exposed her breast. *Amazingly, the lump had disappeared.*

Where had the healing come from—from the spirit inside Nate?

What was it Nana had said? "A Voodoo Queen with full power can heal anything. But every healing has a cost."

Marie only knew that Luella's miracle, Luella's healing, wasn't hers.

Someone brushed against Marie; another touched her hand; more bowed. Followers shuffled, barefoot, making patterns in the earth.

The crowd become one, chanting, whispering, "Maman Marie. Heal me. Maman Marie."

The spirit walked among the crowd. He was there, yet not there. Aged, then youthful. Male, female.

She saw El stroking Brenda's hair, but Brenda didn't feel it. Mimi L'Overture was weeping, holding her beloved baby to her breast.

Marie heard rolling waves.

She felt lost in a new territory—nothing about this ritual was typical, normal. She almost laughed, hysterically. "Normalcy." Ever since coming to New Orleans, nothing had been normal. Ever since El and DuLac had died, nothing had been normal. She couldn't even love a man like Parks, normally. Or care for her child, normally. She needed others to care for Marie-Claire when she couldn't be there.

Everything about her life was outside the bounds of normal.

She was a failure. No, she wasn't.

She reached inside her pocket, pulling out the figurine of Mami Wata. She held it up to the fire, its tail and breasts shimmering, and followers began weeping, wailing anew.

She was different, special. And if she sacrificed herself, she'd be good for no one. Not Marie-Claire, not Parks. Not the hospital. Or herself.

Drums pounded. Bonfire sparks rose like fireflies.

Marie pressed the statue to her lips. It was one thing to be a mother and suppress yourself, another to be a mother and fulfill yourself. What would Marie-Claire want? What would be the better role model for her daughter? The better life for herself? The better life as a woman, as Marie, as a mother? Life, both tangible and spiritually intangible, wasn't easy.

Suddenly, she saw Wata filling Nana with nourishing power. She felt Nana as she'd once been, vital, filled with sacred power.

She saw Nana, younger, ministering, healing, building her community, possessed with exultant glory. She saw Nana mixing roots, herbs, blending potions . . . Nana applying compresses, bandaging wounds, delivering babies.

She heard a kaleidoscope of sounds—urgent voices, whispers *from another time. Voices calling her, demanding that she heed them.*

Nana had been the intermediary between the ancient African faith and the faith transformed by the intermingling of African slaves with Americans, between old and new worlds.

Nana's shape-changing spirit was helping her to rise. Like lightning, "disease eater," flashed through her mind.

"Show me," Marie murmured. "Show me."

The spirit clasped her hands.

She stepped, as Nana had done, through an ancient door.

She saw water rising, creating a vortex. Saw Nana, in its center with a spirit circling her, twisting like a whirlwind, changing faces and form. Male then female. Faces spiraling about Nana—Nate, the Haitian, her face, and a multitude of faces, she didn't recognize. Water cascaded as a tangible mist, shaped and reshaped itself, mimicking human form. She saw two great forces, both prehistoric, linked by mutability.

"Charyn," she heard El whisper.

Charyn. Was that the shape-shifting spirit's name—a name so old or so powerful that only the dead knew it?

Charyn, the statue stolen from Nana's altar.

"Wata."

Nana had worshipped Charyn and Mami Wata. But honoring Wata had come first. When did she start to honor Charyn? How were the two connected?

El chanted, "Hard on women, hard on women."

Nana, now seemingly trapped by the vortex, the ever-swirling spirit, spinning tighter and tighter, shouted, "Every healing has a cost."

Wata murmured, "Give"; Charyn murmured, "Take."

Marie felt power, constructive, destructive power. The vision turned black.

She saw Nana, her hair turning white, her eyes dulling, becoming blind.

Nana fell on her knees, her arms clasping her abdomen. Her belly grew big.

At the water's edge, she saw Charyn, half male, half female . . . saw Nana touching Brenda's pregnant abdomen, and though there was no bleeding, no sucking of flesh, she nonetheless knew that Nana was swallowing diseased cells, swimming through fluids, muscle, and blood.

A police car pulled onto the dirt. *The vision ended.*

A dust cloud rose; women shrieked. The drumming stopped. The man who'd been possessed by Legba straightened his spine, disoriented.

Marie felt bereft, furious. A few moments more and she would have understood better.

The car's front window was stained with dead insects; splattered mud caked the black-and-white's wheels and sides.

The engine died. Aaron staggered out of the car. Barely able to stand, he fell back against the car door.

Deet, skip-hopping from the passenger side, caught him in an embrace.

Aaron shoved Deet, breaking away.

Protectively, K-Paul came to stand beside Marie.

Chest heaving, Aaron's shirt was undone, his pants stained with whiskey. He moved, sliding from side to side, like an unbalanced skater.

Followers stood, wary, moving away from the fire and nearer the forest's shadows.

Spewing spit, Aaron yelled, "Nana's gone and you're still here, Maman Marie. It isn't right. Not right. Damn fucking wrong."

"I'll get the rifle," murmured K-Paul.

"No," she said, touching K-Paul's arm. "He won't hurt me."

Aaron was radiating pain. He tried to advance menacingly, but his stride was off balance. "All you've done is cause trouble, Doc Laveau. Nana stayed alive till you came along. Everything's your fault."

"I didn't cause her death."

"You did. You did something to her. Hexed her. Made her feel shameful. Ashamed."

"What're you talking about? Why was Nana ashamed?"

"Come on, Aaron," said Deet, tugging his brother. "Let me take you home."

Aaron twisted his arm free. "You're a traitor." Deet was stricken. Aaron pointed at his brother, walked backward, then spun around. "You and Doc Laveau, both traitors."

K-Paul stepped forward, steadfastly blocking the path between Aaron and Marie. "You should sleep it off, Sheriff."

"I'm not the sheriff. She," his head tilted toward Marie, "took that from me. Took Nana, too."

"Aaron, you've got it wrong. I'd never hurt Nana."

"Everything was all right, under control. Till you came."

"What control, Aaron? Whose?"

Followers drew farther away, keeping their distance from Aaron.

"I was taking care of her," he said, belligerent.

"You were helping her die."

"We both were." Aaron stumbled, falling nearly flat on his face. Deet caught his brother beneath the arms, righting him.

"I didn't cause Nana's death," said Marie flatly.

"Liar." Aaron lunged.

K-Paul pulled Marie back.

"We, you, caused her to die horribly." Aaron slid down, out of Deet's arms. Dignity gone, Aaron sat blubbering, cross-legged in the dirt. "Such pain. She died in such horrible pain."

Marie knelt before him, caressing his face. "I'm sorry she refused the medicine."

The statue in her pocket was ice cold.

"Aaron," she murmured. "Nana couldn't be saved. Her cancer was too far gone."

"Why didn't you heal her? You could've healed her."

"No. I couldn't have."

"All she ever talked about was the great Maman Marie. Marie Laveau." Aaron's arms were flailing. "'Time for a new voodoo life,' she said. 'Time for the great healer.'"

"What do you mean?"

"You denied her care," said Aaron.

"Shut up, Aaron," said Deet. "Nana had the best care."

Deet's eyes were luminescent with tears; Aaron's were bloodshot.

With sudden clarity, Marie understood that it had been Nana

who'd guided her to DeLaire. Nana who'd called upon the power of her gods to summon her.

"Why didn't you heal her?" whimpered Aaron. "She'd done it enough. You could've helped. You could've healed."

"You're wrong," wailed Deet. "Nana was relieved when Maman Marie came. She felt content to go. She wanted to go."

Aaron, the elder, looked crazy, young. His hands flailed no, and Deet tried to contain them, wrestling his brother to stillness. The two were wrung out, exhausted from playing war. Both were breathing heavily. Deet caressed his older brother's face.

"I love you, Aaron," he said. "But you've got it wrong. Nana wanted to die."

"I don't believe you."

"You don't want to believe me. Nana wore herself out. Taking care of everybody. Even you. Me. You knew that."

"I didn't know," Aaron said, stubbornly.

"You did. That's why the grief's so bad. You knew and yet you still tried everything to keep her alive."

Guilty, his chest concave, Aaron shrank, collapsed in upon himself.

Marie shuddered. She'd seen plenty of terminal patients go through hell, pursuing hope on their children's behalf. For her grandsons' sake, Nana must have held on as long as she could.

"Nana wanted to go," said Deet. "She was worn out. We wore her out." Deet stood. "All of you," he said, stepping menacingly toward his neighbors. "Every last one of you here wore Nana out. You all took until she couldn't give anymore. Couldn't cure anymore. She just held on until Maman Marie came."

Aaron was crying, his back curved, his knees pulled in like a fetus.

Luella, massaging her right breast, murmured, "Maman Marie is our new mambo." She smiled, gaily. "She's healed me."

"I haven't," protested Marie.

"She's going to deliver my baby," Brenda piped, drawing near. "Nana told me so."

"We're all guilty," Aaron said, sitting up, uncapping his flask. "Everybody in DeLaire is guilty."

Tommy took away the rum flask.

"Hey," said Aaron.

Nate pulled Aaron upright. "Time to go home."

"Let it go," said Tommy, soothingly. "All of it, Aaron. Let it go."

Deet rushed forward, pushing Nate's and Tommy's hands away. "Don't touch him. Leave my brother alone."

Fiercely, Deet clung to his brother. "None of you cared when Aaron was paying the price. None of you helped when help was needed."

Followers glanced at each other furtively.

Tommy said darkly, "Let it go, Deet. Take your brother home."

"Damn all of you," Deet cursed, then murmured, "Come on, Aaron. Let's go."

Deet and Aaron took a few steps, arm in arm, toward the car, then Aaron broke free and clasped Marie's shoulders.

"Let her go," said K-Paul.

Marie held up her hand. "No, let him speak."

"Did you think I liked being dirty?" Aaron's voice slurred. "Liked burning the bodies?"

The alcohol smell made her nauseous. She stroked Aaron's face, sorry to see him so vulnerable and weak.

"What else could I do, Maman Marie? They were already dead.

Couldn't help John no more. I'd told him to keep quiet. But he kept saying he was going to the authorities."

"Shut up, Aaron," said Tommy.

"What're you talking about?"

"I didn't want to, Maman Marie—they all made me." Aaron, trying to steady himself, pointed his finger at the followers—the men and women who, in the firelight, dressed in white, infused with emotion, didn't seem so frail.

There were shout-outs, denials: "The boy's out of his mind"; "The wrong was his"; "He's upsetting our ceremony, our healing." The words were like stones thrown at a once-favored son.

If Nana were alive, she'd be appalled. Her beloved community had turned against her grandson.

Gabriel hit the drums. *Boudom. Boudom.* Again and again.

Marie looked at Gabriel. What was he doing? She hadn't given notice for the ceremony to continue.

Boudom.

The other drummers mimicked Gabriel, creating rounds of syncopation, a transcendent, emotional call.

The fire leapt higher, licking the sky.

"What the hell's going on?" asked K-Paul.

Marie began to understand how she'd been tricked, used. This ceremony was never meant to be hers. The DeLaire residents, Gabriel, had intended to use her. As they'd used Nana.

"I told you not to come, Maman Marie," shouted Deet, pushing Tommy away. "All her life, Nana wanted to keep the community alive; but before she died, she said it was time for DeLaire to come to an end. Said Vivco and the DeLaires just kept slavery going, generation after generation."

Tommy shouted, "Shut up, boy."

"Go to hell," answered Deet.

Marie felt entranced. The rhythms were unlike anything she'd ever heard before. Drums were calling older and older spirits.

"Do you see him? Her?" she asked K-Paul. "Do you see it?"

"Are you all right, Marie?"

Charyn carried Mami Wata in his arms, her glittering tail flicking upward. Her teal skin flushing red.

Marie understood. The two ancient spirits were bound to each other in time and space. "Do you see, K-Paul? Two spirits that Nana and the first DeLaire slaves worshipped. Both embody duality. Charyn mimics both genders. Wata embodies human and animal characteristics. But these dualities only signify how ancient their powers, their beings are."

"Marie, what does this have to do with now?"

"As much as Wata filled Nana, Charyn used her up."

"What're you talking about?"

"It's horrible. Wata would've inspired roots, herbs, and organic cures. Charyn, a disease eater, would've encouraged Nana to consume ills."

"What?"

"To take them into her body. Everyone here knew about it. Gabriel," she looked at him, pounding his drums, "called Charyn."

Marie's knees buckled.

K-Paul held her. "We've got to get out of here."

The drums urged, rising and falling like waves. Marie clung to K-Paul. *Her lungs constricted; Wata and Charyn were delving inside.*

She wanted Aaron and Deet safe. Nana, who'd sacrificed so

much, deserved that. "Help Deet and Aaron, please. Get them out of here."

"Are you sure?"

"Yes, go," she gasped. Usually, only one spirit possessed at a time. *The two spirits entering her felt like they were tearing her apart.*

K-Paul and Deet dragged Aaron, held beneath his arms. They'd almost made it to the car when suddenly, Aaron roared, pulling away, fists swinging, hitting K-Paul in the face.

K-Paul dropped to his knees, his hand trying to stanch the blood from his lip and nose.

K-Paul was furious. "Son of a bitch." He ran, crawled toward the makeshift graves. Barehanded, he scraped the surface dirt from the L'Overture skulls. "Is this how you helped Nana? By murdering innocents? You disgusting son of a bitch."

She felt the chaos. Possessed, yet not. Felt Charyn asserting itself.

Hands—seemingly disembodied—were pulling her back toward the bonfire, the ceremony's center.

Aaron screamed, "He was my friend. John L'Overture was my friend."

Hands plucked at her. "Heal us, Maman Marie. Heal." She felt the evil in their clinging need. "What did you all do?" she demanded, her words garbled, catching in her throat.

"Heal us," they answered, demanding grace.

She was drowning.

Weeping, Aaron cradled the skulls.

"I am Marie," she murmured. She had to keep her mind clear.

"I am Marie," she murmured again; and though the power of her name wasn't as strong as the *loas'*, she felt a modest retreat, a breath of clarity.

Hands still held her, pulling her down onto the ground. Touching her body, trying to heal themselves.

Between white dresses and grasping hands, she saw black threads sliding, covering the ground, rushing toward her faster than oil and water.

She understood. The threads were pollutants infecting soil and water. Chemicals that caused tumors, cancers, misshapen bodies and souls.

Inside her, Wata was retreating, Charyn, gaining power. She was hungry, ravenous.

Drumbeats were urging her. Charyn became her. She became him.

Ecstatic followers were howling, the Marie inside her couldn't move. Instead, the black threads were covering her body, entwining her and the followers. Flowing from their bodies were threads of disease—cancerous cells, pus, inflammation—into her.

She could feel the pain they felt . . . feel the disease, fluid, spreading.

When Nana's roots and prayers didn't work, she took the disease into her body. In time, the disease in her birthed the malignant tumors that killed her.

She heard K-Paul yelling, pulling bodies away from her. Then Deet was trying to save her. But as elders were pushed away, they came back, desperate, fighting for life, for survival.

A shot was fired. "Leave her alone."

The drums stopped; whimpering, followers scampered back. *Charyn flew.*

Aaron was standing, holding his gun high.

K-Paul gathered her in his arms. She held on tight, shivering.

Aaron's gun barrel shifting, he shouted, "I can't kill all of you. But enough." He aimed at Tommy and Nate and, finally, Gabriel.

"Why'd we try to hold on to this hell? Why'd we ever trust in Vivco, the DeLaire family? Dumping started again and we all just rolled over. Because we had Nana. Our land, our same old community. Never outgrew the slave mentality. Well, we don't have Nana anymore."

Aaron looked at Deet. "Deet was the best of us. Too bad you came back. I wanted you to get away."

"I couldn't leave you and Nana," Deet answered simply.

"Deet wouldn't let Nana touch him. Did you know that?" Aaron's voice slurred. "Wouldn't let Nana sacrifice one bit of her self for him. Did you know that, Maman Marie?"

"I could've guessed."

"You figured it out."

"Yes."

"Stay back," Aaron warned Tommy, who'd tried to move forward. "I'm tired of lying. Tired of keeping my mouth shut."

A star fell, cutting across the sky.

"John L'Overture wanted to settle in DeLaire with his wife and baby," said Aaron, one hand pointing his gun, the other clasping his abdomen. "When his plants didn't grow, John figured it out. He wanted to notify the EPA that Vivco was dumping again. But nobody—none of you," Aaron screamed at the residents, "cared because we had Nana. Notify the EPA and we feared we'd be run off the land our ancestors tilled.

"I told John he ought to leave—like the others. He didn't have to stay. For those who did stay, it was a hellish bargain. Isn't that right, Gabriel? You were the one who knew how to call the special god—the one without a name.

"Oh, we convinced ourselves that all was well. Nana loved us. Nana had the power. Nana would live forever. A spirit could consume and survive, but Nana was taking it all inside her body, all the poison ... each day she was dying ...

"Deet, you were a better man than me. Everything I did kept the status quo. Kept Nana, you, all of us chained here."

Aaron looked skyward. "Nana's one of them stars. I know it. She is." He stared at the DeLaire residents. "Leave. Die. I don't care which."

Then he fired a bullet into his head.

Screams rent the air. Deet collapsed next to his brother.

Through tears, Marie watched the followers scattering. Selfish, selfish. So much pain they'd caused. So much pain they'd endured.

She stood, sweat draining from her, dirt, traces of polluted oil on her clothes and hair.

In the bayou, she heard car engines starting, then saw flashes of headlights come to life and disappear. K-Paul was on the ground, doing CPR.

Nate was as motionless as a statue. Tommy looked grim, Luella, dispassionate.

K-Paul looked up, shaking his head. No hope for Aaron. He tried to comfort Deet.

Marie turned toward the drummers. All, except for Gabriel, were leaving, their drums strapped on their backs.

The ceremony was over.

Gabriel, his eyes made yellow by the firelight, glared.

His hand touched his necklace. The Charyn figurine, Marie knew. He had no remorse, no care for Aaron. He blew her a kiss.

Religions were meant to be evolutions, too. What had happened in DeLaire that had trapped them in such a demanding past?

Such sacrifice might have made sense in another time, another world.

She saw Nana, Wata, and Charyn—an odd trilogy. Nana's hands were outstretched, begging for understanding.

Marie only knew that her faith, as she practiced it, had never required such self-destruction.

TWELVE

Aaron, bloodied, with half a face, was stretched in the backseat of the ex-police car. Deet sat sideways in the front-passenger seat, his feet planted in the dirt, sobbing. K-Paul bent forward, his arms around him, and whispered in his ear.

Most of the followers had drifted away. Marie stood, alone, in the center of the ceremonial square. Adrenaline and energy had rushed out of her. She was exhausted. Pains radiated down her spine. Her stomach felt uneasy.

"K-Paul," she called, breathless, feeling faint.

K-Paul didn't hear.

She tried to step toward him, but her knees buckled, as if she were a marionette whose strings had been cut. She couldn't stay upright. Her torso leaned then fell sideways.

"Marie!"

Needlelike cramps rippled through her abdomen.

K-Paul's footsteps sounded like a rushing army.

K-Paul cradled her head. Pain choked her throat. *She could hear him talking to her, but she couldn't see him.*

She saw life thriving in the dirt—small creatures, burgeoning grass, and silver-gray moss clinging to rock. She saw death, too, bits of fossil, decomposing leaves, and the L'Overtures' bones.

She tried to breathe through the pain. She gagged; something acrid rose in her throat.

She saw El with sister-friends—ghosts who toiled as slaves, domestics, and prostitutes. Some pregnant, some not. Women who'd tried to make DeLaire home. Mimi L'Overture had tried; Nana, too. Both, in their own way, were heroic.

She saw threads. No, not threads, tiny streams, arteries, and capillaries of the land bubbling black blood, like a blown oil well, widening, becoming a pool ready to swallow and drown her.

Her stomach contracted. She felt the deep connection between the land's health and her own.

She vomited. *Black, viscous oil, solvents mixed with blood.*

"Marie." K-Paul held her head so she wouldn't drown, fall face forward in her own vomit. Projectile vomiting.

She vomited again. Over and over. Her stomach retching, her throat contracting.

As if from a distance, she heard K-Paul insisting, "Hold on. Hold on." She heard Deet muttering, "Like Nana. Just like Nana."

Granules floated in her unnatural vomit. Not food. Not bile. Something more toxic. Like black seeds. Cells.

Inorganic oil and evil, there was no other way to describe it, mixed with her blood and being.

K-Paul held her shoulders, balanced her to keep her from falling forward in the sick sea.

"Do you see it?" she whispered.

"See what?"

"The threads, the streams of black waste."

"No."

Nana was rubbing her protruding abdomen.

Marie buried her face against K-Paul's chest. She felt the strength of him, his arms.

She'd ingested Louisiana, and some of the damage done, to it, by greedy, oppressive people.

"We've got to get you to a hospital."

"Wait."

"No, not this time."

"The pain's lessening. Just get me home, K-Paul. To Marie-Claire. New Orleans."

She looked across the bayou—ferns; willow trees; and swaying, tingling marsh grass. *She felt disease settling inside her like a stone. All kinds of illness—cancerous cells, blood clots, insulin mutations, and viruses flowed into her just as they had Nana. Given time, she, too, would become pregnant with it. Given time, she'd lose her sight, her health, and maybe even her mind.*

She could feel K-Paul's heart beating, the air expanding through his lungs.

Over K-Paul's shoulder, she saw El and Nana. "The world can be hard on women."

"Every healing has a cost."

"K-Paul, get me out of here."

Aaron was dead, and folks were leaving, as if a picnic had come to an end.

Brenda approached. "Nana said you'd care for me. Birth my baby."

"I will. But you've got to come to New Orleans. To Charity Hospital."

"No. My baby can't be born there. Nana said you'd deliver it."

"Then Nana was wrong. Your body and the baby are filled with cancerous oils, cancerous waters. You need a hospital." She turned away from Brenda's distraught face.

"Let's go, Marie. Deet's going to bury his brother here. With the L'Overtures."

She nodded. No investigation. No autopsy or bureaucratic burial requirements. She hugged Deet, kissing his cheek. "Come visit me, Marie-Claire, and Beau."

"I will," he murmured.

"Promise?"

"Promise," he said without looking at her. She knew he'd never come.

K-Paul grabbed her hand. "I want to get you back to the city. Everything's foul here."

"I know," she answered. And I've ingested it, she thought, but didn't say.

"Take me home, K-Paul."

She wanted to hug her daughter and feel her sweet, healing love.

She loved Louisiana, her adopted home. But Louisiana, she now understood, was also riddled with devastation. It was a land that for centuries had been raped and preyed upon. Still, she was part of it. Wed to it. She was the Voodoo Queen. Everything in her life had guided her to this moment, this place in time.

But now it was time to go home.

K-Paul clasped her hand, guiding her back to the Jeep.

"Maman Marie." *The voice was soft, quiet, but she heard it like a shout.*

Marie turned.

Brenda was clutching her abdomen. Water drained down her legs and pooled at her feet.

"My baby's coming. She's coming."

Marie knew it was too soon. Brenda was seven, maybe eight months' pregnant at best.

She and K-Paul reached for Brenda.

They were doctors called to heal. Two lives depended on them.

THIRTEEN

NANA'S HOUSE

PAST MIDNIGHT

Brenda's contractions were still irregular, but she was beginning to dilate. She was in Nana's bed, frightened, holding fast to K-Paul's hand. No mother had come forward; nor father, nor lover. It was as if Brenda and her baby were alone in the whole wide world.

The DeLaire neighbors were all in their homes, squirreled away.

Marie rubbed Brenda's back. She hoped the baby wasn't stillborn, that it was thriving. But they had no medical equipment to monitor either the mother or the child. As a precaution, they hooked Brenda up to Nana's IV. Fluids always helped.

She looked at K-Paul; like her, he was exhausted. "You should take a break," she said.

"No, you. Brenda and I will be all right. Won't we, Brenda?"

Brenda moaned. "How much longer?"

Marie didn't want to tell Brenda she'd be in pain for hours. That a young teen's body wasn't meant to birth a child. Worse, there was nothing she could do to relieve the pain. Nana's medicines were too strong, addicting.

"Marie." It was sweet, compelling. She knew it was Mami Wata.

"Marie."

She squeezed Brenda's hand. "You're doing fine. I'll be back soon."

"Go on," said K-Paul. "Take your time."

"I'm glad you're here, K-Paul."

"It's not easy to get rid of Cajuns." He winked and Marie felt more grateful than ever for his good humor.

✕

"Marie."

Her legs leaden, her body sore, she walked deeper into the marsh. Earth became less firm, became water-cushioned grass.

Nana had been right. She was going to birth Brenda's baby in DeLaire.

Marie walked to the land's edge. Gentle waves lapped against the shore.

Wata lived in water.

Hugging herself, she crossed her arms over her chest and waited. *She was being called to serve the goddess.*

She smelled rot and sorrow. The waters were sluggish, choked with moss and kelp. She felt a heavy breeze stirring off shore.

A storm was coming.

The moon illuminated a path. It was stark, bright, stretching toward the horizon, where water met sky.

"Marie."

Wata wanted her inside the water.

She slipped off her shoes, stripped her clothes, and stepped into the warm Gulf waters, following the light.

Water rose to her calves, to her knees and thighs. *Then she dove, immersing herself beneath water, feeling Wata's grace and touch.*

"Mami Wata," she called inside her mind. "I am Marie Laveau's descendant. Teach me, show me what I need to know."

She floated on her back. Waves kissed her. Her hair and body soaked, she felt wrapped in a watery womb.

She could see stars, the shadows on the moon.

"Here."

She flipped over, treading water.

The mermaid was before her.

"Wata."

Wata opened her arms and Marie swam into the cool, watery embrace.

"Mine the water."

"Yes, it is yours," Marie answered.

"Mind the water."

An explosion of greens, blues, ripped through Marie's mind. She felt fluid, without form. She was Wata, swimming.

"Come." *She was diving deep, breathing inside the waters. Exultant, she saw creatures stirring. Catfish. Shrimp. Alligators floating in brackish waters.*

Yet she could see more clearly than she'd ever seen before. Even polluted, she felt the vibrancy of Gulf life.

"Water goddesses once ruled," said Wata. "We nourished the world."

Marie wanted to shout with joy. Free, unbound, she felt Mami Wata's power. Felt herself a mermaid, swimming, traveling upstream to the Mississippi's start. They reached the cold waters of Lake Itasca, then turned south.

Wata, pregnant with rich soil, was flowing down through America's heart. But as water rushed, as she and Wata swam over rock, granite, sand, the waters became less clear, fouled by pesticides, metals, and solvents. Worse, she felt Wata's pain at being banked, dammed, cut off from her natural course.

Down, down they swam through eddies and currents, twists and curves, until they reached the widening Gulf.

"No place to be," said Wata. "No place to nourish land. Give birth."

She felt Mami Wata's pain. She felt she was dying, just as Mami Wata was dying, fading from the New World.

Disrespect. Forgetfulness. Poisons were undoing the goddess. Unlike Charyn, Wata only served good. She gave and didn't require self-sacrifice.

"I create," said Mami Wata, her voice sounding like music. "I make worlds."

"I understand." Marie felt the womanist connection. Creating life, a fertile world, these were the enduring blessings.

As quickly as she'd come, Wata disappeared. She was no longer inside Marie, no longer in the warm Gulf waters.

Marie felt bereft, as wet and cold as a newborn.

Wata had followed her children from Africa to America, only to have the New World disrespect her life-giving waters.

"Wata?" she called, hoping to feel the spirit.

There was no response, no answering call.

Religions, faiths evolved. Everyone, including herself, had forgotten Mami Wata.

Marie prayed, "Mami Wata, by my ancestress Marie Laveau, by the love given to you by Nana, I promise to honor you. To encourage better care of your waters."

Marie floated, drifting farther into the Gulf.

She felt life—kelp, shrimp, and microorganisms thriving in the water. Sand particles and algae twirled in the water, brushed against her skin.

"I promise," she said, "to honor you. Always. I won't let you be forgotten."

Then, as if all the stars had fallen, she saw diamond specks, floating, twinkling in the water. The entire Gulf was vibrant with light.

Mami Wata rose. Legs fused, her body, sea blue, her hair cascading down her back, Wata spun above the waters, coloring the sky with rainbows. Colors of love, grace, and rebirth.

"*You are me,*" *Wata murmured.* "*See,*" *she said, insistently.* "*See.*"

On the horizon, there was a gathering darkness.

Marie felt dread.

"*See.*" *Water and sky parted, and Marie saw, in the distance, another horizon where a monstrous hurricane fed.*

"*No,*" *Marie screamed.*

Mami Wata pulled her inside the storm. She felt herself shattering inside the violent swirl of wind and rain.

"*Mine . . . mind the waters,*" *said Wata.*

A blessing and a curse.

"*Nature heals.*"

Then the vision disappeared.

The sky cleared. Mami Wata floated serenely on blue waters.

But Marie couldn't undo her terror.

She understood. A ferocious storm was growing, coming to cleanse the Gulf waters, to undo the river's dams.

"Wata, please. I will honor you. But please, keep DeLaire safe, keep Brenda and her child safe."

Wata's head tilted. The approaching storm would free her, wash away poisons in her water.

"Please."

Wata, like all the gods, was passionate; but they were just as imperfect as people. Wata had called the hurricane, but she hadn't considered the consequences.

The hurricane would be a horrific, sawing vortex of wind and rain.

Marie could see it tearing at the vulnerable marsh, see it moving, slowly, destructively, up the coast, toward New Orleans.

She started crying, her tears blending with Wata's waters.

"Mami Wata, protect us. Please. Use your powers to keep DeLaire, Brenda, and her child safe."

She couldn't change the course set by Mami Wata. But she prayed for grace, for charity.

"Please, Mami Wata." Water roughed by incoming wind washed over her face. "Please. Keep DeLaire, Brenda, and her child, safe."

Mami Wata dove deep into her waters.

⁂

Marie swam with all her might. She swam through surf, swam through the soon-to-be storm-tossed waters, channeling fear. The hurricane would hit the Gulf first.

Her mind balked at the thought of the hurricane reaching the city. New Orleans. She couldn't imagine it.

Lungs aching, she stepped onto sand, slipped on her T-shirt and jeans, and started running for her and everyone else's life.

FOURTEEN

NANA'S HOUSE

BEFORE DAWN

"K-Paul," said Marie.

Brenda was on her side, eyes closed, breathing deeply.

"What is it?"

"Katrina. It's a major hurricane. Headed here and for New Orleans."

"We'll have to ride it out."

"I've got to call Parks. How can we let the DeLaire residents know?"

"There's a horn. Down by the docks." Brenda, her face slick, her hands wrapped about her stomach, said, "I'll be all right. You don't have to stay."

"Of course we'll stay," said Marie. "Don't you worry." But she was worried. "Give me your cell, K-Paul. I'll call Parks. Louise and Marie-Claire."

"I'll go. Sound the alarm," he said.

"No, let me do this." She felt guilty because she hadn't correctly interpreted the signs.

Brenda moaned.

K-Paul murmured, "The contractions are becoming more regular." He handed Marie his cell.

"Tell the baby to hurry, K-Paul."

Marie was out the door, down the porch steps. Nana's yard was empty, sad looking. She could smell the wetness in the air.

"Parks?"

"I'm here."

"Marie-Claire?"

"She's fine. So's that dog. Louise's upset because he peed on the carpet."

Marie laughed, then, inexplicably, she started to cry.

"You okay?"

"Get Marie-Claire out of New Orleans."

"Yeah. I know. Weatherman just said 'category five.' Louise is packing Marie-Claire's clothes now."

"Just go," she said. "Leave now. Don't wait. Now."

"You know something."

Parks, who used to doubt her sight, now trusted her implicitly.

"Do you want to say good-bye to Marie-Claire?"

"She's sleeping, right?" *She could see her daughter with Beau curled next to her.* "Let her sleep. Bundle her into the car and just go. As far and fast as you can."

She could hear Parks breathing. "Doc . . . Marie, I love you." He paused. "See you in Baton Rouge?"

"Yes."

IV

Mississippi, the Great River diverted,
Mami Wata cried; so, too, her Yemaya,
And all her sisters.

FIFTEEN

NANA'S HOUSE

MIDMORNING

Stubborn and suspicious, none of the DeLaire residents evacuated. They wouldn't listen to her. She wasn't Nana, so why should they believe her? Why was Katrina worse than any other storm?

"Go," she'd said. "It'll be bad."

"We'll stay," said Tommy. And all the sad-eyed, disease-ridden residents had shuffled back to their homes.

She placed the clay statue of Mami Wata on Nana's nightstand. K-Paul had taken the Jeep to scavenge supplies in town. Humidity was high, and thunder crackled on the horizon. Katrina was coming and Marie guessed she'd come at night. Brenda slept fitfully as her body erratically labored.

Marie wished they were at Charity. She was worried that a C-section would be needed, that the baby would need intensive care.

She held Brenda's hand, praying for the strength to make things right.

"It's going to be a girl," said Brenda, sleepily. "Nana told me so."

"You should rest, Brenda. You've got a ways to go."

"I know. It's gonna be a storm baby. Nana told me so."

Marie smiled. "Nana was right."

Brenda was looking at her with blind trust. It felt as if the two of them were the only people left in the world. Nature was creating a fury. Bayou country would be hurt bad, but the city would be hurt worse.

She needed to survive and return to New Orleans.

※

She thought she heard K-Paul's car. Brenda's eyes were closed. She thought she'd slip outside. Just for a moment. Just to see K-Paul's smiling face.

Gently, she slipped her hand from Brenda's fingers.

Marie stepped outside. She shuddered. The sky was already darkening. Wind whipped the waves and you could hear them crashing onto shore.

Birds had disappeared. Animals had run to ground. There was no sound. No signs of life.

The road was empty. She'd made a mistake. K-Paul hadn't returned. She only wished that he had.

Marie sighed, rubbed the back of her neck. She felt as if she'd aged a hundred years. Coffee. She'd make coffee.

She touched the screen door's handle. A shadow dulled the silver mesh.

Before she could turn, a hand covered her mouth while another hand gripped her waist, hard.

A scream caught in her throat.

"You need to be taught manners." Walker. His pale, translucent hands gripped her.

She squirmed, trying to pull away.

Walker twisted her around, fast and deadly. His hands were now pinching, twisting her throat. She couldn't scream; she didn't have enough air. The constant pressure on her throat was inflaming muscle, tendons, pinching her carotid artery. Soon her esophagus would be crushed.

She summoned her strength, scratching, tugging at Walker's arms and hands.

She thought of Marie-Claire. Her daughter had already endured so much.

"The world can be hard on women."

But it shouldn't be hard on a child.

She fought desperately, but Walker was strong. She let her body relax and focused on calling, "K-Paul."

She closed her eyes, blocking out Walker's albino-faced rage. She was lightheaded, dying.

K-Paul.

Her neck was released. She gasped.

K-Paul slammed Walker into the wall, then, gripping his collar, shoved Walker backward. He fell, tumbling down the porch steps.

Calmly, K-Paul fired his rifle. Twice. Once into Walker's heart, the second time into his forehead.

Blood flowed, staining the ground red.

K-Paul knelt to check for a pulse. The impulse was automatic. He reached inside Walker's pocket and opened his wallet. "Vivco. Head of security."

Marie didn't say anything. She was glad to be alive. She was transfixed by the river of Walker's blood, purple-red, soaking into the soil.

K-Paul, stood, kicking aside his rifle.

Marie thought he was in shock. Doctors saved lives, they didn't take them.

Marie embraced him.

"I heard you," he kept repeating. "I heard you."

"Ssh," she said, holding him closer, feathering his face with kisses. "It's all right. Thank you. Thank you for saving my life."

SIXTEEN

NANA'S HOUSE

EVENING

This is the way the world ends. Wood straining, rain beating like pellets on windows, and a howling wind.

Hurricane Katrina had touched down on the coast.

Brenda's baby was trying to push her way into the world.

There were no voodoo drummers, no special sacrifices for the gods. No faithful followers. No possession.

It was just her. And K-Paul. And Brenda. And a baby eager for life.

In her bones, she knew Parks had Marie-Claire safe in Baton Rouge.

K-Paul was anxious. "We should've gotten the hell out."

"There's no place to go."

The kitchen window shattered. "Marie, I'm not sure this shack can last."

"I don't want to die," Brenda whined, alternating between fear and pain.

Thunder rumbled; outside, they could hear trees and branches snapping.

"Don't push. Not yet," pleaded K-Paul.

Marie saw John, Mimi, and the infant L'Overture. Was this a sign that they'd all die, too?

She stared at the statue of Mami Wata, praying, "Still the waters. Still the storm. Please. Still the waters."

The cottage shuddered, a wind squall threatened to rip the house from its foundation.

K-Paul reached for her across the bed. Clasping hands, they used their bodies to shield Brenda.

Then there was silence, as if the wind had parted like waves, leaving the cottage safe, an island of calm.

"The storm's turning."

Mami Wata had spared them and DeLaire from the brunt of the hurricane.

"'Bout time." Sweat dampened K-Paul's shirt. He felt Brenda's pulse, touched her brow and abdomen.

"Something's wrong. The birth canal's still constricted. Or else the baby's breech. I'm not sure which. Everything feels right, but it's not. Something's wrong."

"What's wrong?" asked Brenda. "Save my baby. Please."

Marie picked up the figurine of Mami Wata. Then she saw El. Nana. Her ancestor Marie.

Heal.

"I am," she said, touching Brenda's abdomen, "Marie Laveau."

Brenda quieted. *Marie could feel the baby beneath her fingers, moving in her mother's body. She could feel the irregular pulse of her heart.*

Medically, nothing was available to save Brenda's child. The baby was premature. Toxins had probably affected her. There'd been no prenatal care.

Brenda clasped her hand. "Save us."

K-Paul was watching her, too, expecting a miracle.

She was Marie. She had to do this—become extraordinary when need demanded it.

She closed her eyes. "Mami Wata, bless me. Make me special."

She kept thinking she'd been brought to Louisiana for a reason. She'd been brought to heal and encourage life.

She murmured, "When medicine fails, faith begins. Pray, K-Paul."

He made the sign of the cross. "I believe in you, Marie."

"Me, too," Brenda whispered, faltering, drained by her labor.

"I believe in me. Marie Laveau. I believe in Mami Wata. The goddess who gave birth to the world with her waters."

Marie touched Brenda's abdomen. Light sprang from her fingertips. She stroked the flesh covering the baby and felt the child move. She murmured: "You need to be strong for this world. The world can be hard. But you'll survive."

She felt the baby turn, ever so slowly, swimming in the birth canal. She felt its tiny fingers reaching toward her palm.

Her body was hot, filled with spiritual power.

Ghosts were at the head of the bed—El, Mimi, Nana.

And, inside herself, Marie could feel Mami Wata. She felt, too, Marie Laveau.

The wind, outside, howled louder; a sheet of rain made the

house shudder. But she believed it was just the storm's fiery aftermath, the hurricane was moving on.

"I believe in you, Maman Marie."

"I believe in you, Brenda. And in my ancestor Marie Laveau. I believe in the sacred waters, the power of Mami Wata."

K-Paul was staring at her, his love for her glowing on his face.

Marie stroked Brenda's swollen abdomen—circles and circles of touch and heat. "Heal, little one. Heal."

She felt the small heart fluttering, then becoming stronger, beating like a tiny, steady drum.

"*It's time,*" Marie murmured. "*It's time.*"

A contraction, like a rippling wave, moved through Brenda. The baby swam.

K-Paul whooped. "Bear down," he shouted. "Bear down."

Brenda marshaled her energy, grunting, bearing down, and expelling her baby.

A tiny, perfectly formed baby slipped out of her mother's body. Slipped out, bloodied and wailing. Slipped out, her arms and legs flailing.

The spirits faded; Mami Wata dove into clear waters.

Brenda crooned, "My baby. My baby."

K-Paul bundled the infant in cloth and placed her on her mother's chest.

Marie felt good.

The hurricane was moving north. Mami Wata had gifted her with grace.

K-Paul embraced her, his chest to her back. She cupped her hands over his. His cheek was pressed against hers.

They watched the baby suckling, heard Brenda vow, "I'm going to be the best mother ever."

Marie smiled. "You'll need some help."

She saw the future. Saw Brenda and her baby, joining her small, but growing family. They were strolling on the Riverwalk. Marie-Claire was the proud big sister. Beau was happy, barking, chasing his tail. Parks was there.

And, of course, K-Paul.

SEVENTEEN

They were driving back to New Orleans. To Charity.

Brenda and her baby were asleep, exhausted, curled in the backseat. At the hospital, they'd do a complete exam to make sure mother and daughter were healthy.

In her heart, Marie knew they were. Mami Wata had helped her perform a healing.

She and K-Paul were both spent, yet, amazingly, adrenaline kept them alert, almost frenetic. It was a high to bring a new life into the world. To save a mother. To escape the full horror of a hurricane.

Yet they were following Katrina. She was whipsawing, lashing her way up the waters to the Mississippi, flowing beside the banks of New Orleans.

"When we get to the city, we should party. Listen to some zydeco. Hurricane Katrina won't destroy New Orleans." K-Paul clutched her hand. "I know you've got to get to Baton Rouge. To get your baby girl. But you can leave Parks. He left you."

"I'm staying, K-Paul. For better or worse, Louisiana's home."

"Staying with me? You're staying with me?" His hand was on her thigh. She lifted it, kissing his open palm. "Maybe. Let's give it time."

K-Paul grinned. He punched the defroster. Humidity was clouding the windows. Next came mist, rain. Cypress and oaks dripped water. They were riding the tail end of the storm, chasing Katrina, heading for New Orleans.

They had to get to Charity Hospital, to help as best they could.

The Guédé, in funeral top hat and tails, were standing beside the road, their heads bowed, their gloved hands, palms flat, crossed over their chests.

"K-Paul, stop."

He slammed on the breaks. "What's the matter? What's wrong?"

Marie got out of the car. Brenda's baby started crying.

Her dream—she'd forgotten the river of bodies.

K-Paul climbed out of the car.

"I see . . . I see . . ."

Transfixed, she couldn't speak.

She blinked and saw bleak, empty streets. Trees, street signs, were down, roofs were ripped off houses. Cars overturned. The hurricane had come and gone.

Something else was wrong.

In her dream, animals and people were floating, dead, in the water. New Orleans's streets were littered with refuse, but clear of water.

"Water needs to go where she needs to go."

"Flooding, K-Paul. The storm isn't the worst for New Orleans. The levees." Despairingly, her voice cracked. "I think the levees break."

"The end of the world."

She looked down and saw water swirling over her feet.

She saw water climbing over grassy knolls, concrete barriers, and bags of sand. New Orleans was like a bowl, filling up with muddy water. Two feet, four feet, ten, twelve.

"Water needs to go where she needs to go."

Riding the waves, she saw Mami Wata, Yemaya, LaSirene, and all the other descendants of Wata.

Dozens of spirit women with mermaid tails—some teal colored; others brown, some with alabaster skin, others full breasted and pregnant.

Marie was in awe of their beauty—a flotilla of women across the spiritual ages, all signifying creation and the beginning of life.

Marie raised her hand, saluting them, and some waved back, others primped, and others swam, and still others spun delicately, as if waltzing. Then, as if on cue, all the water goddesses began crying. Marie shivered at the high-pitched wailing; any second, the sound would break her heart.

Marie understood. "Mind the water, K-Paul. Mine the water."

"I don't understand."

"We're all responsible for the environment. Nature cleanses and renews. But we keep making it harder. Making it worse."

"Like the dead zone?"

"Yes, causing unnatural dying. Unnatural harm."

"Levees, levees . . . levees . . ." the word was humming, whispering like a breeze. "Levees, levees, levees."

Like a woman's water breaking, water would break free of the levees.

Mami Wata was trying to heal herself, give birth.

But there would be such pain. Such cost to New Orleans. Louisiana. Her home.

"It is what it is," she heard.

"The world can be hard on women," she answered. "On men. On children. Animals."

"Harder than you have yet imagined," responded El with cool words that rattled in Marie's mind.

"Harder." What could be harder? How much destruction, disaster could Louisiana take?

※

The Guédé, Mami Wata, and the mermaids had all disappeared; they were replaced by her ancestor Marie, and Nana, and El. The women chanted her name: "Marie Laveau." They were showering her with love, telling her that she was a New World voodooienne, *a medical and spiritual healer.*

"Survive," she murmured.

"Louisianans always do that."

"Even when it's the end of the world? That's what you said, K-Paul. 'End of the world.'"

"Well, I guess it's not going to end in my lifetime."

"Come on, K-Paul. Let's chase the storm. Let's go home."

AUTHOR'S NOTE

For centuries, environmental damage and environmental racism have afflicted Louisiana and the Gulf marshes and waters. Science, spirituality, and historical perspective are all needed by my protagonist, Marie, to understand why New Orleans was so vulnerable in 2005 to Hurricane Katrina and why the levees failed.

In 2009, the National Museum of African Art/Smithsonian Institution mounted a brilliant exhibit honoring the African water goddess, Mami Wata, and the permutations of how her spirit transformed as slaves carried their faith into the New World. The Fowler Museum at UCLA first exhibited the collection of sculpture, paintings, and mixed media and published a glorious book, *Mami Wata: Arts for Water Spirits in Africa and Its Diasporas,* written by Henry John Drewal (and contributors Houlberg, Jewsiewicki, Noell, Nunley, and Salmons).

Mami Wata's core emphasis on fertility, creating new land and new worlds, and celebrating womanist power resonated deeply with me.

Mami Wata, for me, became a symbol for the Mississippi River itself, dammed to serve human needs. Clearly, responsible environmental stewardship means balancing resources with certain and potential damage and caring for the vitality of the environment for future generations.

In *Hurricane*'s metaphorical world, Mami Wata came to symbolize the devastation of the Gulf Coast region, in general, and the dead zone in the Gulf, in particular. Irresponsible environmental stewardship that had made New Orleans and the coast especially vulnerable to Hurricane Katrina seemed, in my imagination, a cry from Nature—Mami Wata herself. Having constricted Mami Wata, her waters were unable to give birth to new land that was essential to creating and sustaining life—both human and animal.

The 2010 BP oil spill compounded problems in the Gulf of Mexico and reinforced my theme of human hubris versus humility in resource extraction.

My protagonist, Marie, doesn't have the answer to solve environmental problems. But she does have faith—a spiritual belief that Nature itself is a good to be honored. She also has courage and optimism to lend her talents to heal a community undone by natural and man-made disaster.

Hurricane ends my contemporary voodoo trilogy. Marie Laveau née Levant has become a quintessential Louisianan. She's become strong enough to keep fighting for the city and state she calls home. She's comfortable with her spiritual power, unafraid of battling injustice, and honored to proclaim her name to the world:

"I *am* Marie Laveau."

She is one in a long line of women, handing *sight,* strength, and love down through the generations.

Sincerely,
Jewell